Also by Judith Hudson
Writing as J.M. Hudson

The Rocky and Bernadette Mystery Series

Temple of the Jaguar
A Mayan Murder Mystery
A travel cozy mystery. A travel writer and a photographer's
first job together in the Yucatan quickly unravels when a body
is discovered in the crocodile lagoon.

Home for Christmas

Book Three in the Fortune Bay Series

Judith Hudson

Welcome to
Christmas at Fortune Bay

Hi everyone,

Home for Christmas *is Louise and Blue's story.*

The ties that bind women together often revolve around family and children. Pregnancy is a life-changing experience that, strangely, is often personal and public at the same times. Miscarrying, or losing a baby, is such a hugely personal trauma that women often choose to keep it a secret. But a woman never forgets, and sharing our darker stories can sometimes help ourselves, and often others, heal.

While those parts of this story were difficult to write, I did have fun with the romance, the tension, between Blue and Louise, and with writing Christmas in July.

Look for some of Louise's Christmas recipes, including Santa's Dark Secret, on my website, at www.JudithHudsonAuthor.com.

I hope you'll join me there and sign up for my Readers Group newsletter for news of contests, events and upcoming Fortune Bay books.

Thank you for reading **Home for Christmas.** *I hope you enjoy it.*

Judith Hudson

The Fortune Bay Series

Available on Amazon as eBook and paperback.

Lake of Dreams
Get this free prequel e-novella when you sign up for my readers group at **bit.ly/freeFB-e-book**

Summer of Fortune
Book One
Maddie wasn't looking for romance. Could a summer of freedom change her life forever?

The Good Neighbor
Book Two
Sean hates to see Frankie and her father estranged. He'd give anything to know where his own daughter is.

Home for Christmas
Book Three
Blue's carried a torch for Louise his whole life, but this time he's not sure he can wait around to pick up the pieces.

Family Matters
A Sequel Novella
Things are at a low ebb for Frankie and Sean. Be sure to read *The Good Neighbor* and *Home for Christmas* first!

Starting Over
Book Four
After a horrific motorcycle accident, Marshall's life seems to be over—until Lily knocks on his door.

Starlight and Tinsel
A Christmas Novella
Star finally gets her chance to shine in this Christmas novella.

Chapter 1

"And the Golden Pretzel Award for excellence in pastry, goes to...Louise Ingstrom."

The auditorium burst into applause as Louise stumbled to her feet. *Yes!* She'd worked damn hard all semester, especially during the last three weeks, often staying late into the evening at the Academy kitchens before going home to her tiny basement apartment to try a new technique one more time before falling into bed.

She squeezed past the knees of her fellow students as they patted her on the back and rumpled her short hair, knocking her tall white hat askew. When she finally made it to the aisle, she took a moment, ostensibly to straighten her chef's jacket and hat, but really to wipe a tear from her eye and swallow the lump in her throat.

These guys were great, but she wished her old friends from Fortune Bay could be here tonight. They would have come, but the trip was three-hours one way, so she hadn't even asked. She'd see them all tomorrow. That would be soon enough.

Squaring her shoulders, Louise lifted her chin and climbed the stairs to the stage. On the platform, Marco caught her eye, grinning and clapping along with the two dozen other instructors of the Seattle Culinary Academy. He'd congratulate her later, privately, but right now, the dean was waiting across the stage, smiling and holding out a hand to shake. In his other hand, The Golden Pretzel gleamed, the spotlight outlining its sinuous curves.

Louise planned to take a month off and go home for Christmas, but you could bet your blintzes she'd be back.

And then, she hoped, the Pretzel would open doors to jobs at the best restaurants and patisseries in Seattle.

An hour later, Pretzel in one hand, Peach Bellini in the other, Louise was celebrating with her fellow students at the reception in the Academy banquet hall.

"Anyone found a job yet?" Pete asked.

There was a chorus of groans around the table.

"I have a job," Monica said with a self-deprecating smile. "At my uncle's bakery, making bagels."

"That's okay," Chin Lee said encouragingly. "It's always good to be employed while you look for something better."

"What about your daughter?" Louise asked.

"My mother's offered to babysit. At least until I can afford daycare."

Monica was a single mom. The image of Louise's sour-faced stepmother Belinda popped her into head. She would walk on hot coals before she'd ask Belinda to do something like that. Anyway, Belinda would probably refuse.

"I have an interview on Monday with Zara's Catering," Big Mike said. "But it's only for the Christmas season. After that, they lay off most of the staff until the spring weddings start."

"Well, it's something," Louise said. He had a wife and baby daughter to support.

He hitched his head toward the statue. "Well, *you* won't have any trouble finding work. Just flash that pretzel and you'll get any job you want."

"It still won't be easy," Louise demurred. But he was right. One thing she had learned at the Academy was that being a pastry chef was a tough way to make a living. She had to try, though. It was the only thing she wanted to do, the logical next step in her career, and her ticket out of Fortune Bay.

Just then Marco, swarthy and gorgeous as a fallen archangel, materialized in front of her. "I couldn't leave without congratulating the winner of the esteemed Pretzel."

She grinned, wanting to throw her arms around his neck, but held herself in check. They always played it cool at the school. Although they were both finished here as of tonight, and he had never been *her* instructor, the academy frowned on instructors dating students. They both planned to move into the local private sector right after Christmas and wanted to leave with their reputations intact. In fact, she had a few job prospects lined up already and planned to email them right away about the award.

Marco took her hand and pulled her in for a chaste, congratulatory kiss on the cheek, whispering in her ear, "See you later."

He released her as the other students crowded around to shake his hand.

"Thank you, sir."

"I really learned a lot from you."

A few minutes later, Marco drifted away, sending her an arched eyebrow on his retreat.

"I guess I'll go," Louise said to her friends.

"Not yet," Chin Lee cajoled.

"I have to, I'm beat, and I have a big day tomorrow. I'm moving out of my flat and heading back to Fortune Bay for December. I'll be back after Christmas, though, looking for work." She laughed. "I might end up sleeping on your couch for a while."

After hugs all around, she caught Marco's eye as she shrugged into her coat. He was dancing with Genevieve, the petite French-Canadian woman who had been Louise's breads instructor. He raised a brow in her direction. Louise returned a slight nod. As she headed into the cold, blustery night, she pulled her hood over her head and smiled to herself, their secret warming her like a loaf of bread, straight from the oven, clutched to her chest.

The trendy food neighborhood surrounding Pike Place

Market had been her home for the past two months. Tonight, cars clogged the narrow street as people poured out of the Market Theatre, heading to restaurants and pubs nearby. Although it was only the first of December, colorful Christmas lights decorated the shops, their festive good cheer reflected in the wet pavement below.

As she walked down the stairs to her basement apartment, she was greeted by a scratchy *meow*, rusty as a garden gate. "Hello to you, too."

The marmalade tabby emerged from his hiding hole beneath the steps to the upstairs apartment and wound his way around her ankles as she unlocked the door. She called him Scrawny because he'd been so, well, scrawny when she found him hiding out of the rain under the steps shortly after she moved in. A real charmer, he'd looked as if he'd been fending for himself on the street for a while. Thin and beat-up, one eye was swollen shut and he had a bald spot the size of a quarter on the top of his head from a recent fight.

He'd been there again the following night and she gave him some tuna water from the can she opened for dinner. The third night she let him in and gave him the tuna.

Now he spent every night inside with her, except when Marco came by. Scrawny didn't like Marco and the feeling was mutual. Some territorial thing between males, she assumed. The cat needed a better name, though. After two months of regular meals, he wasn't as scrawny anymore.

Louise had also noticed that the unnerving scratching in the walls at night had decreased in direct proportion to the dead rodent count at her front door. Charming. She wouldn't miss this apartment and was definitely planning to find something better when she returned to the city after Christmas.

Her roommate Jess emerged from her bedroom with an armload of boxes. "So? How did it go?"

Louise carefully unwrapped the golden statue and set it in a place of honor on the stove.

"Seriously?" Jess shrieked. She dropped the boxes on the floor and grabbed Louise in a hug. "You deserve it, with the hours you've worked. Actually, I think I deserve a medal too, for putting up with your banging around in the kitchen at all hours."

"Well, we both deserve a glass of wine. Tonight might be another late one." Louise yawned. "I'm already exhausted."

"Is what's-his-name coming over to say goodbye. Your mystery man?"

"He's not a mystery. You've met him." Jess was a student at the college, not the Academy, so Marco didn't care if she knew they were seeing each other.

"He comes and goes in the dead of night," Jess intoned like the narrator of a radio show from the forties. "Are you sure he's not married?" She cocked her head. "No, I guess if he was married, he'd be home at night and with you during the day."

"You know how it's been. With him being an instructor, we had to be careful. We didn't want our 'indiscretion' to be thrown in our faces next month when we're both looking for work."

"He hasn't found anything yet either?"

"Apparently not. He has some possibilities, though."

"So, now that you are both finished with the Academy, are you going to live together after Christmas?"

"I'm not sure. We haven't decided what will happen next."

After pouring the wine, Louise looked at the kitchen. It was a disaster, her prized kitchen implements half in, half out of cardboard boxes. Picking up her copper clad sauté pan, she carefully packed it away, wrapping it in newspaper so as not to scratch the delicate surface.

Jess helped for a while, but soon drifted off to bed. When Louise looked up next, it was almost midnight. That wasn't late for her and Marco to meet, they both often worked into the early hours of the morning, but she had expected him to get there a little earlier tonight, this being their last night together for a while.

She succumbed to a giant yawn. Of course, it was Marco's big night, too. He had his own goodbyes to say.

Although she expected him to walk through the door at any moment, she was too tired to wait any longer and, moving a pile of clothing from her bed, lay down and closed her eyes. She could pack her clothes in the morning.

There wasn't that much to pack. Since moving to the city for the course her style had changed from quirky retro finds to stark black and white. The dress code at the academy was severe; their white jackets had to be crisp. Instructors were known to send students home to iron out any rogue wrinkles. No tunics or shirttails could protrude from beneath, and she'd discovered that black pants and long-sleeved, silky black tees worked best under the uniform. Besides, it was fast and easy and, she felt, reflected her new urban life.

She glanced at the clock. After midnight. Where was he?

Marco was different than the other guys she had dated, older, more mature. She bit her upper lip as she remembered inviting him to Fortune Bay for Christmas. It felt risky. She never brought guys home and wasn't sure she was ready to start.

She was always the one to end her relationships before they became too serious. Gently but firmly, that was her policy. So many people had come and gone in her life, leaving without a goodbye, that she had learned long ago to get out before it was too late. Before she gave her heart away.

But she wasn't sure she wanted this relationship to end yet. She was still having fun. There would be time when she came back to Seattle after Christmas to decide how she felt about Marco. So far, they'd kept it casual. No ties, no plans. Just the way she liked it and, she suspected, the same went for him.

Leaving a small light burning by the front door, she took off her clothes and slid under the covers. Exhaustion pressed down on her like a lead blanket and her eyes drifted shut.

She woke when the front door squeaked open, fighting her way up from a deep sleep.

Scrawny mewed, a harsh sound like his throat was lined with sandpaper.

"Out," Marco said. Then, in a softer tone, "Hi Babe, it's me."

Wiping her eyes, she tried to focus on the clock across the room. "What time is it? Two o'clock?"

She sat up straighter in bed, suddenly wide awake. "Where were you?"

She grimaced in the dark. Wrong thing to say. They didn't check up on each other like that. Marco came and went as he pleased, and so did she.

He'd been spending nights—or part of them anyway—at her place ever since that first night six weeks ago when they'd met at a concert at a local bar. She'd recognized him from the Academy, he was swarthy and gorgeous and a little bit dangerous, and she'd been thrilled when he recognized her, too. They started talking and after a few drinks, he walked her home. She invited him in and ever since, he'd come over three or four times a week, almost always late at night.

"A bunch of us went out for drinks. I had some goodbyes to say."

The image of him, darkly handsome, dancing with

blonde Genevieve, flashed through her mind. "You're just leaving the Academy, not the city."

He took off his jacket and hung it on the back of a chair. "Fun night?" he asked, as he undid the silver cufflinks at his wrists.

She pulled her knees to her chest under the covers, smiling as she remembered receiving the award. "It was so exciting. I didn't expect to win."

He tilted his head, a fond half-smile on his lips. "You deserved it."

"I wish we could have celebrated together in public tonight. I guess we can soon."

"Well, I'm here now." He never spoke of their future together, and she understood. She was fine with keeping things light.

He took off his shirt and, as always, she wanted to run her hands over the well-defined muscles of his shoulders and chest. He was an Adonis, with dark olive skin and sultry, almost-black eyes.

He sat on the edge of the bed and pulled off his shoes. She put a hand on his warm back. "Do you think you'll make it to Fortune Bay? I've borrowed a cabin from a friend for the month."

He stood up and undid his belt, then he turned to her and smiled. "I'll try. I have a few things to work out first."

His pants dropped to the floor and he lifted the covers and slid into bed, pulling her against his chest.

She wrapped one leg around his hip. She didn't want to think about the future either. Tonight, she just wanted to enjoy him. They would have plenty of time to talk when he came to visit her at the cabin.

Chapter 2

The headlights of Louise's Jeep lit up the sign, *Welcome to Fortune Bay. W*ithout warning, tears sprang to her eyes and laughing, she wiped them away. Her emotions were flowing so close to the surface. PMS, right out of control.

There was no reason for tears. When she'd left Fortune Bay at the end of September she'd been dying to get out of town. The pastry chef course had been a godsend.

Scrawny moaned from under the seat.

"Almost there, boy." He'd been meowing pitifully every few minutes for the past hour since they'd driven off the ferry. If he was going to hit the road with her, she'd have to get him a travel box.

Rounding the bend, her headlights flashed on another sign, but this one brought a smile. *Last Gasp.* As teenagers, she and Blue had thought it was hilarious when they'd added the *p* to the sign at the abandoned gas station, their pithy social comment on the fate of their dying logging town at the end of the paved road. Blue had left the sign as a remembrance when he took over the property as his home and workshop five years ago.

Windows glowed in the one-room apartment he'd built in the office of the old station. A vintage Volkswagen van was nosed in beside the office, the exuberantly painted body just visible in the twilight. When had Blue bought a camper? She was seriously out of the loop.

Louise was tempted to stop in—to say, *Hi, I'm back*—but that would have to wait until tomorrow. First, she had to go and see her dad.

Forcing her concentration back to the dusky road, she continued a few blocks through town then slowed again as she passed the general store and café. She'd put in ten years at the café, the place she'd always thought of as the heart of Fortune Bay, but by the end she had been ready to move on: first to Seattle for the pastry course, now hopefully to a job as a pastry chef and then, maybe someday, to a business of her own.

The town fell behind as the road snaked along the shore of Majestic Lake, weaving past houses of old friends and neighbors, and crossing the bridge over the creek. Finally, she turned into a narrow driveway that wound through a thick stand of firs and cedars, slowly easing her old Jeep over the ruts and potholes.

At the end of the drive, the headlights picked out the white clapboard and blue shutters of the cabin, but in the dark, she could barely make out the shore of the lake thirty feet away. She had expected the cabin to be cold and dark, but light glowed from the windows. Her old pal Sean had told her he wasn't using it much these days and had offered it to her for the month.

Smoke curled up from the chimney. She hadn't expected him to come by and light the fire but thank goodness he had. The temperature was nudging freezing and the cabin wasn't what you'd call winterized, but she knew how to keep a fire going. She'd manage fine for the month. The privacy would be worth it. She'd lived in Fortune Bay all her life and knew how hard it was to keep everyone out of your business.

Stepping out of the car, the damp air greeted her like an old friend. More like a heavy mist than actual rain, it hung in the air and clung to the rocks and trees. Most people didn't think water had a smell, but to Louise, the aroma of wet cedar and lake water was the smell of home, conjuring memories of rubber boot walks through the forest and teenage kisses in the rain.

She grabbed the overnight bag she'd squeezed between

the boxes packed into the back of the Jeep, then bent over and coaxed Scrawny out from under the seat. Bundling him inside her jacket, he buried his head in her armpit.

She laughed. "Tough guy."

Making her way up onto the porch, she opened the screen door and, at her feet, the welcome mat *ka-flumped* into place. It was possible that she'd hit it with her foot, but she didn't think so.

"Hello to you too, Augusta," she murmured. She'd heard the rumors. They may be true. If she *was* sharing the cabin with a ghost, it was probably better to stay on her good side.

The front door was stuck. She rattled the knob, then put her hip to the solid wood door and gave it a thump. This time the door flew open and she stumbled inside—into the burly arms of a giant.

"Blue! What are you doing here?"

Blueton Humphries stepped back, looking hard and deep into her eyes. This was new. Where was her hug?

"Thought I'd heat the place up for you." Her heart warmed at the familiar gruffness of his voice. "Sean said you'd be back tonight, but I didn't expect you so early." He stooped to look into the furry face that peeked out of the front of her raincoat. "What have you here?"

"Scrawny," Louise said, pulling the cat out for him to see.

Blue laughed, a deep throaty chuckle. "You named him Scrawny? You always were hard on your guys." He took the cat and rubbed him under the chin and within seconds, Scrawny was purring like a muffler-less car.

Setting the cat on the floor, he put his hands on Louise's shoulders, holding her at arm's length. "Jeeze, Louise, you're blonde again."

He ran his hands down her arms and even through her jacket, awareness tingled like phosphorescence in their wake. Louise blinked. This was new too.

Pulling off her beret, she ran a hand through her damp pixie cut. "I decided to go back to blonde. It's a change." She tugged his bushy beard. "But you haven't changed."

Blue didn't respond, just crossed his arms over his chest.

Louise knew him too well to be put off by his taciturn ways and peered around him to get a better look at the cabin. The big front room comprised the kitchen and living room, quaint and cozy, the furniture so dated it would have been considered retro in the city. She eyed the turquoise combination oven and stove with the pushbutton controls, circa 1960. That would be a challenge with all the baking she planned to do.

In the back corner of the room, a fire glowed through the open door of the wood-burning stove. On the back wall, a bamboo curtain hid the doorway to the bedroom.

"Where's the old, flowered curtain?" she asked.

"Sean got rid of that right away when he moved in."

"He didn't live here very long."

"No. Once his daughter Amber arrived, he was out of here pretty quickly."

"I can't believe I missed all that. When I worked at the café, I knew everything that went on in town."

"Why aren't you staying with your folks?" Blue corrected himself quickly when she frowned. "With your dad."

"I got used to having my own place in Seattle. Dad's house is really too small for us all, and a month of Belinda would drive me crazy."

"You're too hard on her."

"I doubt it." She wiggled her eyebrows suggestively. "Besides, I'm expecting company."

Blue's eyes hardened above his curly beard, but the disapproval was gone so quickly she wondered if she had seen it at all. He never approved of her boyfriends but really, despite how close they'd always been, it wasn't his decision to make.

"Help me unload and I'll make you dinner," she said. "I have food in the car."

He walked out the door. "I'll help you unload, but I have plans for tonight."

Really? Blue never had plans. And Louise couldn't remember the last time he turned down a free meal. "Well, thanks for coming by and lighting the stove."

"No problem. You'll need more matches soon."

"I'll get some at the store tomorrow when I stop by your shop. I want to see what you're working on."

He gave her a long look she couldn't decipher.

"You do that," he said, then headed out to the car.

* * *

Louise was back.

After they unloaded the car, Blue stood in the cold, damp night, staring out at the black void that was the lake. He knew he shouldn't have gone to the cabin tonight, but he didn't want her coming back to a cold, dark house. What kind of welcome was that?

It had taken the whole time she'd been away to get her out of his system. Well, mostly out of his system. And he was determined not to let her mess with his head again.

He looked at the warm light falling from the cabin window. Who was he fooling? As soon as Sean had said she'd be staying at the cabin for December, his longing for her had uncoiled in his gut.

It was stupid, stupid and useless because she was already at it again. Had another guy on the hook. Hadn't been back for two minutes before she dragged him out and flashed him like a trophy.

"Expecting company," he mimicked, under his breath.

Some reunion.

Blue pulled his knit cap down over his forehead. He didn't want to go back to the shop. There were problems there, too. Instead, he turned down the shoreline path toward his new house, glad there was one place he could go to get some peace. Free from the women who were messing with his head.

Chapter 3

Louise sidled up to the warm woodstove as she contemplated the pile of boxes and suitcases on the living room floor. Scrawny settled beside the stove and licked a paw, dragging it over his ear, no doubt cleaning off the dust he'd picked up under the car seat. She had to give the boy a better name. *Squatter?* Worse. *Nighthawk?* Too much like a comic book hero.

Feeling strangely deflated, she glanced at the door Blue had closed behind him. Nice of him to come by and light the fire, but why had he made other plans for tonight if he knew she'd be back? She had thought he would stay. Hoped he would anyway. What was so important that he had to run off like that?

Just as well, though. Asking Blue to stay had just been a delaying tactic. She didn't feel like eating anyway. Her stomach had been unsettled for days from the stress of finishing the course.

She dreaded going to her dad's house, but she may as well get it over with. Go over and tell him she wasn't moving back in. He'd be disappointed, but hey, had he checked with her when he married Belinda three years ago? No-o-o.

And seriously, Louise was thirty-four years old. She needed a place her own, especially if Marco was coming to visit. Her eyes lost focus for a minute as Marco's dark, sexy smile filled her mind. She could handle her dad.

She could unpack tomorrow. Tonight, she just didn't have the energy. Despite what her Fortune Bay friends may think, they worked them damn hard at the pastry course. Ten- and twelve-hour days on her feet, and the competition was fierce. Totally worn out, she needed this month to get her energy back so that she could get on with her life.

She wandered around the cabin, opening kitchen cupboard doors and the lid of the blanket box in the bedroom, but there wasn't much to see. A shelf of china figurines of dancing women that must have belonged to Augusta, the original owner of the cabin, and a black and white photograph, curtesy of Maddie. It hung on the wall beside a calendar that said *December 1999*, but with dates that, strangely, coincided with this year.

The view through the big picture window over the yellow Arborite kitchen table was a black hole at night. She glanced at her watch. Only five o'clock. The sun set so early these winter days. She should bite the bullet and go to her dad's. They were expecting her for dinner. Louise's stomach had settled, and she realized she was famished. If there was one thing she could say about Belinda, the woman could cook.

She opened a tin of food for Scrawny and put out a dish of water. As he dove into the cat food, she ran her hand down his back. Then she sprinkled some kitty litter into a cardboard box. "You just relax. I'll let you go out tomorrow."

Blue had left the fire stoked, so she shut the woodstove door, pulled on her beret and went back out to the car. Scrawny would be fine. She didn't plan to be gone for long.

Her friends Frankie and Maddie lived on either side of the cabin and for a moment she was tempted to drop in on one of them instead of going to her dad's. A girl's night sounded like much more fun than facing her father. But she recognized it for what it would be—another delaying tactic. Her friends would still be there tomorrow. She had to deal with her family first.

She drove two minutes back toward town, then inched down her dad's rutted driveway. A rainbow of Christmas lights greeted her through the trees and, as the Jeep pulled into the open, she winced at the garish effect of the gaudy lights outlining the peak, the porch and the downstairs windows. Belinda's color choice. Louise's own mother had always gone with a subtle blend of white and blue. Once again tears pricked behind her eyes.

"Oh, come on," she whispered. Her mother had been dead for seventeen years, why was she upset about it now? Probably the nostalgic effect of the lights on her childhood home. Christmas had virtually disappeared in their house after her mother died. Elise Ingstrom had always made a special fuss about the season, decorating the tree with ornaments Louise had made as a child, baking Christmas goodies and putting up the white and blue lights outside.

There had been the long, bleak stretch of years, then Belinda and Brandy had moved in. Right away, Belinda wanted to do things her way and Louise had resented every minute of it, particularly the way she hijacked their Christmas, not incorporating any of the Ingstrom's family traditions.

Yanking open the car door, Louise stepped out into the misty rain. The front door of the house burst open and Brandy bounded down the steps and threw her arms around Louise.

"We've been waiting for you," Brandy said, her voice muffled in Louise's shoulder.

The porch light came on and over Brandy's head, Louise saw Belinda, silhouetted by the kitchen lights in the open doorway.

"Get in here you two. We're not heating the whole outdoors."

Brandy started for the car. "I'll get your suitcase."

Louise slung an arm around her stepsister's shoulder and turned her toward the house. "Leave it for now."

Once on the porch, Louise pulled off her felt tam and Brandy squealed. "*Ohmygod,* look at your hair!" In her last year of high school, most of Brandy's statements were punctuated by exclamation marks.

Louise laughed and ran her fingers through her hair, releasing it from hat-hair hell. "You've never known me as a blonde. I think it's still my natural color, although it might not be quite so platinum. We'll see when it grows out."

"I love it!" Brandy ran her hands through her own straight, shoulder length, rust-colored bob. "Maybe I should dye my hair, too."

"Not on your life," her mother said. "Now get in here and close the door."

The kitchen was warm and steamy, and Louise inhaled the heady aroma of real food. Ambrosia. She'd been living on pastries and sushi for months.

"Shepherd's pie?"

"And apple crisp. I know, it's not a fancy ganache, or whatever you learned new at school this week—"

"I love your crisp," Louise interrupted. "Where's Dad?"

Her stepmother's mouth tightened and for the first time Louise noticed lines of concern around her eyes. "Watching the game. He's excited you're back."

Louise winced. This wasn't going to be easy.

Nothing had been easy with her father since his heart attack last spring. In fact, it was damn hard to see him struggle like that. To wonder if there'd be another attack. To think about losing him, too.

The gaudy Christmas lights circling the window illuminated the small living room where Henrik Ingstrom sat, dwarfed in his big recliner, watching the football game on TV. Anxiety seized Louise by the heart and squeezed. Each time she saw him he seemed to have shrunken in size.

Quickly she crossed the room and put her hand on his shoulder to stop him from trying to stand. "Dad."

Her father started, then looked up at her and smiled. "Louisie."

She sank into the chair next to him. "Who's winning?"

"Rams, those bums. Don't know what's wrong with our boys tonight."

Louise smiled. "Just an off night."

They sat in silence for a while, watching the players chase the ball around the field. Louise didn't really follow the league, but the banter of the commentators was soothing white noise, the background of her childhood. Her shoulders relaxed and she sank deeper into the overstuffed chair.

"So, are you back for good?" her dad asked, jarring her out of her mellow mood, but keeping his eyes on the game.

Following his lead, she kept her voice even. "I don't think so."

"How long?"

"Probably a month. I'll head back to Seattle after Christmas."

The Rams scored. "Bums," her dad said, and they watched the replays in silence until Belinda called from the doorway. "Dinner."

Henrik aimed the remote to turn off the TV. "They're losing anyway."

The fist gripping Louise's heart squeezed a little tighter as she watched her once-strong lumberjack father struggle to get out of his recliner. Following him into the eat-in kitchen where Belinda and Brandy were loading the table, she pulled out his chair and he carefully lowered himself into it.

"Are you getting enough exercise, Dad?"

"Ya, ya," he muttered. "You and this one here." He hitched his head toward his wife. "Always on about the exercise."

Louise bit her tongue. The doctors had been clear that her father needed exercise if he wanted to regain his strength. Or even part of it. He'd been a tall man, square in the shoulder and big in the chest. Now he met Louise's eye at just under six feet. She had a month to get him started on a healthier regime and vowed they'd go for a walk the very next day.

As she dug into the Shepherd's pie and veggies, Louise asked, "How are you for firewood?"

"We're fine," Belinda said, passing her the salad. "Foster delivered a load and Blue's been by a few times, chopping and stacking. It's all done."

Louise nodded. Just like Blue to slip in quietly when help was needed. She put *bake Blue some cookies* on her mental to-do list.

"After dinner we'll help you take your stuff up to your room," her dad said.

Louise stopped her fork halfway to her mouth. She finished the action and chewed slowly to give herself time to think of a way to break the news to him that she wasn't staying at the house. She choked down the mouthful of Shepherd's Pie but hadn't come up with anything.

"About that. Sean offered me the Murphy's cabin. I've already dropped my things off there."

Three pairs of eyes turned her way, but other than that, no one moved. Or spoke. The silence was palpable.

Then her father asked," Why on earth would you do that?" He looked more surprised than anything.

She smiled softly. "I'm a big girl, Dad. I got used to having my own place in Seattle. I'm happy to be back for Christmas, but I want my own place." No point in mentioning Marco just yet.

As her dad processed this information, Brandy piped up. "Aww. I thought you'd stay here. Isn't Sean staying at the cabin?"

"Apparently not anymore," Louise said. "Fill me in on what's been going on next door at the Murphy's while I've been away." She knew most of it already since her friend Maddie was married to Jake, one of the Murphy brothers, and Frankie and Sean, the other brother, were close to setting a date. The women had been keeping her up to date, but the topic made a good diversion.

"Well," Brandy said with emphasis, warming to the task. "You know Frankie and Sean got together."

Louise nodded, a catlike smile curling her lips. She did indeed. She liked to think she'd been instrumental in helping introverted Frankie over the hurdles of that one.

"But then, bang, right away Amber, Sean's daughter, shows up. We had no idea! Suddenly here's this Goth kid in their backyard. She's a bit younger than me—only sixteen—but even so, that means Sean had to be about that age himself when she was born." Brandie's eyes widened at the delicious scandal of this deduction.

"She has a pierced nose and three holes in each ear and long black hair—obviously dyed, 'cause her blonde roots are showing. They couldn't send her back. Apparently, there was a big scene when her grandad came to get her, but nobody liked him, and she got to stay.

"She couldn't stay in the cabin with Sean though—she didn't really know him at all—so they ended up next door at Stephanie's."

"Steph seems happy to have her granddaughter staying with her," Belinda said, sending Brandy a look. "But it's a big adjustment for everyone."

"Do you like her?" Louise asked Brandy.

"Kind of. More now than at first. We catch the school bus together. She's starting to relax, be nicer. I'm trying to help her out," Brandy added, looking to her mother for approval.

Louise held back a yawn. Finishing school and moving had really tired her out. She'd delivered her news, they were onto the apple crisp, and she found herself counting the minutes until she could go back to the cabin and climb into bed. Hopefully she wasn't getting sick. That would be such a waste of her holiday.

Her dad hadn't said anything since she announced her plans to stay at the cabin, and now, she snuck a look at him. His face looked heavy, pouches hanging under his eyes, his bulldog lips turned down at the corners.

"I'll come by tomorrow Dad. We'll go for a walk."

He brightened a bit. "Okay. I'm not walking too far yet though."

"Maybe just next door to see Stephanie and this new granddaughter of hers."

Her dad shook his head. "She's a tough one, that girl. But Stephanie will get her in line. Just needs some good family time."

Louise stood and pulled on her jacket. "It's been a long day. I think I'll be going." Brandy leaned morosely on the doorframe.

Louise gave her a hug. "Come over to the cabin any time. We'll have a sleep over, although I warn you, there's no TV."

Brandy's face lit up. "That's okay. I just want to hear about Seattle. And Marco."

Louise laughed and swatted her. "Shhh, you." She dropped her voice. "I told you that was a secret."

"Who's Marco?" her dad asked.

"Just a friend." She shot Brandy a wide-eyed, keep-your-mouth-shut look.

Then she gave her dad a hug, holding back a groan when she felt the sharp bones of his shoulder blades under the worn flannel shirt.

She kissed him softly on the cheek. "See you tomorrow, Dad."

Chapter 4

The next morning, Louise groaned as she heaved herself out of bed. She felt terrible, like day-old pizza: dry and crusty outside, but soggy within. The weak light from the window hadn't wakened her and she was shocked to see it was already nine o'clock. She knew she'd been tired, but she had slept for eleven hours.

Pulling on a heavy cardigan and slippers, she shuffled out of the bedroom. She really had to pee but stopped to open the door of the woodstove on the way by and throw a few small pieces of wood onto the glowing coals.

Scrawny greeted her like a squeaky gate. "Good morning to you too," she said.

He was waiting at the front door, back turned, tail raised to the litter box to show her exactly what he thought of that idea.

"Okay, boy. Don't get into any trouble out there." She opened the door and he darted out. A street-smart cat, he would probably do fine—as long as he wasn't carried off by an eagle.

Louise crossed the porch to a door at the far end that led to an old laundry room, now bare except for a painted dresser and deep concrete sink in the corner. From there she continued through another door into a small bathroom. She took in the deep, footed tub with the makeshift shower hanging above it. Calling it modern might be a stretch, but at least everything worked.

After a quick shower, she shook out her short hair, pleased that was all the pixie cut needed. She had no interest in spending time primping these days. Wrapping herself in a big beach towel, she ran through the cold morning air back into the cabin. The stove was doing its thing and had taken the chill off. She'd grown up with a woodstove and a wood furnace, so chilly mornings were no hardship to her. Throwing another log on the fire, she clamped the door shut and went into the bedroom.

Dressing was easy when everything was plainly styled and black or white. She grabbed a turtleneck and leggings out of her suitcase and pulled them on.

Even though she hadn't had anything to drink last night, her head felt stuffed with cotton wool. Red wine was her usual drink of choice, but lately she hadn't been in the mood.

An old electric percolator sat on the counter. It must have been Augusta's because Sean would never use something like that. A search of the cupboards didn't reveal anything better, so she was forced to face her pile of belongings on the living room floor, looking for her Italian coffee maker.

She had to unpack soon anyway. The kitchen was stocked with a combination of Sean's state-of-the-art kitchen gadgets and his Aunt Augusta's vintage implements, but Louise wanted her own equipment ready if she was going to get down to some serious baking.

In pastry school, they had worked their buns off making the prescribed list of pastries: croissants, Profiteroles and Linzer Torte, soft rolls, Focaccia and Italian bread. While Louise thought she might incorporate a few of the recipes into her repertoire, the classes had sparked a deluge of new ideas that she had written in her notebook. Now that she finally had the time, she was dying to try them out.

That was her plan for the month—visit family and friends, make, buy and bake Christmas presents for everyone, try out some of her new pastry ideas, and spend time with Marco. Lots of warm, loving time in bed because that was what they did best. It was really all they'd had time for before but maybe now, when he came to visit, there'd be time to really get to know each other.

For now, though, she'd make a cup of coffee, unpack her things and whip up a batch of Santa's Dark Secret cookies to take visiting with her today. Chocolate chip had always been Blue's favorite and with a double dose of chocolate in these, she knew he'd love them.

Straight espresso—a double shot—was usually her morning drink of choice, but her stomach was still queasy this morning, so she eased back to a latte instead. Marco called lattes "baby coffees" because that's what the children in his Italian family drank. But luckily, he wasn't here to tease her so she could do as she pleased.

She unpacked her kitchen equipment first—clothes and personal items could wait—and started chipping off nuggets from one of the twelve-ounce blocks of Belgian Callebaut chocolate she'd brought with her from the city. She couldn't get quality ingredients like that at the Fortune Bay General Store, or even in Majestic. Assessing the pile of blocks she'd brought, she hoped it would be enough to get through the month. But maybe not; it was Christmas, after all.

An hour later, the old-fashioned kitchen was redolent with the sweet, chocolaty aroma of cookies and three of the baker's boxes she'd brought with her were lined up on the counter, filled with warm gooey cookies. Throwing a log on the fire, she clamped down the damper on the stove, pulled on her tam and warm winter jacket, and stepped outside.

Yesterday's rain had vanished with the dawn and the air was bright and clear. Thirty feet from the porch, Majestic Lake lapped in quiet wavelets against the stony shore. Breathing in the crisp smell of cedar and damp fir trees, she couldn't help smiling.

When she'd left at the end of September, she couldn't wait to get out of Fortune Bay. She'd been saving for years, wanting to make a splash when she got to the city, not be stuck in a minimum-wage coffee shop job. If she wanted to work in a coffee shop, she could have stayed right here in Fortune Bay.

Her eyes sketched out the curves of the misty mountains surrounding the bay. She was eager to get back to Seattle, ready to get on with her life. But for today, she was glad to be home.

The Jeep splashed through the puddles out to the main road where she turned toward town. First on the list of people she wanted to see was Blue. She owed him that honor and wanted to thank him properly for warming up the cabin for her last night.

She swung the Jeep into the parking lot in front of his shop. The gas pumps had been pulled out years ago and the station had sat empty for another dozen years before Blue took it over, using the repair bays for his woodworking shop and converting the convenience store into an apartment.

His rickety old truck was parked on the other side of the lot but unable to suppress a grin, Louise went over to the VW-hippy van parked beside the apartment. Adam and Eve adorned the rear panels, minimally covered by flowers and the vines that coiled around to the sides of the van adding a light, colorful note to the nuclear mushroom clouds and logging clear cuts painted on the sides.

She chortled to herself. She'd forgotten to ask him about that last night. The van should be good for a couple of days of ribbing at least.

Taking the largest pack of cookies from the back seat of the Jeep, Louise approached the big bay doors of the old garage. Plumes of sawdust billowed out from under the half-raised door, along with a belt sander's grinding roar.

Holding her breath, Louise ducked inside. Blue's broad back was bent over a long tabletop. After a moment, he turned off the sander and ran a hand over the surface.

"Hi," a chirpy voice called from the corner. "Can we

help you?"

Louise turned slowly in the direction of the voice. A woman sat on a stool in the corner. A cuddly, colorful aberration in this all-man's workshop, she had on rainbow leg warmers and a long matching sweater that was pulled low over her jeans. A riot of red curls fell over her shoulders and a long red scarf unfurled from her clacking knitting needles, making her look uncannily like a Christmas elf.

No, that would be a list unfurling, Louise thought in confusion. *Who the hell is she?*

Louise turned and raised her eyebrows pointedly at Blue. His face was impassive, giving nothing away. She knew that look. She'd been in trouble with Blue enough times to know when he was hiding something.

He couldn't hide this time, but he was obviously going to try.

Louise pressed her lips together and squinted. She could wait him out.

Blue's cheeks turned pink over the top of his beard and he looked back at the tabletop, brushing some dust off its smooth surface.

"Blue?"

"Hey, Louise. Uh, I guess you haven't met Star."

Louise couldn't seem to get her eyebrows under control. They were nudging her hairline as she turned back to the woman in question. "Star?"

The elfin woman giggled. "Starlight actually, but everybody calls me Star for short. You must be Louise." She hopped off the stool, tucked the knitting under her arm and held out her hand.

Even in her turquoise, platform, leather boots, *Star* was only five-foot four, max, making Louise feel like she'd risen from the land of the giants.

She shook the elf's hand.

"Can I get you some coffee?" Star asked.

Louise blinked and turned back to Blue.

He hitched his head toward his tiny living quarters. "Star lives in the apartment."

Louise took a minute to digest this information.

"With you?" she asked, her voice rising incredulously. She immediately realized how rude that sounded, like no one would want to live with Blue. Or Star. She wasn't sure *what* it sounded like—but Blue? He hardly dated—ever—and except for herself and the Murphy's, he was pretty much of a loner.

"No," he said adamantly. "I have my own place, out of town, down on the point."

Louise frowned and shook her head. She was having trouble making sense of it all. How long had she been away? It was like she'd fallen down the friggin' rabbit hole.

"Which happened first? She moved in or you moved out?"

Star thrust a chipped mug of a fragrant steaming brew into Louise's hand, not Blue's usual sorry excuse for coffee.

"What's this?" Star chirped, taking the box out of Louise's other hand and taking a whiff. "Oooo, cookies."

"They're for Blue," Louise said as Star opened the box.

Star held them out to Blue. "They're for you. Have one. Chocolate Chip. Your favorite."

He took one from the box and bit into it. "M-mm. Really good."

Star's eyes lit up and Louise felt a crazy need to assert her ownership over the cookies. "Santa's Dark Secret."

Star took one too and bit in. "Good name." She held out the box to Louise, but the smell of the coffee had turned her stomach again.

"I just wanted to thank Blue," Louise said. So why was she talking to Star? She turned very deliberately in Blue's direction. "I wanted to thank you for coming by last night and starting the fire."

"No problem," he mumbled.

Even at the best of times, Blue wasn't exactly what you'd call a smooth conversationalist, but Louise didn't usually have a problem with that. She was used to his silences and could talk enough for them both. Now, though, with Star physically and metaphorically wedged between them, she was having trouble thinking of anything to say.

"What are you working on?" she asked, bypassing Star and walking over to run her hand along the tabletop.

"Furniture for the resort dining room. Most of it is already in. I've been putting the final coats of lacquer on over there so they don't smell up the shop. This is the last piece, recycled walnut, for the coffee station."

"It's beautiful, Blue." He looked at her and smiled his meltingly sweet smile and suddenly her old Blue was back.

Star poked her head between them. "It will look so sexy when he gets the finish on it. He's done a couple of others just like it for the reception area."

Louise leaned toward Blue, squeezing Star out of the circle.

"The resort has kept me pretty busy," he said. "In fact, with their expansion plans stretching out for the next couple of years, things are looking good. That's why I decided to move out of the office and into a real place."

"Where—" Louise started to ask, but Star butted in again.

"Lucky for me." *Teehee hee.* Okay, maybe she didn't really laugh like that, but almost.

"My van broke down right outside," Star continued. "I didn't have a dime to fix it. Blue let me park out front for a couple of days but then we had that big cold snap— remember, Blue? —and he offered me the apartment. Too bad he'd already moved out." She giggled again.

Louise stepped back. Could the woman be any more obvious? Or annoying?

She looked at Blue, but he was Mister Deadpan. Then a disquieting thought struck her, and she looked back at Star. Maybe he liked it. Maybe he liked *her*. She was kind of cute, if you liked the Christmas elf thing.

Suddenly Louise had to get out of there. "Okay. Got'ta go. Things to do, people to see."

She was almost at the door when Blue came to life. "I'm glad you're back, Lou."

She stopped, warmth washing over her, and smiled at her old friend. "Me too."

* * *

Blue let out a heavy sigh as Louise ducked under the door and walked away.

"Want another cookie?" Star asked, holding out the box.

He looked at her for a long moment. She meant well.

The morning he'd found her ridiculously painted VW van parked in the station parking lot, he'd tried to look in through the window, but it was all steamed up. So he knocked on the side door instead.

"Just a minute," a scratchy, high-pitched voice called out. The side door slid open and a head emerged from a comforter cocoon, eyes puffy, red curls askew.

"I'm sorry," were the first words out of her mouth. Her lips were a little blue. It had been friggin' cold that night. "My van broke down last night. Blowing black smoke out the back. It just chugged to a stop and I coasted in here."

"Too bad." As always, he'd been a sparkling conversationalist. Here was a bona-fide damsel in distress and all he could come up with was, *Too bad.*

Turned out she had no money. *No* money. He couldn't fathom what she'd planned to do for gas if her van had kept running. Apparently, she'd had a great summer though. Or so she said.

Well, he couldn't let her sleep in the van, not with the weather changing like that. He was just moving out of the office, so she moved right in. A couple more days, and she'd landed a job.

He didn't really mind her hanging out in the shop. She just knit in her corner most of the time, and if he got tired of listening to her talk, he just turned on the band saw or the belt sander.

But now Louise was back. He'd almost laughed at the look on her face when she saw Star in the shop. Good to let her know he wasn't just pining away, waiting for her.

And he had truly thought he wasn't, thought he'd gotten over her, until Sean said she was coming back.

What Sean hadn't said was that she had a new guy. Louise had gone out with a lot of guys but they never stuck, and usually Blue didn't worry. Not much, anyway. But this time, he was worried. This time she was bringing the guy home to Fortune Bay.

Chapter 5

Starlight. *Gag.* Who names their kid Starlight?

Sort of suited her though, all twinkly and bright. But she was pushy too, not afraid to butt in. Acting like she belonged in Blue's shop. Now that Louise was out of the workshop, she could think of a million things she'd have liked to have said to Blue, if Starlight hadn't stuck her face in the middle of their conversation. First thing would have been, where are you living?

But there'd be plenty of time to get together for a drink or three and talk over old times in the next month. Without *Starlight.*

It wasn't as if she expected Blue to be a monk, for heaven sake. It's just that he sort of was. Or had been. He'd always been there as a backup date when she needed one—as she'd been for him. But obviously, things had changed. That was okay. She had Marco and didn't need a backup anymore. Now she and Blue could just be old friends.

She pulled the Jeep into her dad's driveway and stopped beside the house. It was Friday. Brandy would be at school. She'd seen the disappointment on her sister's face the night before when she'd told her she wasn't moving home. She really loved Brandy, loved having a sister. She'd make it up to her. Plan something special for just the two of them.

Belinda worked three days a week in the school office and, unless things had changed, she'd be home today.

Louise grabbed a box of cookies and went into the house. Belinda was furiously scrubbing the sink. Probably wasn't even dirty, but she always went into a flurry of work when Louise walked in, as if she had something to prove, and forcing Louise to speak first.

She gritted her teeth. "Hi, Belinda."

As if Louise's words had thrown a switch, the other woman stopped scrubbing and turned around. "Hi, Louise. Didn't hear you pull in."

Ya, right. "Is Dad here?"

Belinda hitched her head toward the living room. "Where else would he be?"

Louise nodded, kicked off her boots and walked into the living room where her dad was in the recliner again, watching a game show on TV. *A game show.*

"Hi Dad. I brought you some cookies."

A small box. She wasn't sure cookies were on his diet. Hopefully Brandy would eat most of them.

He made a move to get up, but it was just a gesture. He quickly slumped back into his chair.

"Thanks Honey."

Louise blinked back tears. She hated to see her big, strong dad reduced to this, but forced a smile and put a cheery note in her voice that sounded, to her ears, far from natural. "Are the salmon running yet?"

"I don't know." Her dad's eyes flickered to the window.

"It's a beautiful day. Let's go for a walk and see."

His eyes were back on the TV. "I told you, I can't walk very far."

"I know. Just over to the creek. See if the fish are back."

She took her dad's arm and hauled him out of the chair. "Didn't the Doc give you some exercises to strengthen your legs?"

"Ya, I do them sometimes," he said as they walked into the kitchen. Behind his back Belinda shook her head. Obviously, he didn't. They'd work on that too.

Louise slipped into her jacket and turned to find her dad struggling to get his arm into his coat. She took it from him and held it up so he could get his arms in, then lifted it onto his shoulders. Belinda stood helplessly—uselessly—in the kitchen, watching. Why didn't she step in and help?

As they walked out the door, Belinda said, "Take your stick."

"Don't need the damn stick," Henrik muttered as Belinda reached into the closet and came out with a wooden cane with a flat hook on top. He snatched it out of her hand and shuffled out the door.

As Louise hurried out after him, she caught the pleading look in Belinda's eyes.

Henrik stood on the porch, bleakly surveying the yard. "Too damn much work."

"It doesn't look too bad," Louise said. The grass and weeds leading down to the water looked a little rougher than usual, but their yard had never been a showplace. "I'll get the lawn chairs into the shed later. Come on, let's go."

Her dad reached for the railing and she took his other arm to steady him as he walked down the three steps to the ground. He seemed less steady now than he had when she'd left in September, but once on solid ground, he straightened his back and headed to the trees at the edge of the yard with a purposeful stride.

A path led through a grove of tall firs and maples. Around their bases, thick ferns and summer grasses lay decomposing on the ground, beaten down by the recent rain and frost. Moisture sparkled on the undergrowth in the weak December sun. Fallen leaves crunched under their feet. Soon Louise heard the gurgle of water and a minute later, they came out at the creek.

In summer, the water was ankle deep and you could hop across from stone to stone, but now the river rushed in swirling rapids over stones and fallen branches. Here and there, where the water was shallow, you could see the red backs of powerful Sockeye salmon as they twined through the current between the rocks.

Henrik walked to a still pool at the edge of the boiling

water and stood with both palms on the top of his cane, staring down.

"There they are," he said, in a hoarse whisper.

In the quiet eddy below them, three big silvery fish twisted sinuous figure eights in the small pool, gathering strength for the final leg of their journey.

After fighting the rapids up the river from the open ocean to the lake, instinct had led them to the creek where they had been born. Somewhere ahead, they would find a shallow spot with a gravel bottom in which to lay their eggs before they died.

An eagle called, a tremulous descending whistle, and Louise scanned the overhead branches for the bird. The stark white head stood out against the dark evergreen boughs twenty feet down-stream where the bird sat on a branch over the river, his laser sharp eyes focused on a struggling fish. It swooped down silently, his wingspan equal to the height of a man, so near that Louise could see individual feathers on the white head and the strong, hooked beak. With a flash of white tail feathers, it beat a steady path to another perch further down the creek where it would wait to feed on the spent salmon. Cruel, but also a promise of renewal. Louise felt re-charged by this show of strength and determination.

She and her dad didn't talk as they watched the salmon fight their way up the creek. Occasionally they nudged each other and pointed out a strong exposed fin as a fish made a run at the rapids, smiling when they made it, groaning when they failed, knowing they'd try again.

Finally, her dad started coughing, a dry hacking cough that didn't sound good. A chill wind blew up the creek off the lake. Louise felt the dampness seeping into her boots and buttoned her father's jacket up to his chin.

"I'm glad you're home, honey."

"Me too, Dad. Time to head back?"

It took them much longer to get back than it had taken them to get to the creek. Her dad's pace was noticeably slower, his breath wheezing, and Louise slowed her steps to match.

Belinda was waiting at the kitchen door and whisked him inside. "Lunch is ready. Then maybe a little lie down?" She took the cane and helped him out of his jacket. "Will you stay, Louise?"

Louise felt emotionally drained by the walk with her father and was more than willing to let Belinda take over. "No thanks, I think I'll head back to the cabin. I still have unpacking to do. I'll see you tomorrow though."

Henrik slumped into a chair, obviously exhausted. Louise gave him a kiss on the cheek, and he responded with a weak smile. She pressed her lips together to hide her distress, not wanting him to see how worried she was.

Belinda followed her to the door. "Thank you for taking him out. He doesn't have much stamina and fights me when I suggest we do anything."

Louise looked at her stepmother thoughtfully. She'd never been a fan of Belinda's. After her Louise's mother died of cancer, twenty years ago when she was fourteen, she and her father had lived a lonely existence, each pulling into themselves, going their separate ways, living their separate lives. But she'd stayed with her father because he was her dad, and if she'd left, he would have been totally alone.

Gradually they had both recovered. Her dad had mostly stopped drinking and Louise had been doing okay. Then suddenly, three years ago, he'd married Belinda, almost overnight, and she and Brandy had moved in.

Belinda was much younger than Henrik, about the age Louise's mother had been when she'd died. Belinda was divorced with a teenage daughter and in Louise's mind, seemed to be grabbing a good thing in her dad when it came her way.

Louise bonded with Brandy right away. The sweet fourteen-year-old idolized Louise from the start, but Louise's relationship with Belinda had gone from awkward to downright hostile in the three years they'd lived together. Louise had stayed, not wanting to give up her rights to her dad and her childhood home, using the time to save enough money to make her move.

By last September, when she'd left for Seattle, the strain between them had become too much. In her mind, the break had been final. She was not moving back.

"I'll be back tomorrow morning to take him out again."

Belinda nodded, her shoulders relaxing slightly. Then she looked Louise in the eye. "Thank you."

"You're welcome," Louise replied awkwardly.

Visiting her dad left her all churned up, so when Louise found herself sitting in the Jeep, staring out the window, she did what she had always done when she wanted to talk. She drove next door to Stephanie's house.

Chapter 6

While Louise was growing up, the Murphy's sprawling house under the giant maples had been her second home. As a child, she would cross the creek and follow the path through the woods to the Murphy's yard. There was always room for another child at their table and as an only child, Louise had loved the noise and commotion of their boisterous family. Blue was often there too, as well as the Murphy kids, Jake, Sean, their older sister Colleen and her friends.

As far back as she could remember, Louise had been buddies with Blue and Sean, racing through the forest, building rafts on the lake in summer and generally getting into all kinds of wholesome trouble. And Stephanie had always been there with a plate of butter tarts or cookies and milk, to refuel them between adventures.

Louise let herself into the quiet back sunroom, crammed with wicker furniture and tender overwintering plants. She knocked on the kitchen door and stuck her head inside.

Stephanie's back was to the door, two, big, masculine hands planted on her ass.

"Excuse me," Louise squeaked, ducking back out onto the porch and leaning back against the door. *How awkward.*

Steph's laugh, rich as dark chocolate, echoed onto the sunporch. Stephanie threw open the door, seemingly unperturbed at being caught in a bit of noon delight. "Louise, come in."

Behind her, Max Finster beamed at Louise. Max had moved to town last summer to bring the faltering Fortune Bay Resort back to life. Louise knew he and Steph had been seeing each other but knowing and seeing are two different things.

Grinning sheepishly, she stepped inside. "Sorry to interrupt."

Stephanie swamped her in a big hug, the best welcome Louise had received so far. "You aren't interrupting. Welcome home."

Stephanie was almost as tall as Louise and in earlier times would have been called statuesque. Big, dangly earrings hung beneath her chin length, salt and pepper hair.

She pulled back and gave Louise a kiss on the cheek. "Max was just going back to work. We had lunch."

Louise's cheeks fired up again as she imagined what might have preceded their lunch. But why shouldn't Stephanie have a boyfriend? An amazing woman, an artist, her husband had died almost four years ago. She shouldn't have to spend the rest of her life alone.

Not that she was ever alone in the big old house. Sean had lived with his mother since his dad died, but he'd moved out last summer, into the cabin. Then his daughter Amber arrived, and Sean and Amber moved back in with Stephanie, although apparently, he was spending a lot of time with Frankie now. So many changes in the few months that she'd been gone!

Max extended his hand. "Nice to see you, Louise. The café hasn't been the same since you left."

She shook his hand. "How are things going at the resort? Still planning to open for Christmas?"

"Things are back on track," Max said, his eyes sparkling. "I hired an extra crew in October, and we are planning to open for a couple of weekends at Christmas, just to try everything out. The grand opening will be at Easter, but the bar will be open Friday and Saturday nights starting next week."

"Wow, finally. Some place to hang out right here in

town."

"I'm counting on the locals to keep the bar going until the real opening. That said, I'd better get back to work."

He gave Stephanie a kiss on the cheek, grabbed his hat and coat and headed for the door. "Sean and Blue are working over there this afternoon. You should drop by."

"I will. If not today, then soon."

When the door shut behind him, Louise turned to Stephanie who now had the grace to blush behind her smile. Louise felt a subtle shift had occurred in their relationship, from almost mother-and-daughter to something more like friends. "So. Max, eh?"

"We're just spending time together, two lonely old fogies."

"Funny, that's not what it looked like to me."

"Coffee? Lunch?" Stephanie asked, clearly changing the subject. Something simmered on the stove, filling the air with a tantalizing mix of Middle Eastern spices. "I have a pot of lentil soup going there."

Louise thought of the cabin, how cold it probably was by now, and definitely with no pot of soup on the go.

She held out the last box of cookies. "I can't stay long though. I have lots to do at the cabin. Thanks, by the way, for letting me stay there for the month." Sean might be the cabin's current tenant, but Stephanie was the actual owner, having inherited the building from her Aunt Augusta when she died.

"It's mostly sitting empty these days so you might as well keep the fire going. Sean is either at the resort, at Frankie's or here with Amber."

Louise blew on a spoonful of soup she'd scooped out of the pot. "I still haven't met her. I can't believe all the changes. Years went by and nothing seemed to happen, then I leave for a few months and it's like a tornado blew through town."

Stephanie laughed. "I think Amber is the biggest change. She's quite a handful but a good kid. I think we got her just in time, before her grandfather had a chance to ruin her life, like he did her mother's."

"Sean sounded happy when I spoke to him."

"He never wanted to give her up, but Amber's grandfather, Lacey's dad, insisted. Actually, Sean's dad insisted too. But in the end, Lacey never put Amber up for adoption and the poor child lived all these years with that terrible man."

"And her mother?"

"Died. Drugs. Amber got a dose of reality much too young. We're doing our best to help her adjust to her new life here."

"I can't think of a better surrogate mother than you."

"And how about you?" Stephanie asked as she put a bowl of soup on the table for Louise. "You sticking around?"

"No."

"I thought not." Stephanie looked at the table for a moment, then looked back up. "Have you been to see your dad?"

"We went for a walk this morning. Not far, but it's a start."

"Belinda tries, but he gives her a terrible time."

"Really?"

"It's not uncommon for men to turn their anger on their wives when they suddenly feel they are not the men they used to be."

"Well," Louise said, "I'm here now and I'll try to help them over this hump."

"Good. And how was the course?" Stephanie sat down across the table from Louise.

"It was great. At the end, I won the trophy."

"Honey, that's wonderful!" Stephanie reached across the

table and grasped her hand. Louise teared up. She'd missed Steph and realized that while grappling with the changes she found on her return, she hadn't told her family, or Blue, about the Pretzel. Steph was the only one who'd asked.

"So, what are your plans."

"I am going back to Seattle after Christmas, to look for a job. The Golden Pretzel—"

Stephanie's eyebrows raised in amusement.

"Hey, don't laugh. That's what the award is called. It's very prestigious and should open a few doors."

Stephanie managed to control her expression. "I'm sure it will. Did you keep your apartment?"

"No. Not sure yet what I'm going to do about that. I have a friend there I might be able to stay with for a while." Now it was her turn to blush.

Stephanie's gaze sharpened. "A male friend?"

"Yeah." Louise concentrated on her soup. Tried to keep it casual. "He's probably coming to visit. You can meet him then."

Everyone would meet Marco then. But now that she was back in the familiar surroundings of Fortune Bay, she had to wonder if he'd like it, if he'd fit in, if inviting him had been a mistake.

* * *

Normally Blue would have chosen a hand-rubbed French polish to finish a tabletop rather than a thick layer of acrylic polymer, but Max wanted the dining room tables at the resort to withstand constant spills and wiping and still come up shining. So acrylic it was.

Dipping his brush into the can, he applied the finish to the last edge of the table then moved on to the next one. The bank of French doors to the lake were wide open but the fumes were still intense. When he finished, he'd close the doors and let the tables cure in the warm room, glad he could leave and escape the fumes rather than have sixty square smelly tables cluttering up his shop.

Sean breezed into the dining room. "It's freezing in here."

Blue glanced up but didn't feel that comment required an answer. Sean grabbed a stool from the bar and pulled it over to where Blue was working and perched on top, hands thrust in his pockets and shoulders hunched against the cold.

"Don't you feel it? How can you work in just a t-shirt?"

"Maybe because I'm actually working, not playing on the computer all day."

Sean always looked sharp, hell even his jeans looked like he'd ironed them. Blue knew the marketing plan Sean was drawing up was crucial to the success of the resort and to all of their futures, but he wasn't about to tell him that.

"So, she's back," Sean said.

Again, a statement that didn't merit a response. They both knew who Sean meant, and Blue was kicking himself for the hundredth time—make that the millionth time—for spilling his guts to Sean about Louise all those years ago. Granted, Sean had kept the information to himself. Blue had to give him that. There was, after all, a guy's code of honor. They may have let Louise tag along, well, forever, but somewhere around eighth grade they'd stopped telling her absolutely everything. Especially where Blue's feeling for her were concerned.

He'd worried once or twice over the years, when Sean was really angry or when Louise did something really hurtful, that Sean would just out and tell her. But he never did. Guy's code.

But the jerk was still sitting there staring at him. Finally, Blue blurted out, "Yeah. But she's not staying. She has a boyfriend."

"Jeeze, man, you have to step in. All the more reason if she's not planning to stay. This might be your last chance to tell her how you feel."

Ever since Sean and Frankie had gotten together, the guy thought he could hand out advice on relationships. Okay, he'd always been better with women than Blue. A friggin' golden boy in fact. But in this case, he didn't know what he was talking about.

"Didn't you hear me? She has a boyfriend."

Sean snorted. "How long is that going to last?"

"Sounds serious this time."

"How do you know?"

"She looked serious. Says he's coming to visit."

Sean shrugged. "Your life, your loss. It's friggin' freezing in here." He walked through the wooden arch Blue had carved with swimming salmon, out of the dining room and back to his office.

How could Sean possibly understand? Sure, he'd had his problems, but Blue couldn't remember Sean ever being rejected by a woman. Not like Blue, who, idiot that he was, had carried a torch for Louise even though she'd made it clear years ago that she wasn't interested in him as anything more than a friend.

He'd been a big kid and when he started to grow, he got even bigger, carrying a lot of extra weight. Baby fat, his mother called it. She thought that explained it, made it better, but to a thirteen-year-old boy with raging hormones, calling it baby fat only made things worse.

Unlike the other kids, Louise had never teased him. They were friends and that's all that she seemed to see, not his big awkward body. And for that, he'd loved her ever since he could remember.

She grew too, like a colt, with long legs that were built for speed. Even at thirteen, she took his breath away.

The problem was that as they grew up, she still only saw

him as a friend. Nothing more. A confidant she felt comfortable talking to about her next crush. And although she always picked the worst possible guys, she didn't want to hear about it from him. So he just stood by and watched, there to pick up the pieces every time she crashed.

And crash she did. Time after time. But she rebounded quickly and each time he told himself that the guys must not mean that much to her. If they were good looking and had a fast car, that seemed to be all that mattered.

He wondered what kind of car this guy drove. And if this time it was worth waiting around to pick up the pieces.

Chapter 7

The buzz of an incoming text woke Louise from a sound sleep that left her struggling to swim to the surface. She smiled groggily at the text on her phone. It was from Maddie. *Are you back? Why haven't I seen you?*

She texted back. *I'll be right over. Call Frankie.*

She had returned from Stephanie's at two-thirty in the afternoon to find Scrawny sitting guard on the mat outside the front door, looking perfectly at home.

"You survived," she said, scooping him up and rubbing his ears as she let herself in. Once inside, though, he struggled to get loose and went straight for his dish.

She popped a log in the stove and opened the damper, then lay down on the bed—she couldn't have kept her eyes open for another minute and—*yikes!*—now it was five-thirty and already dark. She must be coming down with something to be so tired.

She found her medicine bag in the clutter of debris in the bedroom and rooted around for the bottle of vitamin C. Popping two with water, she took stock of her cookie inventory. Running low, but still enough perfect ones to fill one more white cardboard box. She checked herself out in the mirror. *Loving this haircut.* A quick ruffle and she was ready to go.

The framed black and white photograph that hung on the wall beside the mirror had probably been taken in the nineteen-forties or early fifties. A woman who must be Augusta grinned out the side window of an old car with a split windscreen.

Sean had told her about his encounters with the ghost of his Great-Aunt Augusta last summer when he'd lived in the cabin, small incidents that were corroborated by Maddie and Jake who had both lived there too at various times. They'd assured her the ghost of Sean and Jake's great aunt had a noticeably maternal bent.

"Are you still here?" Louise murmured as she gathered up the cookies. "Will you look after me too?"

And damn if the lights didn't flicker. She looked at the dark window but didn't hear any wind outside.

"Okay then," she murmured and, grabbing a flashlight, she turned off the lights in the cabin, leaving one burning on the porch.

The shoreline path ran past Frankie's, then the cabin, then Maddie's house, continuing around the bay past Stephanie's, finally ending in the village of Fortune Bay. In good weather, it was the quickest way to get from one house to the other, considering the length of their driveways.

It wasn't actually raining tonight, just the light mist that passed for good weather in December in Fortune Bay. The round beam from her flashlight bobbed along the well-worn path that ran along the shore and to her left she could hear the soft rustle of waves on the gravel beach.

Soon she emerged from the trees, into the field where Maddie and Jake had built their new house. At their wedding last summer, she and Blue had been paired up as bridesmaid and groomsman, and now the memory of dancing the first dance together under the trees swirled back around her. He'd been so handsome in his suit—she'd been amazed at how well he'd cleaned up—and when he'd taken her in his arms she'd been, well, slightly overwhelmed by the sheer size of him. Blue was built like a linebacker and made her feel small and delicate—no mean feat with her at five foot ten. What had happened to her soft, pudgy friend? When had he turned into this hunk of a guy?

Jake's old dog Rex let out a faint woof when Louise climbed their back steps. As she knocked on the door, he rubbed up against her and she gave his head a pat. Then a heat-seeking missile from out of nowhere almost knocked her off her feet. A puppy, probably five months old and already eighteen inches high at the shoulder, bounced and leapt and licked her face, demanding love.

Laughing, Louise let herself into the big country-style kitchen, then stopped for moment just inside the door. Maddie sat at the dining room table with Sarah, Jake's seven-year-old daughter, Maddie's head of paprika curls bent close to Sarah's over her homework. Dinner—it smelled like chicken—bubbled on the stove.

Louise softened at the sight of such quiet domesticity. She knew Maddie had worried she'd end up alone when her daughter Jenny went away to college this year, and now here she was with a whole new family. After the struggle of raising Jenny alone, Maddie deserved every ounce of happiness.

Sarah looked up from her work and squealed, "Louise!" Jumping out of her chair, Sarah ran over to hug her around the waist.

Louise ruffled her hair. "I swear you've grown another foot."

Sarah straightened to her full height. "Two inches since last spring," she proudly announced.

Louise looked Maddie over as she came toward her and yup, her face was noticeably fuller. Maddie was pregnant. She had told Louise on the phone a few weeks ago. Louise looked for a telltale bump but apart from her obviously fuller breasts, she wasn't showing yet.

For someone like Louise, who was not what you'd call well endowed, that part of pregnancy would be a bonus. But that wasn't the hand she'd been dealt. A series of events in her teens, culminating in a brutal miscarriage, had conspired to leave her a loner. The doctors had told her it was doubtful she could ever conceive. So, she'd moved on.

What else could you do?

Maddie gave her a warm hug. Gone was that emotionally distant, isolated woman who moved to Fortune Bay a year and a half ago. Love and marriage certainly agreed with her.

Louise stepped back and looked her over

"You're not showing yet."

"I have a few weeks yet."

"How far along are you?"

"Almost three months. I'll be glad to hit that twelve-week gateway. They say after that the morning sickness lets up and your energy comes back. I'm convinced the two things are related. Surely being sick as a dog every day saps your strength."

Louise grinned. "Sounds like fun. Sign me up. But you look wonderful."

"I feel wonderful, except for the nausea. This is the way to do it though, not like when I had Jenny. Although Mark and I stayed together for six years after Jenny was born, I already knew when I was pregnant that it wasn't working. The stress while I was carrying her was horrible. Now, with Jake, it's totally different. We really wanted to have a child together." Maddie turned all soft and googley-eyed. "None of the tension or worry. Only the joy."

The kitchen door opened behind them and Frankie came in, shaking water droplets off her raincoat like a dog.

"It's pouring now," she said. "I walked. Stopped by the cabin—I thought you'd wait for me. It'll be fun having you next door."

Maddie nodded. "The three of us right in a row."

Frankie hung up her jacket and Louise gave her a long hug. Then she held out a bottle of wine to Louise, saying to Maddie with a wincing smile, "Sorry, but you can't have any."

"I know. I don't mind. I probably couldn't keep it down anyway. Louise brought chocolate cookies. They look amazing. I'll hide them until after dinner. You're both staying, aren't you?"

The phone rang and Maddie answered. "Mm-hmm." She shot Frankie and Louise a look. "Yes, they are... Okay. See you later."

Putting down the phone, she turned to the women. "Jake says 'hi.' He figured you'd be here, so he went over to Sean's place to watch the football game."

"Sean doesn't really have a place. He's always at my house or Stephanie's," Frankie said.

"Now I feel guilty for taking the cabin," Louise said.

Frankie shook her head. "Don't. They never watched the game there anyway. No cable. They probably went to Stephanie's. Amber's into football too, or seems to be. Or maybe she just likes to have a non-verbal guy-way to hang with Sean. They are still feeling their way into their relationship."

"And how about you?" Louise asked Frankie as she opened the wine. "How do you feel about suddenly becoming a step-mother?"

"I'm not really Amber's step-mother. For one thing, Sean and I aren't married and for another, Amber's pretty clear she doesn't need a mother. Have you met her yet?"

"Haven't had the pleasure."

Frankie raised her eyebrows and nodded wisely. "Hm-m-m."

Louise grinned. "Can't wait. I hear she's a firecracker."

"That would be one way to put it." Frankie scooped her straight brown hair back over her shoulders.

"Time for a trim?" Louise asked. "Or are you letting it grow again."

Frankie laughed. "Sean wouldn't let me go back to the braid, and I wouldn't want to. I think I'll let it grow some more before I get it cut again though. Last time was pretty traumatic."

Neither of them had mentioned her own hair and Louise ran her fingers through it. "Notice anything different about me?"

Frankie looked her up and down. "I'll say. This all-black is a new look for you."

Maddie nodded.

Louise frowned. "What about my hair?"

Frankie and Maddie kept straight faces for another few seconds, but then looked at each other and burst out laughing. "Stephanie warned us, so we agreed to wait and see how long it took for you to mention it," Frankie said. "It looks amazing."

Maddie nodded. "Very cool. So urban. Is that your real color?"

"Who knows? I had it black for so long I can't remember. I'm going to let it grow out a bit and see. Whatever color it is, it'll look cool with frosted tips. But I think I'll keep it short for a while."

"How long was it black?" Maddie asked.

"Since I was fifteen. It was a Goth thing."

Her two friends burst into giggles.

"You were Goth?" Maddie asked.

"More Grunge, I guess. It wasn't a really well thought out statement, more a reaction to my Mother's death."

Her friends sobered immediately. Louise grimaced. "I kind of overreacted."

Frankie put a hand on her arm. "There is no 'overreacting' to the death of a parent. I was only five when my mom died. I hardly remember her at all, but it still had a tremendous effect on me and my Dad. I can't imagine what it must be like to be a teenager and have your world ripped apart like that."

"It was rough for a few years, but then ..." Louise shrugged. She rarely talked about those years. "So, yeah, Grunge, or whatever. Torn clothes, black hair, heavy eye make-up, Doc Martins."

Maddie and Frankie laughed. "I hope you have pictures," Maddie said.

Louise smiled, glad to let the moment pass. "A few. The thrill wore off after a few years. Then I got into more colorful retro styles—"

Frankie rolled her eyes. "You can say that again."

"But this look works with the white chef's gear, and I'm kind of enjoying my new urban lifestyle."

Maddie's face fell. "So, you're planning to go back?"

"Definitely. I won an award—"

"Wow!"

"No kidding?"

"It should really help when I go back and I'm looking for a job after Christmas."

There was an awkward silence, then Maddie said quietly, "We were all hoping you'd come back and stay."

Louise bit her top lip and winced. "I know. But you have to understand. You two are new here. I've been in Fortune Bay all my life. I finally got away. You don't know what it was like to grow up here and never see the rest of the world."

"I haven't seen as much of the world as Frankie," Maddie said. "But from what I have seen, Fortune Bay is the best."

Louise knew Maddie had a rough time growing up. "But I've been here *all my life.*"

"What was it like growing up here?" Frankie asked, pouring two glasses of wine and a mineral water for Maddie.

Louise laughed. "Pretty darn great, actually. I was a tomboy, hung out with Blue and Sean. Rode our bikes from dawn 'til dusk, built forts in the forest—all that kind of stuff. We used to drive Jake nuts. He was two years older and we tagged after him and his friends. The Murphy's house was our second home."

"So why do you want to leave?" Maddie asked.

"It was great when I was *a kid*. I worked at the café for ten years—more, if you count high school. There has to be something better. I want a change, some excitement."

Maddie and Frankie exchanged a look, then, with innocent smiles on their faces, rested their elbows on the table and their chins in their hands and looked expectantly at Louise.

"And you found some 'excitement' in the city?" Frankie asked.

"What's his name?" Maddie added.

"Yes, okay, I'm seeing someone." Louise felt nerves start to jump in her stomach. She'd often regaled them with comically embellished stories of dates gone awry but had never before had a possibly-serious relationship to discuss with her friends.

"His name is Marco and he's a chef, one of the instructors at the Academy. But he finished there yesterday and is going out on his own. I might stay with him, for a while at least, when I go back."

"For a while?" Maddie asked.

"We haven't been going out together for very long. In fact, we've hardly gone *out* at all. We weren't supposed to be dating. It's *verboten* for instructors to date students." She thought of the hot nights spent in her tiny room in the Seattle apartment and heat sparked in her belly.

"How long have you been seeing him?" Frankie asked.

"Almost two months. Pretty well the whole time I was away."

"Two months? That's a long time for you. And you're not ready to pull the plug yet? Must be serious."

"More serious than most, I guess. He's a bit older, and gorgeous. But it might be time to call it quits."

Maddie looked confused. "Why?"

Frankie rolled her eyes. "Louise thinks that if she gets too close to someone, something terrible will happen."

"It's not that exactly," Louise said.

"I know," Frankie said gently. "More like you don't want to get hurt."

Louise looked at her sharply.

"Sean might have mentioned something." Frankie mumbled.

"Yes, well, I learned that lesson early. When I was in my teens first my mom died, then I fell in love with a guy and *he* died." She waved her hands, as if it wasn't important. "It's just easier this way." This was something she never talked about and she didn't plan to start now.

Maddie and Frankie exchanged a look and Frankie asked, "So this new guy, is he a pastry chef too?"

"No, a culinary chef. A chef chef. He's heavily into *charcuterie*, spiced and smoked meats."

"Deli meats?"

Louise grinned. "To the uneducated masses."

Maddie's skin turned pale. "Can we talk about something besides food?"

"Sure," Louise said. A beat passed and they all took a drink, then she said, "So what's up with Star?"

She had promised herself she wouldn't ask, but it just slipped out. What Blue did with his time was his own business and besides, she was with Marco now.

"She seems nice," Frankie said cautiously. "Fun to be around."

Somehow, coming from ultra-serious Frankie, this didn't really sound like a compliment.

"She seems kind of flakey," Louise said. "I mean, seriously? Starlight? And how could she *completely* run out of money right in front of Blue's workshop?"

"It is kind of hard to understand," Maddie agreed.

"Are they dating?"

Frankie frowned. "I'm not sure."

"I think he let her rent the office just to be nice," Maddie added.

Nice. Maddie was so naive. Although this *was* Blue, and he *was* very nice, he was also a guy and in Louise's experience, guys always had an ulterior motive that usually involved sex.

"Well, good for him," Louise said, trying to put some enthusiasm into her voice.

Good for him.

Chapter 8

The next day Louise pulled out her course notebook. It bristled with papers and post-its and big red stars indicating recipes she wanted to work on after the course. Tinker with. Make her own. But today as she leafed through the book, she was looking for something special to bake for Christmas.

They'd made *Stollen* in class, the German yeast bread with almonds and dried fruit and a marzipan filling, but it hadn't quite satisfied her Christmas cravings. She wanted the recipe for the Christmas bread her mother had made, the Scandinavian version, flavored with cardamom. That was the taste she remembered.

Tomorrow, when she went back to her dad's house, she'd look for her mother's recipe book.

Putting on the kettle, she spooned coarse ground coffee into her French-press. While she waited for the kettle to boil, she saw a small wooden box she hadn't noticed before sitting on the counter. Small enough to sit on the palm of her hand, the carving on the top looked like a local scene. It looked old enough to have been Augusta's. Picking it up, she saw that the box was so full of recipe cards that the lid didn't quite close. When she opened the box, the smell of fragrant spices drifted out. She sniffed again, detecting in the mix the strong, smelling-salts aroma of cardamom.

One card stuck up an eighth of an inch past the others and her hand automatically plucked it out. Written across the top of the card in a spidery hand were the words, *Swedish Coffee Bread, Sven's mother's recipe.*

She read through the list of ingredients: yeast and egg, sugar and flour, nuts, dried fruit and there at the end, cardamom. She'd brought a few spices with her, but that wasn't one of them. A quick scan of the cupboards, however, revealed, front and center, a bottle of the green seedpods. Twisting open the lid, she took a sniff. Her eyes sprang fully open as the sharp aroma rushed through her sinuses.

She set the yeast to proof in warm water and prepared her ingredients, painstakingly peeling the papery husk off the cardamom pods and grinding the tiny black seeds to a fine powder with her porcelain mortar and pestle.

While the dough was rising, she started a batch of Swedish rusks, tiny buns, also flavored with cardamom, that were split in half after they were baked, then second baked to crunchy goodness. Not too sweet, they were just what she felt like today with coffee for breakfast. She made a quarter recipe to try it out and when she tasted one and checked the recipe, she realized it didn't include salt, so she added 'a pinch of salt' to the card.

By noon, the kitchen smelled like warm spice and the rusks and coffee bread rings were cooling on racks on the counter. She still had one more visit to make, so she loaded another box with the last of the cookies, filled the extra space with rusks, and headed out to the car.

After her mother had died, The Fortune Bay General Store had been her refuge in town. She'd worked there, stocking the shelves all through high school, helping the cook in the café on weekends and eventually, when she was in her twenties, she took over running the café. Without Fiona, the owner of the store, and Stephanie, Louise didn't know how she would have survived those difficult years.

At the sight of the short, slight woman behind the counter, Louise's heart warmed. A baggy colorless sweater hung on her narrow shoulders and a pencil stuck through the knot of hair on top of her head. Fiona didn't look a day older, or younger, than she had twenty years ago when

Louise first started working for her at the store.

Fiona's normally gruff expression softened into a smile when Louise came through the door and she came out from behind the counter to give her a warm hug. "I heard you were home. Wondered when you'd get around to paying me a visit."

"Home for a while," Louise said, and handed her the box.

Fiona lifted it to sniff. "Smells like Christmas." She may have had Scot's blood in her veins, but she'd been married to a Swede for forty years.

Louise smiled. "Just trying out a few things."

"We could use you back baking for the café." Fiona glanced over her shoulder and lowered her voice. "The new girl is good, but her baking leaves something to be desired. People are grumbling."

Louise grinned. "Always nice to be appreciated. I'll have to check it out."

She walked over to the arch in the wall beside of the till and poked her head into the café to take a look. A counter with six twirly red stools took up most of the room. After all the years she'd spent filling coffee cups and plates from behind the counter, she felt she was on the wrong side of the looking glass, looking at the person who had taken her place.

"Starlight."

It wasn't a greeting, more of an accusation. Of what, though, she wasn't sure since she'd left the job of her own free will. Still, seeing the little elf behind the counter felt like a slap in the face. Like she'd been replaced.

"Hi, Louise." Star was her normal chirpy self, seemingly unaware of the effect her presence at the café had on Louise. "What can I get you?"

"Nothing." Okay. That was harsh. "Just stopping by to say hi."

"Must feel weird to be back."

"You can say that again."

"Here. Have a muffin." Using tongs to take one out of the glass cake server, Star wrapped it in a napkin. "On the house."

"Thanks. Um, I have to run. Things to do..."

Louise backed out of the café into the store. Fiona was busy with customers, so Louise gave her a half-wave and left.

Standing on the stoop in the raw, damp air, she bit into the muffin, chewed for moment, then leaned over and spat the mouthful into the trash. The rest followed.

Sawdust.

Somehow that made her feel significantly better.

Across the road, a big carved sign welcomed visitors to the Fortune Bay Resort. Having seen virtually everything Blue had ever made, she recognized the sign as a piece of his work. He'd outdone himself this time. A Bald Eagle sat on a treetop with mountains and the lake in the background and the resort's name carved in flowing script. The man was an artist in wood.

Louise crossed the road and walked down the driveway, through the trees and into the resort parking lot. The property used to be part of the old mill site, but the mill had closed seven years ago. The rest of the mill site was a waste land, buildings gone, most of the debris burned or hauled away, Scotch broom and blackberries taking over. But the mill had never built on this piece of land, a forested point with water on both sides.

Max had situated the main building of the resort to take advantage of the view of the mountains and the bay, which was now even clearer since the fire in October had burned down the trees between the parking lot and the lake. New trees, dogwoods and other native ornamentals now grew where the burnt stumps had been. Someone was on the ball getting them in so quickly. They'd be small but blooming in time for the spring Grand Opening.

The outside of the main building was finished West Coast style, all warm cedar and local rock, with tall windows overlooking the water. Although it was Saturday, the parking lot was filled with tradesman's vans, including Blue's old, flat deck truck. Louise climbed the steps and grabbed the bronze handle of the tall glass door, surprised by how easily it swung open.

The lobby was a hive of activity, men and women, each on a mission, all hurrying in different directions. A cathedral ceiling soared a full two stories, held aloft by giant wooden beams, and a river-stone fireplace took up most of one wall.

Voices she recognized drifted through the square arch of a doorway where salmon, carved into the wood, swam up one side of the doorway and down the other. Blue wasn't kidding when he said the resort was keeping him busy, apparently with carving as well as furniture making.

In the dining room, Sean and Blue were deep in discussion and didn't notice her as she stood in the doorway. Louise stared at her two old friends. Being away for even this short time had made her aware that they had all grown up.

And Blue, well, her heart skipped a beat as he lifted a solid wood table up over his head and put it down in an empty space on the floor. She thought back to how he hadn't hugged her when she'd arrived or when she stopped in at the shop. She wanted a warm, welcoming bear hug from this man, and felt a little lost without it.

Then she frowned. Why *hadn't* he hugged her when she got to the cabin? She wasn't imagining the distance between them. It was real. Were his feelings hurt because she'd been so preoccupied with the pastry course? Or did it have something to do with Star?

Then Sean said, "Well, it's time you stopped mooning and did something about it."

"About what?" she asked.

Both men turned toward her. Blue looked guilty as sin, but Sean scarcely missed a beat. With his angelic features, he'd always been the best liar in the group. "Hi. Welcome back."

Louise was exactly the same height as Sean, but he had never been intimidated by that. He walked over and gave her a hug, then reached up and ruffled her newly blonde hair.

She laughed, then gestured around the dining room, a large open room with exposed rafters and two outside walls composed of sets of French doors leading onto a wraparound deck. "This is great. Are you really going to be ready to open for the weekend before Christmas?"

"Actually, we have to have the mess cleared out by the fourteenth. There's a Christmas fair booked for that weekend," Sean said.

"I haven't heard about that."

"We've invited a bunch of local artists and artisans to set up booths in the dining room before we load in the chairs. I've been promoting it all the way to Seattle. I'm hoping it'll be a big event. Kind of a sneak peek at the resort."

"Great idea." Louise cocked her head. "You really are cut out for this job."

Sean's face broke into a broad smile. "I love it."

He looked happy, not just smiling because it was his go-to way of dealing with things but truly happy. With the job, and Frankie and Amber, it all seemed to be falling into place for him.

She turned to Blue. "Are you taking part?" He was standing silently off to the side, arms crossed over his broad, checked-shirted chest and she just wanted to bust her way through the solid wall he'd seemed to have thrown up between them.

"I'll have a table with some carvings. Max insisted. He

wants to show them off since I did so much of the finishing work here at the resort. He bought my carving of a bear and plans to auction it off. Give the money to the fire department. They really saved his neck the night of the fire."

Louise shook her head. "I feel like I've been gone for a year, so much has happened."

"You haven't met Amber," Sean said.

"I'm dying to."

"Come for dinner. Not tonight, there's a meeting at the fire hall. Tomorrow night. Both of you."

"Where?" she asked.

"My Mom's. Amber lives at my Mom's now so I'm there most of the time."

"I'll bring something. Veggies?"

Sean shrunk back in mock horror. "Oo-oo. The great chef. I don't know if I can compete."

Louise punched him in the shoulder. "See you at six." She turned to Blue. "You going, big guy?" And would he bring Star? Were they a couple now?

"Sure. If you two are cooking, I'm in."

Max walked into the dining room, deep in discussion with an assistant. When he saw Louise, his eyes lit up. "We'll finish this later," he said to the young man, and hurried over to greet her.

"Louise." He took her hand and tucked it into his arm, drawing her away. "What do you think of the resort?"

"It's amazing. I mean, last summer when I was working across the road at the café, I watched it grow from a muddy hole in the ground into an actual building. But when I left, it was still pretty rough. I had no idea it would turn into this."

They stopped at the wall of French doors that linked the dining room to a porch that ran the length of the building. Max said, "In summer we'll open this up and let the customers eat on the deck. Breakfast by the lake. It will be fantastic." His eyes shone. She could tell he didn't see the rain dripping off the eves, but instead, soft morning light and fish jumping in the lake.

"Sounds wonderful."

"Wait until you see the kitchen."

He towed her across the large room to a pair of swinging doors, each with a round window at eye level. He threw open the doors with a flourish and Louise blinked, almost blinded by the white tile and gleaming stainless-steel counters and appliances inside.

"State of the art," Max said proudly.

"I can see," Louise said as she slowly walked in, head pivoting from left to right.

"Oh," she breathed. "A twelve burner Vulcan cook top with double ovens." She was having palpitations, thinking about the old turquoise range at the cabin that she'd used this morning. She ran her hand lovingly along the brushed steel front. How many Stollen could she bake at once in this baby?

"You bet. Nothin' but gas," he said, bursting with pride.

"And here." He tugged at her arm, but she had trouble tearing her eyes off the ovens.

"The pastry area," Max said, and her eyes snapped to the stainless counter in front of her.

"You have a dedicated pastry area?" Her voice was hollow with awe.

"When we're up and running next spring, I plan to have all breakfast pastries, breads and desserts made in-house. Now I just have to find someone to bake them."

He was grinning from ear to ear. "You know, I always loved your baking when you worked at the café. Now that you're a real pastry chef, they must be through the roof. I want you to come and work for me."

Louise's throat dried up and she felt the blood drain from her face. "Oh no, it's too soon. I just graduated last week. You have to work your tail off for years to get a job in a kitchen like this."

"I trust you, Louise. If you could run that café by yourself, six days a week for all those years, you, and one or two staff, can run this end of the kitchen."

"One or two staff..."

"To start. We'll see how you manage. We can hire more if we need to."

Her knees gave out. There were no stools in the kitchen, so she sank onto the cool tile floor.

Max hardly seemed to notice, he was stalking the room, pointing to the empty shelves and talking a blue streak.

"I've ordered everything we need, it's being delivered next week, although of course there might be other things that you need. No problem. Make a list. Our new investor is very understanding," he chuckled. "He wants this place to be a success, and that means a dynamite kitchen."

"Your new investor?" Louise was having trouble keeping up.

"Philip Alvarez. Frankie's dad."

"Right." Frankie had phoned Louise in Seattle when she reunited with her father, but the details hadn't really sunk in.

"And the chef?"

"Don't have one yet. Any suggestions?"

"Not off the top of my head."

"But what about you as pastry chef? What do you say?"

Max was looking at her with a smile on his face. Louise realized she was sitting on the floor and pushed to her feet.

"It is a fabulous offer, Max, but I don't have enough experience. I just finished the course. And I'm not planning to stay in Fortune Bay. I'm going back to Seattle."

Max's face fell. "You don't need to start right away. I can hire the baker in Majestic to supply us for the week we are open between Christmas and New Year's, but I was hoping..."

Louise shook her head. "Sorry, Max. You're going to have to find another pastry chef."

Chapter 9

Louise ran her soapy hands over her shoulders and let the hot water beat down on her back, thankful everything worked in the cabin's hokey little bathroom.

She'd been home for four full days and Marco hadn't called. She'd texted him yesterday and he'd shot back a quick note—he was moving, busy packing, he'd let her know when he could come—but that was all. She slid her hands over her soap-slicked breasts. They were tender and swollen. Sometimes she felt so horny right before her period—and this seemed to be one of those times.

Closing her eyes, she imagined she wasn't alone in the shower, that a man was there and running his hands over her body. Strong hands rubbing her breasts, soft lips kissing her neck and his big brawny body pressing her into the tiles.

Wait a minute. That wasn't Marco. He was scarcely any taller than she was, and certainly not brawny.

Louise opened her eyes and reached for a washcloth, a faint smile tugging one side of her lips. It had been years since she'd fantasized about Blue and, *oh my god,* had he ever grown into the role. She couldn't help noticing, the night she'd arrived when she'd fallen into his arms. He'd always been bigger than she was, but when had all that extra weight turned into muscle? He used to be quiet, shy and awkward, but now he seemed strong, silent and, well, kinda' hot.

Gruff and growly, sure, but he'd come by to warm up the cabin for her. That was so Blue.

Her brows pulled together as she remembered how he'd seemed to shut her out, that first night, at his shop and then again at the resort. She didn't know why. He was her oldest friend and it hurt that he didn't seem to want to hang out anymore.

Okay, to be honest, she hadn't called him much from Seattle and, come to think of it, not at all for the last month. But he hadn't called her either. Why was she always the one who had to reach out?

There was that one time, when they were teenagers, that he *had* reached out, and she remembered with chagrin how clumsily she had rejected his advance. But it was right after Tony, her first love, had died. She was broken, in a black fog, not in any shape to start a new relationship. And, well, it was Blue.

He'd understood, or seemed to, and had backed right off. He had probably only been trying to comfort her anyway. After that, luckily, they'd gone back to being buddies, best friends really, because she couldn't think of a better friend. Sean was great, but that was different. He'd always have her back—just look at how he came through with the cabin—but they weren't confidants. Not like she was with Blue.

But other than that one time years ago, there had never been anything sexual between them—except maybe at Jake and Maddie's wedding last summer, when they were dancing together, and she thought...

But no... It turned out to be nothing. She must have imagined that. There never had been anything between them, which made these thoughts she was having about him now just plain weird. Her hormones barking.

But he was certainly looking buff these days, that she couldn't deny. They'd both grown up while she wasn't looking.

She climbed out of the tub and towelled herself off, noticing again the soreness in her breasts. Pulling on a robe, she made a quick dash through the icy morning air, across the porch and into the cabin, shutting the door behind her.

Then she stopped, and thought. Sore breasts. Upset stomach. She raced to the calendar on the wall.

Her last period had ended immediately before that night she'd brought Marco home from the concert. Their first date. She'd just had her hair bleached and hacked off short and was feeling her oats: urban, sexy and free. Marco was older, brooding and totally hot. A deadly combination.

Looking at the calendar now, she realized that was over six weeks ago. Her face froze into an open-mouthed mask, an icy ball of tension forming in her stomach. She'd never been late before, but with finals and packing and moving back home, she'd lost track of the time.

She slumped onto a kitchen chair. Could she be pregnant? They'd told her when she'd miscarried that it probably couldn't happen again. Too much trauma and scarring.

Hot tears pricked the back of her eyelids. It had taken years to get over that devastating loss, the loss of her potential future family, but she'd come to terms with it—she really had. Had finally gotten on with planning a different life, a life that centered around her job rather than a family of her own.

It could still be stress. And PMS. But she knew enough to recognize the signs.

She stood up abruptly and went into the bedroom. She couldn't be pregnant. They had been careful. Pretty careful. Hugging herself, she rubbed her upper arms, trying to chase away the chill.

Not now. She had places to go, people to see. Plans for a new life far away from here. Plans that did not include a baby.

But it could be true. She had to find out.

The bathroom was freezing. Louise sat on the closed toilet seat and stared at the stick in her hand, too worried to turn on the electric heater. When the plus sign appeared on the pregnancy test, she stopped breathing as panic grabbed her heart and started to squeeze. The plus sign was clear, no question about that. Maybe she had it wrong. Maybe plus meant...

She grabbed the box— *Pregnant.*

Her head spun. She was going to black out. She blew out a spent breath and inhaled deeply into her oxygen starved lungs. It couldn't be true. Kids weren't anywhere on her radar. She had plans—and none of them included a baby.

She was numb, didn't know what she felt, just knew that this spelled the end to her dream of a job in the city, maybe a bakery of her own. She had wanted a place that served coffee, where people hung out with friends or sat writing on their laptops. The heart of a community, like the Fortune Bay Café, but not the Fortune Bay Café. Something urban. Something different. Something that was hers.

And Marco. *Oh no.* A harsh new anxiety dug in its claws. They had never talked about anything permanent, and they had certainly never talked about kids. She wasn't even sure he wanted her to move in with him when she went back. It had all sounded like a grand adventure in her mind: get a place together, both find new jobs, see if it worked out between them. And if not, she would strike out on her own.

She stopped short at the end of the flight of ideas she'd raced along so many times before. It had all changed in the space of a heartbeat with a plus sign.

The indicator stick in her hand shook, whether from nerves or cold she wasn't sure, but she couldn't hold that damn stick any longer. Wrapping it in toilet paper, she threw it in the garbage. She didn't want anyone to see it before she decided what she was going to do.

What could she do? Pregnant again, and with no more idea of how to handle it than when she was sixteen. That time, with her family disintegrating around her, losing that baby may have been for the best. Not that she'd felt that way at the time, of course. The memory still followed her, a black cloud that was always there, sometimes just out of sight, sometimes overtaking her without warning.

When it had happened, she had been desolate, desperate. The doctors had told her she probably couldn't have another baby and the experience had been so horrendous, she had totally believed them.

This was so unfair. She'd come to terms with it. Made other plans for her life. Plans that did not include a baby.

Her mind shied away from the obvious solution. She shuddered. She couldn't terminate the pregnancy. Such a clinical term for such a desperate act. But she couldn't keep it either. Could she? Maybe she had to. She was thirty-four years old now and thirty-four-year-olds didn't give away their babies.

Dammit. She was screwed.

She made a cup of herbal tea and sat at the kitchen table, staring out the window as dark clouds scudded over the lake and her tea grew cold. This explained so much. The mood swings, the tears. Why her morning coffee didn't taste good anymore.

She checked her phone. No calls from Marco. She lay the phone on the kitchen table beside her and stared at it.

If he called, would she tell him?

The baby was his. She had to tell him.

What would he say? They had never talked about children. Hell, they'd never talked about anything. If she was honest with herself, theirs was strictly a nookie relationship. She didn't really know him at all. But he was older. Maybe he wanted children. Maybe he'd throw his arms around her and say he was thrilled, that of course she had to come and live with him in the city.

Unfortunately, that didn't sound likely.

Scrawny made his presence known at her side with a

loud meow. She scooped him up and automatically set him on her lap and ran her hand over the thick silky fur on his back.

She wasn't sure she wanted to live with Marco anyway. He didn't seem like the paternal type. Look how he treated the cat. She could see him saying he would help with financial support ... But would that be enough?

She rubbed her fingers up and down her forehead. It might have to be. But then, where did that leave her?

Glancing at the clock, she saw it was already five. The afternoon had slipped by and she was due at Sean and Stephanie's in an hour, although the last thing she wanted to do was spend the evening in a room full of happy people. The party was for her though, and there were bound to be a lot of questions if she didn't show up.

She'd promised to take veggies, so she turned on the oven and peeled all the root vegetables she'd bought, chopping them into large chunks. After tossing them with olive oil, salt and pepper, she arranged them on a baking tray and put the tray in the oven. Her hands worked automatically as she ran over the ramifications of her situations. Or tried to. Her brain felt like an old cd player. Stuck, repeating one word.

Pregnant.

In the bedroom, she pulled on a slinky black top and studied herself in the mirror. Definitely bustier than normal. She actually had cleavage, something she'd never been able to say before.

Her knees buckled and she sat on the bed with her head in her hands, pressing the heels of her palms into her eyes. Cripes. How could she be pregnant?

She knew how. That night of the concert, she and Marco had gone back to her place and she'd invited him in. He was so devilishly sexy, she couldn't resist. He'd taken her in his arms and kissed her—and she'd surrendered. That's what it was, surrendered to his dark brooding eyes, sweet lips and even sweeter words.

She hadn't been on the pill that first night, but they'd had a condom and, always more worried about being safe than not getting pregnant, she figured that was enough. *Obviously not.* She'd gone on the pill again right away after that, hoping they would be together again, but it must already have been too late.

What in heaven's name was she going to do?

She sat and stared at the stove, running over the same questions again and again, but nothing became any clearer.

Then the buzzer went off. Time to go. She ran a line of dark liner around her eyes that made her face look even paler than before, and slipped some silver hoops through the lowest piercings in her ears.

Then grabbing the dish of veggies, she headed out the door.

Oh my God.

Chapter 10

Blue slipped off his muddy boots and left them on Stephanie's covered front porch. He'd been coming to this house since he was a kid and he knew the rules. No muddy boots in the house. No running on the stairs. No girls in the bedrooms.

Stephanie had hit them with that last one when they'd reached their teens. It had seemed weird to them all at the time because Louise had always been one of the guys, but Steph had been right. Sometime during those teenage years, things had changed. Blue began to notice that Louise was a girl and after that he got a boner—he smiled, that's what they'd called it—every time he saw her. And all he could do was groan. Silently, he hoped.

She was so friggin' beautiful, it was hard not to touch her—and agony when he did.

He still felt pretty much the same way. Over the years he'd developed coping strategies that helped him keep a physical and psychological distance, but they'd been shot all to hell when he and Louise had been thrown together at Jake's wedding last summer.

They danced the first dance, then another and another, and the proximity, the atmosphere and probably the beer had loosened his control. He'd reached for her then and he thought she'd reached back.

Nothing had actually happened, though. At the end of the night they went their separate ways, but it had left him thinking, *what if?*

The next thing he knew, she was leaving for Seattle, so he must have imagined that her feelings for him had changed that night. It wasn't the first time he'd been fooled where Louise was concerned, and probably wouldn't be the last. Because every time he thought things were changing between them, Louise would meet a new guy and she'd be gone. Never for long, they were all losers, but Blue would be back at square one.

The sound of soft laughter floated down the hall from the kitchen to where he stood lost in thought. When she left for Seattle he'd promised himself he wouldn't wait, wouldn't pine, but like the sucker he was, he hadn't been able to stop thinking about her. Every friggin' day.

And now she was back and she was doing it again.

He squared his shoulders. Well, *he* wasn't going to do it again. Not this time.

* * *

Louise slipped into Stephanie's kitchen through the back door with Maddie's family, hoping no one would notice her. The last thing she felt like was a party tonight.

Sean and Blue were already there, Blue leaning back against the antique oak sideboard, nursing a beer. He nodded, but didn't send her a smile. Something was definitely up.

Sean, playing host, put a glass of wine in her hand, got a beer for Jake, a soda for Maddie and Sarah, then went back to filleting the salmon. Louise put the veggies and cookies she'd brought on the counter and went over to stand with Blue, out of the way. She was not up to joining the fray. Sean and Steph could handle the dinner prep without her.

She gave Blue a soft nudge with her shoulder. Star hadn't come—at least not yet. Louise was glad, but she didn't have the energy to try to figure out where she stood with that.

Blue's dark eyes searched her face. He knew her so well, she was sure he could read her mind. *Pregnant.* She couldn't think about anything else.

"So, what do you think of the resort?" Sean asked, dragging her back to the party, his hands flying at incredible speed as he chopped veggies for salad.

Louise tried to put some enthusiasm in her voice. "Fabulous! And Blue, your work there is wonderful."

"Isn't it?" Stephanie said. "It really defines the place. Those salmon swimming around the doorway into the dining room? Perfect." An artist herself, Stephanie always appreciated the visuals.

Blue's cheeks reddened. "Thanks," he said, and took a slug from his bottle of beer.

Louise carried the glass of wine around the room like a stage prop. Once or twice she brought it up to her lips, but didn't drink. *Pregnant.* Everyone would notice if she turned down a glass of wine though, and she wasn't ready to answer their questions.

A teenage girl slunk into the kitchen. Had to be Sean's new-found daughter, Amber. Louise sucked in a sharp breath. It could have been fifteen years ago and Lacey walking into the room. Under the rebellious trappings, Amber looked just like her mother, but her long black hair had been straightened and colored to within an inch of its life, the ends thin and wispy from over processing, and at least half a dozen piercings ringed her nose and ears and, oh yes, one on her eyebrow too.

They'd all been so self-involved at that age that Louise had never realized that while she'd been going through her own crap, Sean and Lacey were too.

"Amber," Sean exclaimed. His face radiated happiness, but the girl held herself tightly, as if wishing he hadn't noticed her. Hadn't singled her out. As if wishing she could hide. Louise knew just how she felt.

"You haven't met Brandy's sister, Louise." Sean turned to Louise, his eyes shining. "My daughter, Amber."

Amber's shoulders relaxed slightly and she gave Louise

a tentative smile. Striking blue eyes—definitely Sean's daughter—contrasted with the harsh black hair, and Louise could see the blonde roots growing in. She could be such a pretty girl if she ditched the black hair. But Louise remembered her own teenage rebellion too well not to cut her some slack. Heck, she'd only gone back to her original blonde herself last month.

Sean and Amber were clearly not comfortable with each other yet. Both still trying too hard. But he looked so darn happy it brought tears to Louise's eyes.

She smiled and held out her hand. "Hi Amber, I've heard so much about you."

Amber looked surprised. "Really?"

Louise laughed. "You're big news in this family."

Amber blushed, touched her hand, and Louise let her go.

"Cool hair," Louise said, wanting to touch base with the girl.

"Yours too," Amber said shyly.

"Thanks, I just did it. Cut and color." She ran her hands through the short crop. "I had mine black for years too. Just wanted a change."

Amber nodded shyly, withdrawing again. An interesting friend for Brandy. She'd have to keep tabs on those two.

Everyone sat around Stephanie's big square oak table to eat, and when questioned about her pastry school experiences, Louise offered stories about her culinary disasters, the chocolates that wouldn't harden and pooled on the plate and the Profiteroles that burned to a crisp while she was across the room, struggling to roll out some sticky dough. She got through the evening as she always did, hiding behind a veil of words. She probably talked too much, she certainly felt manic, but no one seemed to notice.

Finally, the evening was over and as Louise stepped onto the porch, she was met by a deluge of rain. Great.

She'd walked from the cabin along the path to Steph's.

Blue was right behind her.

"Can I catch a ride?" she asked.

He grunted a reply Louise took as a *yes* and headed to the truck, waiting in the cab with the engine running until she'd said her goodbyes.

The truck's headlights shone tunnels of light down the driveway as they pulled away. The silence hung heavy between them. She wanted to ask him what was wrong, but couldn't. Instead, she asked, "Where are you living?"

"The Macy place."

"The log house on the point, down the road from the cabin?"

"That's the one."

"I've never been in there."

He shot her a look. "You can come by some time."

"When did you move there?"

"Month and a half ago."

She shook her head. "I didn't know."

"No, well, we didn't talk much while you were gone."

He said it like an accusation. She could have thrown it back in his face—*You could have called me too you know*—but she didn't have the energy.

The truck turned down her driveway. The lights were on inside the cabin.

"I could have sworn I turned them off," she murmured.

"Did you lock the door?"

"Duh, no. It's Fortune Bay."

"I'll go in with you," he said, cutting the engine.

She slipped out of the truck. "I'm sure it's okay." She didn't want him to come in. Didn't want to be alone with him anymore tonight. He knew her too well, would know something was up, and she didn't want to explain. Not yet.

"I'll just wait then. Until you're inside."

There was no moving Blue when he'd set his mind on

something, so she ran through the rain, up onto the porch and let herself into the cabin.

No one was there of course, except Scrawny who was dying to get out, so she waved to Blue from the bedroom window. He sat in the dark, looking right at her. Hadn't he seen her? She waved again.

Finally, the truck growled to life and he backed down the drive.

Louise felt strangely unsettled as he drove away. She'd been looking forward to having the cabin to herself this month, but she'd discovered she felt lonely living alone. She would have loved to talk to someone about her situation— she didn't even want to think the word—but didn't know who to turn to.

Although she'd been tired at the party, now that she was back at the cabin her nerves were jumping under her skin and her mind was spinning like tires in the mud. And she was starving. She'd been so preoccupied at Stephanie's, that she had hardly eaten any dinner. Now she poured herself a glass of milk and cut a big slice of *Sven's Mother's Coffee Bread.*

Who was Sven? She tasted the cake. Not bad. Good texture. The spice mix was pretty good, but the flavor was flat. She would add more cardamom next time. And salt. She copied the recipe from Augusta's card into her binder of recipe notes.

"So, Augusta," she murmured. "Fine pickle I've got myself into. A baby? Scares the hell out of me. I haven't thought of myself as a mother for a long time. Don't get me wrong, I love children, always have. In fact, I wanted a bunch of children at one point, but had pretty well given up the idea." She inhaled a ragged sigh. "Maybe it's not too late.

"I've never thought of myself as the traditional type, but I never saw myself as a single mother, either. I'd really like a dad in the picture, and I'm not sure Marco's the one."

She added the extra ingredients in pencil to her copy of the recipe and read it over.

"No time like the present to try this out. I'm not going to get any sleep tonight anyway."

Pulling one of her large Pyrex bowls out of the cupboard, she greased the inside. She'd unpacked her own utensils and packed away most of Sean and Augusta's in boxes and stashed them in the attic.

Luckily, she'd picked up more fruit and nuts when she went into town for the pregnancy test. At that point she hadn't really believed it could be true, figured she'd be carrying on as planned.

Oh, shit.

She pushed thoughts of the future into a dark corner of her mind and immersed herself in the soothing process of baking bread.

Soon she was up to her elbows in a billowing, sweet smelling dough. The rhythm of kneading settled her nerves. Rain fell soft as cats' paws on the tin roof over the porch and the woodstove pumped out a protective cocoon of heat.

"Did you ever have children, Augusta?" She glanced at the picture on the wall by the attic stairs of the young woman waving gaily out the window of her 1940's Ford. She didn't seem to have a care in the world.

"How can I have a kid now? I don't have a foundation. No job, no income, no support. No plan that makes any sense anymore." She could almost imagine Augusta sitting at the kitchen table on one of the odd assortment of chairs, nodding.

"One child, maybe, I could do on my own. If I had to. Because..." She hesitated, worried that voicing her fears out loud might make them true. "I'm not at all sure Marco will stick it out."

She turned the dough and pushed into it with the heels of her hands. Turned and pushed, turned and pushed, setting up a rhythm.

"In fact," she said softly, "I'm not sure he's coming to visit at all."

She forced out a harsh breath. "Isn't that the story of my life? If I've learned anything, it's that you can't count on people to be there for you. I thought Mom would always be there. We used to bake and talk, and she'd tell me about places we'd go together, how she'd make my dress when I graduated high school...

"I could tell her anything. I could tell her this, if she were here, and she'd tell me it would be okay. She'd have known what to do. You knew her. She totally took care of me and my dad—until the cancer came. She only had two months.

"Dad never was much of a talker, but after that he clammed up completely. Went to work, brought food home, but if you looked in his eyes, he wasn't there. And we never talked about mom anymore.

"Blue and Sean and Stephanie were there though. They pulled me through. And Fiona. She made sure I ate when I worked at the store, and that someone drove me home if it was dark. They were totally there."

She slapped the soft dough out onto the counter, sprinkled it with flour and continued to knead, pushing the heels of her hands into the warm mass, already alive with a soul of its own. She gave the mound a half turn, folded it over and pushed her hands into it again using her height to put her body weight behind the motion.

The sound of rain hitting the windows became more insistent, sharp ice crystals tapping the dark windowpane. When the dough felt smooth and elastic under her hands, she put it in the bowl, turned it over to grease the top, and covered it with a linen towel. Setting the bowl on an end table near the woodstove, she settled down with a cup of tea and her notebook to look over her notes while waiting for the dough to rise.

She preferred what she called an organic form of note taking and her book bristled with clippings and scrawled notes that all made perfect sense to her. When the dough doubled in size, she punched it down and kneaded in the dried fruit and nuts. She could already tell from the warm yeasty smell that this batch would be better than the last.

She turned on the timer, curled up on the couch, pulled a woolen blanket over her and let the black fog swallow her up.

Chapter 11

"If I wanted coffee bread, I would have made it myself," Belinda said.

Louise ground her teeth and forced a smile. "Your sweet breads are great, but I'm trying out new recipes and can't possibly eat it all myself. Do you know what happened to my mother's recipe book?"

Louise had been worried that Belinda had thrown it out, but now she pointed to an upper kitchen cupboard.

"They're in there, in the binder on the top shelf."

Belinda was five foot four, tops, and could never reach the binder on the top shelf. It was dead storage. An insult to her mother's memory. Not that Belinda remembered her mother. She'd moved to Majestic, the town at the head of the lake, years after Louise's mother had died.

Louise had never understood what her dad saw in Belinda, although it was clear from the start what Belinda saw in him. A meal ticket. They looked ridiculous together, her dad so tall and Belinda so short. Not like her mom who had been tall and willowy, a real Scandinavian beauty.

Louise reached up and pulled down the tattered binder. Opening it on the kitchen counter, a lump grew in her throat at the sight of her mom's clear, round handwriting. She flipped through the colored dividers on the side, *Meats, deserts, breads,* and opened it to the one marked *Christmas.* There was her mother's recipe for *Christmas Stollen.*

"Can I take these?"

"Sure. I never use them. Your dad might like it if you made some of them for him sometime though."

And why hadn't *she* ever made them for him? *Typical.*

Louise put the binder by the door. "Is he ready to go?"

"I'm here. Keep your shirt on."

Henrik hobbled out of the living room leaning on his walking stick, his outdoor shoes already on his feet. Louise knew how long it took him to get them on, but now when she came by, he was always ready. It was a good sign. Attitude was important. She couldn't say he was any better yet—it had only been five days—but when she got there he seemed eager to go and she liked to think he had lost some of the drag in his step.

"It's a nice day," she said. "Cold though. You'll want a hat."

There are two kinds of winter weather in the Pacific Northwest: warm and wet or clear and cold. The previous night had been clear, the moon shining brightly, and the thermometer had dipped below freezing. In the shadow of the tall trees, the puddles were milky with a thin layer of ice.

They crept at a snail's pace down the gravel drive to the forest trail to the salmon creek which over the past few days had become their daily walk. Now, white corpses of many fish lay under the water on the creek bed where they had died after following their instincts and returning home to spawn.

"I hope they died peacefully," she said. "But I've always wondered, what do the other salmon think as they swim over the bodies of their fallen comrades?"

"Probably don't even notice," Henrik said, leaning on his stick and looking into the clear water. "Salmon aren't known for being particularly introspective."

Louise laughed. Joking was a good sign too.

The living fish were still fighting the current. She knew just how they felt, fighting forces that sometimes—often—felt too strong to overcome. Their silver backs undulating in place in the clear water, you'd swear they were just holding on. Then suddenly one would make a run for the small rapid, throwing themselves over the rocks, sometimes leaping into the air, sometimes being washed back down only to start the process again. But they knew where they were supposed to be, in the pool where they were born, and they would do anything to get there.

She wished she could talk to her dad about the baby, ask him what she should do. But she knew what would happen if she did—the pressure would start for her to stay in Fortune Bay, and she couldn't bear that. She was happy to help him now while she was here for Christmas, and hoped Belinda would continue to walk with him after she had gone, but watching her father like this, so weak and tenuous, was eating away at her. He'd always been a strong man. She'd watched him fall and pull himself up after her mother died. It wasn't fair he should have to struggle like this again.

"Do you ever think about grandchildren, Dad?"

He looked at her, surprised. "Why? Have you found yourself a guy?"

She laughed. "No. Just thinking about Maddie and Jake and the baby, I guess."

"Yeah," he said wistfully. "Stephanie is one lucky woman, all those grandchildren. What's she got now? Five?"

"Six, if you count Jenny and the new one coming."

"Well, honey, I guess I'll have to wait for Brandy to grow up. I resigned myself years ago to the fact that you're not exactly the mothering type."

Louise stopped in her tracks and watched her dad shuffle down the trail.

Was that's what he really thought? "Why not?" she asked, catching up with him again.

"Well, you never stay with one guy long enough for paint to dry, honey, never mind start a family."

"Maybe I just haven't found the right guy."

"I'd agree with that. You really know how to pick 'em,

Louisie. None of them seemed like the marrying kind. Just as well. I can't think of one of them I'd want you to marry."

"Well, and I didn't." What else could she say? He meant well, or at least she didn't think he meant what he'd said as an insult. She hadn't thought her dad had paid any attention to who she dated, but thinking back over the list, she had to agree.

"I know the guys with attitude might seem more interesting, but often it's just a lot of flash. If you're looking for a mate for life, you have to look deeper than that. I've been lucky to find two wonderful women."

"How could you compare Belinda to Mom?"

Her dad looked at her and his blue eyes sharpened. "Belinda's a good woman, and she loves me. I could never have gotten through the past few months without her. I'd like you to give her a chance."

Louise didn't want to upset her dad, so she zipped her lips, but she didn't see her and Belinda becoming best buds anytime soon.

* * *

Not the mothering type. That stung.

Louise punched down the pillowy mound of Challah dough, the recipe for the Jewish egg bread she was testing.

Were that what people thought of her? Not true. She was a simmering cauldron of maternal juices these days.

The soft dough stuck to her fingers and she sprinkled more flour on the counter and put her back into kneading the dough.

Brawny certainly thought she was motherly. She'd changed his name. Now that he was filling out, 'Brawny' seemed more appropriate. He was a big bruiser and obviously a scrapper. The scab on the top of his head was gone and new fur was covering the bald spot. But he had a marshmallow center and right this moment was weaving figure eights around her ankles, purring so loudly she could hear him over Bruce and the E Street Band that were blasting out of Sean's state-of-the-art sound system tucked under the staircase.

She slapped the dough on the floury counter.

And look at Sean, suddenly a father and no one suggested that he wasn't fatherly enough for the job. Everyone just stepped right in and lent a hand when he needed it. The Murphy's were great that way, and she knew they would do the same for her. Because they always had.

Even Maddie, with her horrible childhood with terrible role models had managed to do a good job of raising Jenny alone. Sarah loved her too and Louise was sure Maddie would do just as good a job with the new baby.

So why did her dad think *she* couldn't do it?

Her mother had been a wonderful role model. Louise's memories of her early years were filled with sunshine and fun. Of course, they couldn't have all been sunny days, but that's how she remembered them. Playing in the forest with Blue and the boys next door, riding their bikes in a pack on the quiet country roads, her mother bringing them snacks on the porch, her long blonde hair pulled up in a ponytail, her old straw hat frayed around the brim.

She'd been gentle but firm, loving and fun. Louise could do that. She was fun. And she was a diva in the kitchen. Would make wonderful, healthy meals for her children. Her mother's death had left a yawning hole in her heart center that she'd patched the best she could. But maybe, just maybe, she could have a family again.

While the dough was rising, she found her mother's old recipe for gingerbread cookies and mixed up a batch. They'd had a quick course on royal icing at the Academy and she loved the smooth shiny look of the glaze—when it was done right. But she needed more practice before hers would pass the test. She had ideas for painting red or blue designs with food grade colors on a white glaze, and if she put a hole in the cookies and tied a ribbon on top, they could be edible Christmas tree decorations. Children would love them.

Who isn't maternal?

She put the Challah in the oven and threw another log in the woodstove. Taking her recipe binder over to the couch, she found herself staring into the flames, memories swirling around in her head.

At fifteen, two years after the death of her mother and her father's withdrawal into the bottle, she'd been open and vulnerable and visibly rebellious. She dyed her hair raven black and had ringed her ears with piercings.

Her dad didn't seem to notice. Steph was the one who dosed her ears with antibiotic cream when they became infected. She raised a hand to the rim of her ear, feeling the small scars where eventually she'd let most of the holes close over.

That's when she'd met Tony. He was new in town. She could remember the first time she saw him at school. He slouched into the room, his eyes fell on her and **BAM!** That was it. They had fallen together like long lost lovers.

After a few months of afternoons of ditching school and hanging out alone together at one or the other of their empty houses, she discovered she was pregnant. It filled her with hope. She'd embroidered their future together into a fairytale pipedream. She could have another family, a family of her own. Her and Tony.

She knew now, though, had known for years, that they had been too young. It would never have worked out like it had in her dreams.

Anyway, she didn't want to think about Tony now, but couldn't help wondering if this pregnancy was a second chance, a sign that it wasn't too late to try again. Try for a family of her own. She'd be thirty-six next spring and after what the doctors had told her when she lost the first baby, she was almost afraid to believe it could happen. But it might be her last chance for a family.

Was Marco the right guy to start a family with? Did she have any choice? He'd never shown any indication that he wanted children—or even a permanent relationship for that matter—and she had a niggling feeling that he wasn't going to be thrilled. The one good thing about Marco was that if it didn't work out between them, she wouldn't be too badly shaken. She'd survive.

But she didn't want to think about that now either.

When the golden, braided Challah loaf was cooling on the rack and the cookies were out of the oven, Louise suddenly ran out of steam. It was dark outside, but only five o'clock. The early sunsets at this time of year made the evenings seem interminably long.

Grabbing a cookie, she collapsed on the couch in the living room and stared at the TV. She hadn't tried it yet but wasn't hopeful. From the size and old-fashioned wooden cabinet, she figured it must be a remnant of Augusta's days. There was no remote—too old for that—so she dragged herself off the couch and turned the knob to *ON*. All she got was static.

She turned off the TV and pulled her phone out of her purse. "What do you say, Brawny? Let's see if anyone's called."

Nothing. Nothing from anyone but most notably, nothing from Marco.

"Maybe I should call him again. That's what you do, isn't it? You tell the father."

Brawny left his warm spot by the woodstove and jumped up beside her on the couch with an encouraging *Plur-rp.*

"If you say so." She punched in Marco's number and waited while it rang. And rang. And went to voice mail. Why wasn't he answering? Now she needed to think of something to say.

"Hi Marco. It's me." Her mind went blank. "I need to talk. Give me a call."

Still blank.

"Bye."

Weak. But what she had to say wasn't something you could leave in a message. *Hey Dad, guess what?*

No, she had to speak to him. Preferably in person.

She slouched on the couch, the dark rainy evening stretching long and lonely ahead of her. She was tired of her own company, but the idea of spending time with anyone else, anyone who didn't *know,* wasn't appealing.

Except for Blue.

Louise straightened up on the couch. She still hadn't seen his new place. A visit might be just what she needed to pull herself out of the doldrums. Putting the warm loaf and some cookies in a bag, she grabbed her rain slicker from the hook behind the front door, slipped her feet into her rubber boots and sloshed through the rain to the car.

Chapter 12

Louise knew where the McGee place was. Old man McGee had been considerably older than her dad but at one point they'd worked together at the mill. Although he'd retired years ago, Mr. McGee had lived in the log house out on the point until two years ago when he'd gone into a senior's home in Majestic. After that, the house sat empty. She wondered what kind of arrangement Blue had made with him, or whoever managed the place.

The lane was unmarked, but Louise knew every driveway on this road from her years of exploring the back roads on her bike. It was pitch dark and pouring rain as she drove down the narrow lane. Even in the shelter of the overhanging branches, her wipers had a hard time keeping the windshield clear.

Blue's beat-up flat deck truck was parked in front of the log house. Smoke curled from the chimney and an inviting golden glow emanated from the downstairs windows, like that kitschy little town Belinda always set up under the Christmas tree. Louise bundled the bag of warm baked goods under her raincoat and raced for the porch.

The skimpy overhang didn't offer much shelter from the rain, but she huddled underneath as best she could and knocked on the door. She could hear football on the TV inside. Blue had been a tackle in high school, not really a heart throb in those days but effective on the field.

Suddenly she felt awkward. He'd been acting strange lately, distant, and more than once she'd wondered if he and Star might have something going on. She could see where someone like Star could find him attractive. Single. Eligible. Hot.

Just because there wasn't another car in the drive, didn't mean Blue was alone.

* * *

The first half of the game had just ended when Blue heard the knock on the door. His first thought was that someone was in trouble because no one ever came knocking on his door. If they wanted to see him, they went to the workshop where he had lived and worked for the past five years. That was how he liked it. If he wanted company, which he rarely did, he knew where to go to find it.

He swung open the door. A figure in a dark green raincoat huddled under the stoop roof. Although a deep hood hid most of her face, he knew instantly who it was. His shoulders stiffened even as his heartbeat quickened.

"Louise."

"Hi. You said I should come by so...here I am."

She didn't push her way in, just stood on the porch, waiting. It wasn't like Louise to hold back. If she wanted to come in, she came in.

Something had shifted in their relationship since her return, but he wasn't sure what. It wasn't the distance he had hoped for, although there was certainly a new restraint between them. At the same time, though, a current of energy flowed between them, stronger, more intense than before. He felt kind of sick with it most of the time.

She shivered and he realized she was still standing in the rain. "Come on in."

As she stepped past him, he inhaled the aroma of fresh baking and spices that wafted in with her.

Shaking off the rain, she shrugged out of her raincoat and boots. Her eyes quickly scanned the room. "You alone?"

Then they settled on the TV. "Who's winning? The TV

at the cabin is toast."

"Seahawks," he said. That was one thing about Louise—she usually did enough talking for them both. He never had to try too hard. Could just be himself.

Tonight, though, she seemed a little awkward. But then, she'd never been to his house before. He should probably say something.

"My new place."

She looked around with interest. "Renting?"

She set a paper bag on the wooden counter that separated the kitchen from the living room and pulled out a braided loaf of bread, the source of the enticing aroma.

He looked up. She was watching him. She'd asked a question. "Renting. No. I bought it."

"What?" she squealed, grabbing him by the arm and giving him a shake. "You bought a house and didn't tell me?"

"It happened kind of suddenly. McGee died—"

Her face fell. "Aww."

"In September. I got to know him a bit the last few years when I visited my mom in the home in Majestic."

"How is your mom?"

Blue's expression shuttered. "About the same. She only knows me some of the time now."

Louise lay a hand on his arm. "Hard for you."

She'd been with him five years ago when he'd had to put his mom in the home and she'd seen how it had torn him apart. But as his mother's dementia progressed, he couldn't care for her on his own.

So he'd sold the house to Frankie, whom none of them had known at the time, and used the money to pay for keeping his mom in the best protected accommodation in the valley. That was when he moved into the station. But Louise knew he'd always felt he should have been able to do more.

"Yeah, well, I got to know Mr. McGee on my visits. His son lives in Portland and rarely came to visit, and often my mom isn't very responsive, so Mr. McGee would drift into the room and we'd talk."

"I'm sure he loved the company." Everyone loved Blue, if they hung around long enough for him to open up.

"He was a great old guy. I learned a lot from him about what the area was like when he got here in the 1950's. He bought this cabin and put in hydro and plumbing, pretty basic but it made my job a whole lot easier when it came to renovating. When he died, his son sold me the place. He gave me first refusal because of how much he appreciated me spending time with his dad.

"I was happy to take it. Living at the station was getting to me. Had been for a quite while. I wanted a real home."

Louise started to snoop, opening light-colored maple cupboard doors and running her hand along the cool, figured granite countertop.

"The view is great here on the point," he said.

"I bet. I didn't think this place would look this good inside. I love it. Stainless appliances? Did you do much work when you moved in?"

"Not much. New kitchen cupboards, new stove and fridge, new tub and toilet. Refinished the floors."

Her eyes widened.

"I haven't gotten to the front porch yet. Probably won't 'til spring. I have to jack it up, then I want to extend the roof."

"You've been busy."

"Yeah, I guess. Besides the work I've been doing for the resort—which is paying for all this—I haven't had much time to just sit." He looked at the TV where the Seahawks were starting the third quarter. "Want to watch the game?"

Louise brightened. "Want to try my Challah?"

Blue pulled a wooden cutting board out from behind the

breadbasket and a bread knife out of the rack and set them in front of Louise. As she sliced thick pieces of soft, sweet bread, Blue opened the refrigerator to get out the butter.

"I love the kitchen," she said.

"I made it for you."

He froze and, although he couldn't see her, he heard the silence behind him as she stopped cutting the bread. A big, fat, pulsing silence.

He hadn't meant to say that, but that was the picture he'd had in his mind while she'd been away and he'd been working on the house. He'd been building a kitchen for Louise.

Stupid. What did he think? That she would come back after the course and move in here with him?

That's exactly the picture he'd had in his mind. Not a plan really, not even consciously recognized, but he realized now it had been there all along.

He turned around and forced his mouth into a stiff grin. She was looking at him with eyes too big in her pale face. "I knew you'd be coming with bread some day."

Her worried look vanished and was replaced by a self-satisfied laugh. "That was a good bet. I brought cookies too." She pulled a cookie out of the bag and set it on the counter.

Blue turned away, found a plate in the cupboard and busied himself piling bread and cookies on the plate while Louise got the milk out of the fridge. Anything not to look at her. She looked perfect in his kitchen.

"Just like old times," she said as they headed back to the living room. "Eating cookies and milk while we watch TV."

Blue put the plate on the coffee table and sat back in his spot on the couch, beside the end table where his beer still stood. Louise put down the cookies and settled in beside him.

Right beside him.

Christ. He should have known she would curl up on the couch. She always did. He should have sat in the chair. It would seem weird to move now though and she didn't seem to think anything of it, was just thoughtfully tasting a slice of the bread.

"I think this is really good. It's a new recipe so I wasn't sure. What do you think?"

She swiveled to offer him a bite of her piece. He took a bite, feeling awkward as hell, but when he looked at her, her eyes were on the game.

"O-o-h-h. Good catch."

He was obviously the only one who thought it was weird so, after a few minutes and another cookie, he started to relax. Just old friends watching the game.

This went way back. Not just the cookies and milk, but the years they'd sat on the couch together watching after school programs and football. Louise had been blond then too, until she was sixteen. The year that everything changed. That horrible Christmas when their world imploded. The winter she died her hair black.

Now it was blonde again. And what did *that* mean? Short and edgy. Urban. That described her whole look, black on black clothes, not like the colorful clothes she used to wear. Everything was changing again.

Louise swung her legs up onto the couch and nudged her back into him, wiggling her shoulders to find a comfortable spot. Without consciously thinking about it, he stretched out his arm along the back of the couch, around her shoulders. Suddenly his pants didn't fit right. He adjusted them as unobtrusively as he could.

So. Here they were again, snuggled on the couch, her leaning on him for support, him wanting her and not able to have her. It was déjà vu all over again.

He put his hand on her shoulder. She blew out a sigh and the bluster went out of her. She wasn't herself.

"Hey, Lou, what's up."

Her laugh sounded shaky. "Nothing. Everything's great."

"Come on, I know something's up."

Something hot dripped onto his hand and he craned his neck to see her face. *Christ, no. Not tears.* Something was definitely wrong.

Louise dashed them away with the back of her hand. "Just being stupid."

He pulled her back into a hug, wrapping an arm across her chest and she melted against him with another big sigh.

"I feel so safe here with you." She twisted to face him and slid her arms under his fleece vest, hugging him tightly and laying her head on his chest.

He put his chin on top of her head. Probably breaking up with the new guy. She always came crawling back to him when that happened.

"I'm scared," she whispered.

"Scared of what?"

She gave an anguished laugh and tears spurted from her eyes like from a squirt gun, wetting his shirt.

"Hey, what's wrong."

"When I'm with you, I feel like a kid again."

Not the response he was looking for, but he'd take it if it meant he could keep her in his arms.

"I'm pregnant."

"What?" All the air went out of him like he'd been punched in the gut and in a reflex action he pushed her away so he could see her face. It was red and runny, but she looked totally serious.

She closed her eyes and more tears leaked out. "I didn't mean to tell you. It's not your problem."

"Are you sure?"

"Yes. I'm sure. I've taken the test."

Tears were streaming down her cheeks. He shifted her

to one arm, reached into his back pocket, no easy feat with her basically on top of him on the couch, and pulled out a clean white handkerchief.

She laughed through her tears. "You're so old fashioned. Who carries a handkerchief these days?" But she took it and gave her nose a brain-rattling blow.

"The father...?"

She blew loudly again and wiped her eyes. "Marco. The guy I was telling you about."

"Does he know?"

"No. I just found out. I haven't told him yet."

Blue set her upright on her own side of the couch, desperate for some space. He couldn't think. She was crushing him under her heel like a bug again and didn't even know it. Why hadn't he stuck with the program and kept his distance. How had she ended up on top of him on the couch anyway?

He straightened his pants. The erection that had left them askew had vanished. "What do you think he'll say?"

Her voice was very small. "I don't know." Then she squared her shoulders and put on a watery smile. "He'll be excited. I know he will. I can't wait to tell him."

Blue didn't entirely buy it. "When's he coming?"

"In a couple of days." She blew her nose again, looked at the hanky and offered it back to him.

"Keep it."

She grabbed his hand. "Don't tell anyone."

He gave her a hard look. "Have I ever?"

They sat for a while in silence. The Seahawks won. He didn't really remember how.

Louise took control of the remote. "Can we watch a movie? I don't want to go home."

"Sure." Hell, why not? He was already sunk. All that bull about him getting over her while she was gone? That's exactly what it was—bull.

Jake was having another kid; Sean had found his daughter; and Louise was having a baby. Just not with him.

Why, after all these years, was he still fooling himself? Everyone else was settling down and starting a family. Wasn't that part of the reason he'd bought the house? Getting ready, in case it happened for him, too. But as always, he'd picked the wrong girl.

In a small shaky voice that was nothing like the old Louise, she said, "I don't know what I'm going to do, Blue. I had a plan: finish the course, come home for Christmas, then go somewhere, Seattle, California, I don't know, *somewhere,* and really get started."

"What's wrong with here?"

Louise laughed and he was glad she couldn't see his face, see how much that hurt.

"I'm trying to get *out* of here. I've had it with working at the café. Seeing the same old faces; making muffins every morning. I want something new, new faces, a new adventure."

"What about Marco?" If he'd been looking her in the face, he never could have asked.

Another shaky sigh and Blue's abs tightened as he struggled not to wrap his arms around her.

"I guess we'll see when he gets here."

Louise wiggled backwards on the sofa in that way she had until she was backed right up against him again. *Christ.* And there was that bulge in his pants.

But he lifted his arm and she wiggled her shoulders into the spot that was reserved just for her. Might as well have her name on it because no other woman that he'd gone out with—and there hadn't been many—had fit together with him like this. Only Louise.

She didn't sound very sure about this Marco. Blue just bet he was another of her unavailable loser boyfriends. He hadn't liked Tony either, but at least he really seemed to care about her.

Blue was no psychiatrist, but he'd always felt that ever since Tony died, every guy she picked was all flash. She pretended she was a good-time girl, but he knew it was just a defense against whatever was chasing her. She never let anyone get too close. She was always the one who called, 'the end'.

It was as if after the trauma of her teenage years, first her mother dying, then Tony, she always picked guys she couldn't really care about. Guys who weren't there for the long haul. Guys who couldn't hurt her if they left. Had she done that again with Marco? He didn't know whether to hope so or not this time.

She fell asleep and his arms crept around her, his hands lightly, protectively, cradling her belly.

Louise was having a baby.

Chapter 13

Stephanie heard a rumble on her back porch, then a light tap. The door opened and Blue poked his head into the kitchen.

"Hi, dear. Take off your boots."

He disappeared for a moment back into the porch, then shuffled into the kitchen in stocking feet, looking like a world-weary version of the boy she used to know. But he wasn't a boy anymore. He'd grown into a thoughtful, caring man, one who didn't deserve to be so heavily burdened.

Stephanie pulled her housecoat tight at her waist. "Sean's not here. I think he's at Frankie's."

"That's okay." Blue sat heavily on one of the wooden chairs.

A wooden stretcher pinned taut with a piece of white silk lay on the big oak table. She'd had a design in her head for days and had been planning to sketch it onto the silk, but that could wait. She pushed the stretcher aside to make a spot for them to sit. "Coffee?"

"Thank you. I didn't get much sleep last night."

She poured them both a cup, then sat across from him. "What's keeping you awake these nights?"

Blue rubbed a hand down his face and tugged on his beard. Then looked at her with pain in his eyes. "Louise is pregnant."

Stephanie pressed her lips together and nodded. He stared into his cup. "It's the other guy."

She covered his hand with one of hers for a brief moment. "I know."

"I don't think I can take it anymore." His unsteady voice nearly broke her heart. This gentle giant had been carrying a torch for Louise since they were playing forts in the woods together, and she'd been unaware she'd been stomping on his heart the whole time.

"What are your choices?" Stephanie asked mildly, although she had a few ideas on the subject herself.

"Give up. Walk away."

"That's one choice." She took a sip from her cup.

"My only choice," he said into his cup.

"Not necessarily."

He looked up at her. "He's the father."

"In name only, so far. Unfortunately, Louise's choice in men has not always been the best."

"Losers."

Stephanie hid a smile. "Well, yes. Usually." But not when she chose Blue for her best friend. "So, he may not be, you know, the one. Has she told him?"

"I don't think so."

"Well, then, the game's not over."

Blue didn't answer, but he squinted and she could see the wheels turning in his head.

"Have you ever told her how you feel?"

"No. Well, once in high school, but," he looked away and mumbled, "the timing was wrong."

"High school? Come on Blue, what's holding you back?"

"I'm afraid I'll lose her. I'm afraid she'll run. She's not good on commitment."

"She's been your friend—"

"Best friend."

"—for twenty years."

There was silence, then he said, "Longer."

"That's a long commitment. Her longest. Don't you think it might be time to step it up a notch?"

Blue's cheeks turned pink above his beard. "That's what Sean said."

"Does he know?"

"Not about the baby. But he knows how I feel."

"Well, he might be right. Promise me you won't give up without telling her."

Blue sighed. "I'll try, but I don't know if I can."

* * *

Blue was gone when Louise woke up on his couch the next morning. He'd left without even making coffee—but still, she must have been out cold not to hear him walk right by her where she slept.

Last night, snuggled on the couch together watching TV had been just like old times. Eventually she had fallen asleep with her head on his shoulder, but when she awoke in the middle of the night, he was gone. He'd put a pillow under her head though, and had covered her with a wool blanket before he went upstairs to bed.

Louise hadn't had any reason to go home so she'd closed her eyes and drifted back to sleep, but not before wishing she could take her blanket and pillow and go upstairs, climb into bed with him and hold onto his big solid warmth.

She was glad she hadn't. That would have been so wrong.

She made herself at home, brewing a cup of Tummy Time Mint tea and toasting a piece of Challah bread. She dug around in the fridge and found a jar of Stephanie's famous fig jam and ate standing in the kitchen, leaning against the granite topped counter.

The tension that had tied her shoulders in knots since she received the positive pregnancy result had finally eased now that someone, Blue, knew.

The sun shone through the kitchen windows and her breath caught when she saw the magnificent hundred-and-eighty-degree view of the lake and the mountains beyond. She could imagine the porch he'd build in the spring and sitting there with him on warm summer mornings and evenings, watching the sun rise and set on the lake.

Then the confusion about her future hit her again and her stomach curled into a knot. Where would she be next summer? Not here with Blue. Would she have a baby—would the pregnancy hold? Because she'd done the math. If she could hold onto this baby—and for the first time she really wanted to try—she'd be a mother sometime in early July.

Tears sprang to her eyes and she gave a self-conscious laugh as she wiped them away. Then sighed. But she wouldn't be here. Hopefully she'd be somewhere with Marco. Maybe Seattle, or California. She'd heard him mention San Francisco. Off on a whole new adventure.

If only she was as comfortable with Marco as she was with Blue. It had been so easy to tell him that she was pregnant, knowing that all she'd get from him was unconditional support.

From Marco? She had no idea, and the thought of telling him was tying her stomach in knots.

When she finished her breakfast, she rinsed out the dishes and drove over to her dad's house for their daily walk. After that, she spent the rest of the day in the cabin, kneading, rolling, measuring and thinking. She told herself she wasn't hiding, just processing her new situation, but she knew she was lying to herself.

She was making notes in her recipe binder when the phone rang. Even before checking the caller ID she knew it was Marco. Her stomach rolled queasily. They hadn't spoken for almost two weeks, and now, although she'd been waiting for his call, her hand hovered over the phone.

Then it rang again, jangling her nerves, insisting she answer.

"Hi." She tried to put some cheer in her voice, to sound normal, but she wasn't sure what normal was any more.

"Hey, Babe. How's it going." *He* sounded normal. Light and breezy, like his mind was on something else.

"Great. Everything's great." Silence. She stared out the window into the dark. "How are things going with you?"

"Great here too. Lots to do. Things to wrap up."

At the Academy? "Like what?"

"Looking ahead. Trying to set a few things up for after the holiday."

"Well, great." *Great.* Was that all she could say?

"Cool," he said.

He was cool, too cool, and suddenly it pissed her off. "I was offered a job."

There was a pause and she felt a spark of satisfaction at finally getting his attention. "Where?"

"Here. In Fortune Bay. At the new resort."

"Are you going to take it?"

"I don't know."

He didn't sound very interested. Didn't sound like he cared if she came back at all. Now she did feel like throwing up. "Are you coming to visit?"

"About that. I'm not sure when I can come. I've got irons in the fire." His laugh sounded false. Evasive. "Maybe next week."

Nausea rolled over her, but she wasn't sure what was causing it this time. Seeing him? Not seeing him? Telling him?

Like a random *blip* on a computer screen, a thought flashed through her mind. *Maybe I don't have to tell him.*

For a moment she felt light, free, like a butterfly fluttered in her chest.

Then she crashed back to earth. She had to tell him. They were having a baby.

But that sounded wrong. Maddie and Jake were having

a baby. Louise was just pregnant.

She had to tell him, but not on the phone.

"Next week would be great. Please come." She tried to put some warmth in her voice. "Come for Christmas. It'll be fun. I have this cute little cabin on the lake all to myself."

He didn't answer right away and her heart turned into a hard, hot ball in her chest. She didn't want to do this alone.

Finally, he said, "Sure Babe, I'll try. Sounds like fun. Call you in a few days."

She disconnected feeling— disconnected. Slightly queasy, she went back to work, trying to concentrate on updating her notes.

There'd been no, "I miss you," from either of them. Certainly no, "I love you."

Had they ever said that? She didn't think so. She hadn't expected it either, not considering the brief time they'd been together. In fact, she would have run as fast and as far as she could if he'd said something like that.

The sad truth was, if it wasn't for the fact that she was pregnant, she'd probably be running now. It was about that time. The time she usually ended her relationships.

She picked men who were fun, for the moment, always vaguely aware they would never work out. Or, in the odd case, she had ended it because they were getting too serious and she thought it just *might* work out. Either way, she was out of there. Managed to stay friends, most of the time, but still out.

After what had happened with Tony, she'd always felt safer keeping a bit of distance. She never wanted to go through that again—the loving and then the losing. Raising her hopes and having them shattered. Never again.

At the time, she'd already been fragile, having barely gotten back on her feet after her mother's death two years before. It had almost killed her when Tony died and she lost the baby, all in one fell swoop. She could never go through that again.

In fact, she was trying hard not to think of this pregnancy as a baby at all, didn't dare hope it was true. After the miscarriage, the doctors had told her she might never be able to carry a baby to term, and all these years she'd believed she had blown her one chance to have a child. Now she was afraid that if she dared even *think* about it as a baby, this chance might vanish as well.

Louise was still holding the phone after Marco's call when she heard a vehicle pulled up outside.

Chapter 14

At the rumbly sound of a truck motor outside the cabin, Louise mumbled a curse. Whoever it was, she didn't feel like company tonight.

Car doors slammed and voices sounded, loud in the quiet night. The chatter of women's voices accompanied by one deep male voice. Footsteps thumped up the porch stairs. Louise sighed and opened the door.

Like two drown kittens, Brandy and Amber stood on the porch in front of Blue. They fell silent when they saw Louise, both girls peering out at her from smoky, kohl-ringed eyes. Somehow, tonight, the effect came off more as Children-of-the-Damned than young-sophisticates.

Louise looked at Blue. "What's going on?"

"Found them on the side of the road on the edge of Majestic—hitching."

Brandy's eyes were round. Belinda had expressly forbidden her to hitchhike. Louise wasn't sure if her fear was the result of something that had happened earlier that evening or at the thought of what was to come now that she'd been caught. The narrow road from Majestic ended at Fortune Bay, so hitchhikers were usually picked up by someone they knew, but that didn't mean it was without its dangers, especially on a cold rainy night.

Louise swung the door wider and a sharp wind whistled in. "Well then, come in. And don't bring the whole lake in with you."

Jeeze, now she sounded like Belinda.

"I'm going to go," Blue said. "I'll leave this to you."

"Thanks for bringing them home." She was glad Blue had found them and not someone else.

Louise closed the door behind the girls. Brandy stood on the welcome mat shaking with cold.

"Come on. I'll get you some hot chocolate."

Amber glanced at Brandy, her face expressionless. Brandy nodded and they both stepped silently into the room.

"Take off your coats."

"I think I'll keep mine on," Brandy said in a tiny voice. "I'm pretty cold."

"Nasty night to be standing on the side of the road." Louise hoped for a reaction, but Brandy just nodded and went to warm her hands by the woodstove. Amber stood in the living room area.

"Sit down," Louise said. "This will take a couple of minutes."

"It's okay. I should probably go." Amber glanced at Brandy, but her friend's eyes were fixed on the woodstove.

"Sit," Louise said firmly. Amber slipped off her jacket, hung it over a kitchen chair and sat on the couch, defiance clearly etched in the squint of her eyes. She'd obviously been in trouble before and planned to brazen it out.

Louise poured milk into a pot and set it on the stove. "So how did you end up on the side of the road on a night like this?"

Amber answered. "We were out with friends."

Um hm. Under her winter jacket, Amber's white lacey top clearly showed her black bra, and Louise could see her pierced belly button in the inches of space between her top and tight leggings. No wonder she was cold.

"Anyone I know?"

"No."

"I know most of the local families," Louise persisted. Truth was, she was out of the loop, but she still wanted names.

Brandy offered up her childhood pal. "Drake

Bolkowski."

"So, how's Drake doing?" Louise asked.

"Fine." A silence followed that juicy tidbit.

Louise put three mugs of cocoa on the kitchen table along with a plate of cookies. "Come and get it."

She took a seat. Brandy came over and joined her, still in her jacket. Louise wondered what she was hiding underneath. Amber followed her lead and drifted over.

When they'd each sipped their cocoa and had a cookie in hand, Louise asked, "What really happened?"

Brand's lips trembled, then she said, "We had to get out, the party was getting too crazy."

"It wasn't that bad," Amber bluffed. "I've been to worse."

"It was bad," Brandy said softly.

"Why didn't you call Dad? Or me?"

"I couldn't call Dad—we were supposed to be at a party at Melissa's—all girls. Not a party where we were the only girls."

So, innocent Brandy had stumbled into a Friday night party of teenage boys who were no doubt all showing off to impress the girls. "Were they drinking?"

Amber nodded. "Somebody had a mickey of rum."

"And beer and pot." Brandy added.

So, a full-fledged party. No wonder Brandy was shaken up.

"Not all the boys were as nice as Drake," Brandy whispered.

She'd had a good scare, Louise thought. Not a bad thing if she came out unscathed.

"You could have called me. You can always call me."

"You're not always here."

Right. Thank you, Blue.

"I was this time. It sounds like a bad scene. I know how that can be. You were right to get out. It can go from bad to worse in a flash. Did you ever hear...?" Louise glanced at Brandy and her sister nodded almost imperceptibly.

She'd never told Brandy the story, but it would be hard to come of-age in Fortune Bay and not hear the cautionary tale of Tony and Louise. Odds were, Amber hadn't heard it, though.

It wasn't something Louise ever talked about, but now, tonight, it was so near the surface she couldn't *not* tell them the story. It might be time to free those devils, and perhaps stop it from happening again.

"When I was your age I was kind of a wild child. Goth." She smirked, trying to lighten the tone.

Amber laughed. "Goth?"

"Look who's calling the kettle black." Louise gave Amber's raven hair a gentle tug, eliciting a twitch at one corner of her mouth.

"I bet you were pretty," Brandy said. Louise's heart melted. Brandy had always been her number one cheer leader.

"I was pretty awesome, if I do say so myself, and I had the coolest boyfriend in the school. He was a year ahead of me in school but two years older. Had his licence and a car of his own. He had just moved to town in September and we hit it off right away."

"Didn't Dad say anything about you going out with him in his car?" Brandy was having trouble comprehending this alternate home-universe scenario.

"It wasn't long after my mom died and he was still pretty upset. So was I. That was probably why I clung so tightly to Tony." She stopped, surprised when her eyes filled with tears. "That was his name. Tony."

They were all silent for a moment, then Amber said, "My mom died too. Last year." She took a shaky breath. "Then my grandma died, last summer. That's why I came to find Sean. Dad."

Amber's pain was obvious in her tight shoulders and mournful eyes. Louise reached out and covered the girl's hand where it rested on the table. "It sucks."

Amber nodded, lips pinched.

Louise gave her head a shake. "So, anyway, Tony and I were hot and heavy into it by Thanksgiving and the week before Christmas we went to a party."

Blue's party. Blue had seen it all unfold, and she suddenly realized he had never talked to her about how it had affected him. It must have, though. It was his party.

"Tony was drinking; I don't know how much. He was a nice guy, a musician with a gentle soul, but he drank. Too much. He was nice to me, though, at a time when I needed someone, so I let it slide. A stupid thing to do," she said with emphasis, eyebrows raised as she looked from one girl to the other.

"Anyway, this night of the party, Tony'd had a few drinks before he got there and when the beer was gone, he decided to go on a beer run to Majestic. You can't get alcohol in Fortune Bay."

The girls nodded knowingly. Maybe not so innocent after all.

"Of course I went with him. It was a terrible night, kind of like tonight. It had snowed the day before but most of it had melted when the rain started to fall. There was slush on the road, but it was cold enough that the rain was freezing on the windshield. Tony put the car into a skid on those curves near Majestic. You know the ones?"

Brandy nodded.

"He did it on purpose, he had it under control. I thought it was pretty funny. At first. Then he did it again and I started getting kind of nauseous from the beer and all." And probably because she was six weeks pregnant. But that was a story for another night.

"Tony was going too fast when we hit the curves just

outside Majestic. On the first curve, the car went into a skid, heading sideways down the road. Everything seemed to move in slow motion. I had time to see the scared look on Tony's face and register that he'd lost control of the car. He jerked the wheel the other way and yelled *Christ!* His last prayer before we hit the next curve and flew off the road.

"His hands were clutching the steering wheel and he turned his head away from me to look out the driver's side window. The forest was flying toward us. In the snow, everything seemed kind of blurry and dream-like. Snowflakes drifted down in slow-motion, branches were covered in a fluffy layer of white and, for a moment, I thought we'd land softly. That we'd be okay."

The two girls were wide-eyed, unblinking. Louise could see the scene as clearly as if it were yesterday. She had replayed it for months afterwards behind closed eye lids, and it still sometimes played in her dreams.

She shuddered, and shook her head. "My door swung open and I flew out. Hit some bushes and banged my head. It knocked me out cold.

"I woke up with a splitting headache. I didn't know where I was. At first I thought that the flashing lights were just from the pain in my head—but it was the first ambulance pulling away.

She stopped talking. The next few days were a jumbled memory. The hospital, her dad. Blue and Stephanie taking her home.

Amber cleared her throat. "Tony?"

This was the first time in all those years that Louise had told the story aloud, and she had gotten so caught up in the telling, she'd forgotten the girls were listening.

Wiping the tears from her cheeks, she bit her lips together and shook her head. "He didn't make it."

Both Amber and Brandy were crying, makeup running down their cheeks. Louise laughed through her tears and plopped a box of tissues in the middle of the table. They each took one and grinned self-consciously as they wiped their eyes.

"I don't want that to happen to you. Don't ride with strangers or friends who have been drinking. Call somebody. Your dads, Stephanie, me, Blue. Someone. Promise me you will."

Wide-eyed, they both nodded their heads. Most of their eye makeup was gone, wiped away by the tissues, and except for a bit of redness, their eyes looked back to normal.

"Now," Louise said. "Finish your hot chocolate and I'll take you home."

* * *

When she got back to the cabin after taking the girls home, Louise made a pot of herbal tea and took it over to the big armchair by the woodstove. It had been quite a night.

As she sipped her tea, Louise mentally patted herself down, checking her feelings. She expected to find them raw and oozing and was surprised to discover she was calm and strong instead. After years of holding the hurt inside, her world hadn't caved in when she'd told the story.

Talking about Tony had been cathartic and Louise felt buoyant with relief. She should have done it years ago. That wasn't the whole story, but it was all the girls needed to hear right now. The rest was still too painful to tell.

What did Blue remember? He was the only one, other than her dad and Stephanie and the doctors, who knew that she had been pregnant and miscarried. But being so lost in her own dark world, she had never spared a thought for Blue's feelings, a fact that now grew to an ache of embarrassment in her chest.

No, worse than embarrassment —shame.

She had taken him for granted for all these years, after

he'd done so much for her.

How many times had he shielded her over the years? And of course, the big debit she owed him, for the way he'd taken care of her when she'd been so devastated, first by her mother's death then by Tony's.

She had taken him for granted and that had to stop.

* * *

It was a god-awful night on the road, Blue thought, as he headed for home.

When he'd seen Amber and Brandy by the side of the road, hitchhiking in the freezing rain, the horrors of that long-ago night came back like a cold hand clutching his heart.

Blue had never liked Tony. He was a little bit older and thought he was so cool. To be honest, the whole school thought he was cool. But he'd stolen Louise—was the first guy she'd gone out with—and then he'd almost friggin' killed her.

Blue took a deep breath and loosened his hands on the wheel. That was many years ago and he'd thought he'd let that part go. The guy had died. Wasn't that enough? But when he'd seen the girls on the road tonight, it had all come back.

Blue was the one Louise called from the hospital, and he'd been the one who, in the following weeks, held her on his couch while she cried.

They were sixteen, and she had turned to him. She'd cried on his shoulder, softened in his arms, sat on his couch after school, her head on his shoulder, watching *Full House* and reruns of *Saved by The Bell*.

He remembered waiting weeks for her to get over Tony. And then finally, her tears had stopped and she was still there, curled up beside him as his body quivered and burned when they touched. Then one day, he tentatively nuzzled her neck and she turned to him. He kissed her and—heavenly God! —she kissed him back.

Then she was lying on top of him on the sofa in his mom's living room. He ran his hands up and down her sides, on top of her clothes and then right along her cool bare skin—he could still feel the silk of it—pouring kisses down her long neck and fumbling with the buttons on her shirt until, miracle of miracles, it was undone.

Then, just like in a movie, he flipped on top of her in one smooth move and, lying between her legs, he was in heaven. He wasn't big clumsy Blue anymore. It was finally happening; they were together. She had chosen him.

Then she started to cry. Big, wet, noisy sobs. She buried her face in his neck—and they were back to square one. Like the snakes and ladders board game they'd played as children, he'd struggled to the top row of the board only to slide down the longest snake, back to square one.

"I can't, Blue. I can't," she'd sobbed.

"I know. I'm sorry." He pulled her up until they were sitting again, still holding her but now just patting her on the back, awkwardly trying to shift the lump in his pants.

That was almost twenty years ago. What was wrong with him? He'd tried to get past her, tried dating other women, but the feelings just weren't there and eventually, one or the other of them would call it quits.

And now Lou was back, and having a baby. And he wanted her more than ever.

This time, Marco was in the way. Blue would bet the house that *that* wouldn't last. Her relationships never did. But he felt like a jerk butting in before she even told the guy. Before they had a chance to try to make it work.

But when it all fell apart, like he knew it would, he was taking his turn at the wheel because, deep inside he just knew, if he had the chance to tell her—to show her what she meant to him—to show her how much he loved her—she would choose him.

And if not, then for once and for all, he'd know it would never work out.

Chapter 15

Louise had spent the last two days trying out recipes, telling herself she wasn't hiding—just processing the new information. But tonight, the women were meeting at Maddie's. Maddie had told her Colleen would be there too and Louise was excited to see her. Besides being Maddie's sister-in-law, and Sean and Jake's older sister, Colleen had been the closest thing Louise had had to a sister growing up.

She planned to wow them with her latest creations— Profiteroles, light-as-air cream puffs with two kinds of sauce for the women to rate, and individual chocolate-mint cheesecakes with tiny candy canes anchored to the top with a crown of chocolate ganache.

She figured she had processed as much as she could on her own but wasn't yet ready to tell her friends. She was worried that, physically, she couldn't hang onto this baby and didn't want to tell anyone else until she was sure.

Rain lashed the kitchen window and the temperature hovered at zero as the weather gods fought it out between rain and snow. A treacherous night out on the roads, but Maddie only lived next door so between the rain and all the baking she was bringing, Louise decided to drive.

"Will this weather ever let up?" Louise said as she stepped into Maddie's kitchen. "Frankie's right behind me."

"Have you seen how high the lake is?" Maddie asked, taking the bag from Louise's hands as Frankie hustled through the door. "Soon it'll be up to the path along the shore." She took a sniff as she carried the bag to the kitchen counter. "Smells like chocolate."

"Santa's Dark Secret cookies. Double chocolate."

"Perfect."

"And samples of a few other recipes I'm trying out. I want feedback."

Just then Colleen swept in from the living room. "I thought I heard your voice. Come here and give me a hug.

"You'd think we lived a hundred miles away instead of only on the other side of the lake for the amount we get over here," Colleen said. "But it's great to see you. I want to hear all your news."

Frankie sniffed the bag. "M-mm. I'm so glad you're back."

Colleen laughed. "I'm not sure I'm glad, not if you're baking. I don't need any more inches around my waist. I haven't lost the weight I put on having our last little guy."

"And he's how old now?" Louise had never paid much attention to the details that all the moms seemed to remember.

"Two and a half." She smiled and Louise didn't have to ask if she was happy. It showed on her face.

"Alex and Jake took the kids over to Stephanie's to give us a break."

"Nice guys," Louise said. "They're the best."

"We are pretty lucky," Colleen agreed. "But how about you? Any closer to domestic bliss?"

It was obviously a joke, Colleen's fall back sarcasm, but it all seemed so overwhelming right now that Louise couldn't come up with a snappy comeback. She just smiled and shrugged.

"I hear you're really pumping it out over there," Frankie said, peeking into the other bag. "Can we eat these or just look at them?"

Glad for the distraction, Louise started laying out the baking she'd brought on a platter Maddie supplied. The women groaned when she brought out the four individual cheesecakes, then groaned louder and laughed when she opened the box of cream puffs.

"This is serious," she objected. "I need your honest opinion. These four have a chocolate spice sauce. Cinnamon and a pinch of cayenne. And these have an orange-chocolate crème sauce."

"So, we have to eat one of each?" Colleen asked.

"Eat and comment. Honestly. These are new recipes and might need some work."

"How can you possibly eat everything you bake?" Maddie asked perusing the selection on the platter.

"I can't. That's why you're all getting baking for Christmas."

Frankie placed a bottle of wine on the table along with three glasses. They had always joked that their gatherings were just an excuse to buy a good bottle of wine, and usually between them they drank more than one. There was no way Louise would get away with pretending to join in tonight the way she had at Stephanie's party. With a sigh, she realized it was time for full disclosure.

"I'm glad to have the three of you alone tonight." She rubbed her damp palms on the thighs of her jeans.

Maddie's forehead wrinkled in concern. "What is it, honey? Something wrong?"

"No. No. Well...no."

Maddie sat down and turned to Louise. "We have all night."

"Well, there's not really much to say," Louise said, then she ground to a halt, not sure where to go from there.

"After I finished the course, I had a lot of plans." She paused again.

Frankie looked at her carefully. "What do you mean, '*had* a lot of plans'."

There was no way to sugar coat it. "I'm pregnant."

Frankie's mouth fell open. "What?"

Maddie's face lit up. "Oh, Lou."

Colleen, for once, was speechless.

Louise laughed, a quick embarrassed laugh. "Yup. Pregnant."

Frankie sputtered. "Who? What? When?"

Maddie reached out and took her hands. "Are you happy?"

Tears came to Louise's eyes. "Yes, I think I am." She wiped the tears away and laughed again. "But tell me this teary part doesn't last the whole nine months."

Maddie smiled, her own eyes suspiciously bright. "It doesn't."

"Who is the father?" Colleen asked.

For some reason Louise hesitated. But that was ridiculous. "Marco. The guy I was seeing in Seattle."

"The instructor at the Academy?" Frankie asked. Louise nodded.

"Does he know?" Maddie asked.

"No. I just found out since I got home and I haven't told him yet. I wanted to wait until he comes to visit. No one knows. Well, no one except Blue."

The other women exchanged a look.

"What?"

"Nothing," Maddie said. "What does Blue think?"

I have no idea. "Well, you know Blue. He doesn't say much. But he's been great." She thought about how comforting it had been to watch TV together on the couch in the dark. How he'd covered her with the cozy blanket as she slept. "Great."

"When is Marco getting here?"

The knot in her stomach pulled tight. "Probably any day. Now, how about those cream puffs?"

* * *

They had been introduced to Royal Icing at the Academy, but Louise had not been blessed with a steady hand so she decided to practice on the gingerbread cookies she'd made the day before from her mother's recipe. She filled the piping bag with the runny white icing and tried to outline the cookies, but her hand was no steadier than it had been at school and the first few were a squiggly mess.

She'd seen Stephanie use a mahl stick once when painting a particularly delicate passage and it didn't take much imagination to fashion one herself out of a dowel with a rubber thimble she found in a kitchen drawer stuck on the end.

Holding the piping tool in her right hand, she used the mahl stick in her left to form a resting bridge to steady her hand. Now, when she rested her right wrist on the stick, the line of icing flowed smoothly around the edge of each gingerbread cookie.

Much better.

The first dozen still looked like a kindergarten class project, but eventually she started to get the hang of it. When she finished this batch, she'd let them harden overnight and then, tomorrow, fill in the space with more of the runny white icing.

Once *that* icing had hardened, then came the fun part, painting on the decorative designs. It was a long process, but the result would be worth it.

While she worked, she couldn't help thinking about the fact that her friends now knew that she was pregnant, and she couldn't help wondering if she'd done the right thing. The circle was widening. How long could her pregnancy stay a secret? She particularly didn't want her dad to find out. That's when the pressure to stay would start.

They were her best friends, almost family, but she hadn't meant to tell them yet because it wasn't a done deal. She had a few weeks to go before she'd breathe easy. After all, the doctors had told her the odds were slim that she would get even this far.

A knock sounded on the door and Louise's hand jerked, running the bead of icing off the cookie and onto the plate. She scooped up the blob with her fingertip and licked it clean.

The door opened and Brandy peeked inside. "Can we come in?"

"Of course. Who is 'we'?"

"Amber and me."

Louise went over and gave her a hug. She'd missed Brandy while she'd been in Seattle. In the three years they'd lived together, they had bonded like sisters.

Amber slid furtively into the room as if trying not to displace any air in the process.

"Hi, Amber."

The girl looked out from behind her long black bangs and mumbled a response that could have been, *hi.* Her shy, almost-frightened manner was totally at odds with her harsh, almost-frightening looks. But it struck Louise that possibly it wasn't so much surly as self-protective. And for some reason, maybe because she'd been a scared teenager herself once, Louise wanted to help Amber feel more comfortable in her new life.

"Have some cookies. Take these ugly ones. I'm ruining as many as I get right." Louise laughed as she set a plate of gingerbreads in front of the girls, the icing wiggly or running right off the side instead of carefully following the shape of the cookies.

Brandy grabbed one and bit the head off the man, then she took another and handed it to Amber.

"They're delicious," Brandy said.

"Good. The cookies are my mother's recipe. And I'm finally getting the hang of piping the icing." Louise picked up the piping bag. "I'd better keep going before the icing hardens in the bag."

While Louise worked, Brandy told her about school

and her friends. Every few minutes Louise looked up and smiled. That was all the encouragement her sister needed. Amber nibbled on a cookie, following the flow of the piping bag with rapt attention.

Finally, by the time Brandy stopped for a breath and another cookie, Amber had sidled up to the counter where Louise was working.

"Tomorrow I'll fill this rim with icing," Louise explained.

Amber nodded, her eyes on the cookies.

"Want to try it?"

Amber's head jerked up. "Me?"

Louise smiled. Amber was skittish as a young deer. "Sure. It's not rocket science. You couldn't do any worse than I did."

Amber looked at the tray of cookies and back at Louise. Then she shoved the last gingerbread leg into her mouth, pushed the sleeves of her oversized sweater up to her elbows and held out her hand for the bag.

Louise didn't know how Amber could see past the veil of black hair that covered her eyes, but she carefully outlined the first cookie with a steady hand. When she finished, she glanced up at Louise, her face brightening in a shy smile.

Louise grinned. "Beginner's luck. Do another one."

The second turned out as clean as the first. Brandy came over to see. "Wow, you're a natural."

Amber offered her the bag, but Brandy declined. "You can do it. You're doing a good job."

Brandy took a carton of milk out of the refrigerator. "Are they all going to be plain white?"

Louise showed her a page of designs she'd sketched out. "I have lots of ideas. I'll finish them tomorrow"

"Will you still be able to eat them?" Brandy asked.

"I'm using edible paints," Louise said.

Amber moved on to another cookie, following the edge with a sure hand.

"You can paint yours if you like," Louise said, winning another smile.

Brandy moved in and held Amber's hair away from her face. "I bet you could sell hundreds of these at the artisan's fair." She sucked in a breath. "We should get a booth."

Louise laughed. "But then we'd have to *make* hundreds of cookies."

The girls looked at each other, barely containing their excitement.

"We're on Christmas holidays," Brandy said. "We could help."

Two pair of eyes glowed at the prospect. Louise thought for a moment, opened her refrigerator and looked at the baked goods piling up inside. It was getting kind of crazy. Her friends and family could never eat it all. A bake sale would be one way to work on her recipes and not drown in Christmas baking.

"Okay. But you two have to help."

"We will."

"With the baking and minding the booth."

She pulled out a pad and started taking inventory. She already had two Stollen. Better make three more. No, make that four. Many of the people around the lake were of German and Scandinavian heritage and few made their own Christmas bread anymore. And there could be other people there, too. Sean had done a lot of promotion and people were curious about the resort. He'd said there'd be an article in the Seattle paper next weekend.

Louise put her hands on her hips and looked at the turquoise stove and oven combo. "I don't know if this old oven is up to the challenge."

"We could bake some of the cookies at our place," Brandy said. "And Stephanie would probably let us use her oven too." She gave Amber a nudge.

"I don't know if I should ask..." Amber's voice trailed off.

"I'll ask Stephanie," Louise said. "She'll be happy to help." Especially if it kept Amber occupied.

"Gingerbread men," Louise said as she wrote it on the list.

"Or sugar cookies," Amber said shyly. "My Grandma always made sugar cookies at Christmas. One year my Mom came home, and we decorated them together. That was a long time ago though..."

Louise jumped in. "Sugar cookies it is. Stephanie has more Christmas cookie cutters. She used to pull them out every year."

"We sprinkled them with colored sugar," Amber said, her blue eyes swimming.

Louise said, gently, "Great idea."

She smiled at the girls. "The show is only a week and a half away. We'd better get busy."

Chapter 16

Louise let herself into Stephanie's back porch. Through the window to the kitchen she could see Steph at work framing a large canvas on the big oak table.

Stephanie looked up, smiled and waved her in.

Louise took off her jacket and hung it on the back of a chair. "You look busy."

Stephanie's face flushed with pleasure. "It is so exciting. Max wants this big painting and quite a few others for the lobby and dining room at the resort. I've never sold anything before." Her brows contracted in a thoughtful frown. "I hope it's not just because, you know..."

Louise shook her head, not wanting her thoughts to go there. "Your work is fantastic. We've been telling you that for years. You should be selling in galleries. Are you putting any pieces in the Artisan Show?"

"I'm having a table with some of my smaller pieces. I'd love to sell one or two."

"I'm thinking of getting a table myself. Well, me and the girls."

"Brandy?"

"And Amber. They came by the cabin when I was decorating gingerbreads and got all excited about making cookies to sell at the show."

Stephanie's eyebrows went up. "Amber? Excited?"

Louise nodded as she poured herself a cup of coffee from the carafe on counter. "Amber was really pretty good with the piping tool. She has a steady hand. Said baking cookies was something she'd done with her grandmother. It seemed to be a good memory."

Stephanie's face softened. "She doesn't have too many

of those. I'm glad you've struck a chord."

"Apparently, they made cutout sugar cookies shaped like Santas and things. Do you still have those old cookie cutters we used to use?"

Stephanie put down the framing hammer and opened a high cupboard over the refrigerator. "I think they're up here."

"I was wondering if, once you have your paintings out of the kitchen, we could make some of the cookies here. I worry that old stove at the cabin isn't quite up to the job."

"Well of course."

The women looked around the room, at the paintings stacked against every square foot of wall space.

"But why don't you see if you can use the resort kitchen," Stephanie said. "I'm sure Max would be happy to let you give it a test run."

"As long as he doesn't think it means I'm changing my mind about being his pastry chef."

"He offered you the job?"

"He did, but I turned him down."

Stephanie looked skeptical. "That sounds like a pretty good job."

"Yes, but I don't plan on staying in Fortune Bay." *Especially not now, when I need to be with Marco.*

"Well." Stephanie picked up the hammer and turned briskly back to her frame. "Ask him anyway. He can only say no."

"When are you loading in the paintings?"

"Early next week. Max plans to spend the week on the final decorating touches, including the Christmas decorations. He wants to have everything ready for the opening of the bar next week and the show next weekend. He has a few rooms booked on the weekend as well, mostly for the press."

"Let me know if you need a hand with your paintings."

"Thanks, you're a darling, but if you're planning to have a booth of your own, you'll already have your hands full."

"I think I'll head over and sign up for the show. I'll talk to Max about using the kitchen, too." The thought of the bright, new, empty kitchen had Louise licking her lips as she walked back out to the car. What she wouldn't give to try it out.

A few minutes later, Louise parked at the resort between a painter's van and a furniture delivery truck. Inside the lobby, Max had set up command central at the beautiful maple reservation desk. Under Blue's talented hand, even this was a work of art, and Louise ran her hand along the front edge of the top, imagining how his hands had gently peeled back the bark to expose a smooth wavy edge to use as a decorative feature.

Max looked up from his clipboard and his face brightened. "Louise. What can I do for you?"

"I want to register for the show, if there's still room."

"Sure. For your baking? That would be great. Actually, I wanted to talk about hiring you for a little job. I'm having a brunch for family and neighbors here Christmas Eve morning. I want you to cater the event. Sean's volunteered to do bacon and eggs, but I thought I'd see if I could talk you into bringing some of your fancy Christmas baking."

"I'd love to. How many people are you thinking?"

"Around fifty."

Louise laughed. "That's some family brunch. But no problem. In fact, maybe we could make a trade."

"Trade what?"

"I was wondering if I could take the kitchen for a test run, do some baking for the show. I'm really entering for the girls, Brandy and Amber. I think Brandy's interest is more in the sales end and eating the cookies, but Amber seems really eager to help with baking and decorating the cookies."

"Really? That's great. I know Steph's been kind of worried about how she was fitting in here and has been trying to find something she was interested in to fill her time. But you know how it is, it can't be something Grandma suggested."

"Not at that age. Steph thought you might let us use the kitchen here for a couple of days right before the show. I could give you some feedback on how it's set up, maybe tweak the arrangement if necessary."

"That would be great. And then you'd do the brunch on Christmas Eve?"

Louise smiled. "I'd love to."

"Good. You can sign up for the show with Sean."

Sean's office was off the dining room at the far end, and Louise stepped into the kitchen on her way by. The crisp white tiles, stainless counters and appliances all gleamed in beams of sunlight streaming in through the windows. She couldn't wait to get started.

A rumble of voices drew her back out to the dining room as Blue and Star struggled in carrying a long narrow table, the coffee station he'd been working on the day she dropped by the shop.

Louise hurried over. "Let me help."

Blue pushed her aside with his elbow. "We don't need any help."

Star put down her end and rested her hands on the top to catch her breath. "Maybe you don't, but I could use a hand."

"Not you, Louise," Blue said firmly.

"Oh come on, I can help."

Blue put his end down and stood with his arms crossed stubbornly over his chest. "Not you."

Star looked at her with sympathetic eyes. "Bad back? Too bad."

"Who has a bad back?" Sean asked sticking his head out

of his office.

"Louise."

"Since when? Oh, great, the coffee station. It's a beauty." Sean came over and nudged Star aside. "Let me give you a hand."

Louise shook her head as the men carried the heavy table over to the wall. She had always been as strong as Sean—used to beat him regularly at arm wrestling. And she was fine, but she could see Blue was going to be a bear about this.

And he might be right. Maybe if she started taking better care of herself, it might help to make this pregnancy last.

As the men nudged the table into its spot, Star said to Louise, "Sore back? I could give you a massage." She wiggled the fingers sticking out of her fingerless knit gloves and giggled. "They say I have magic fingers."

Not in a million years. Louise gritted her teeth and smiled. "Thanks, but really, I'm fine."

She turned to Sean as the men walked back toward them. "I wanted to talk to you about the show."

"Sure. Come into my office," he said, leading the way to a door off the dining room, just past the kitchen.

"Now, where is the list?" His fingers flew over the computer keyboard. "We're into the countdown. I've been working until ten every evening this week on details for the show and the opening of the bar, as well as for the soft opening."

"Sounds crazy. I want to book a table." As she said it, she felt a buzz of excitement.

"Great. Christmas baking? We have nothing like that."

"Brandy and Amber are giving me a hand."

His face brightened. "Amber wants to bake?"

"Apparently, she made Christmas cookies with her grandma, and she was pretty good at decorating when she and Brandy dropped by the cabin. Max said I could use the hotel kitchen for a couple of days before the show, take it for a test run. I don't think the old oven in the cabin's quite up to the job and the freezer there is just a block of ice."

"Sure. Anything. Thank you for letting Amber help."

Louise laughed. "Hey. They talked me into it."

"Did Max speak to you about the Christmas Eve brunch?"

"He did. I'll do it."

"Good. I can check that off my list." He pulled another list up on the screen.

"I hear you're the grill cook for the occasion," she said.

"It'll be fun. We've hired a few local people to serve."

"It *will* be fun. But I won't keep you. I have a ton of work to do myself."

Louise drove straight to her dad's house. Brandy and Amber were hanging out in the kitchen, making grilled cheese sandwiches. They turned eager faces toward her when she walked through the door.

"Good. You're both here. I booked the table for the show."

The girls squealed and high fived.

"Time to go shopping."

* * *

That evening, Louise painted blue highlights on the Royal iced cookies. Part cookie, part Christmas tree decoration, the results looked like Delft china

Absorbed in her work, she was startled when the text signal bleeped on her phone. She thought it could be Frankie, wanting to come over, but when she saw it was from Marco, her heartbeat accelerated. So lulled was she into life in Fortune Bay that she had almost forgotten about this bit of unfinished business. A bit of business that could change her life.

Hi Babe. Juggling job offers. Don't think I can get away. Talk soon. Marco

Louise put the phone in her pocket and stood for a moment contemplating the ramifications of the message. Of course she had to talk to Marco—yet she felt relieved that he wasn't coming. Wasn't that wrong? This little Christmas cocoon she was living in was too easy, too soothing. It wasn't real. Wasn't solving her problems.

Marco didn't seem eager to see her though. Sends a text? Coward! All her instincts screamed this wasn't the way to start a serious relationship. Although what did she know? She was the poster girl for keeping it casual

Chapter 17

Late the following afternoon, Frankie stopped by the cabin to pick up Louise and together they walked to Maddie's for tea.

A misty rain had set in, bringing with it warmer weather. The lake was calm as glass as they walked along the shoreline path. Moisture dripped off the fir trees and a few late mushrooms poked their heads through the thick moss that covered the ground between low growing salal.

Walking the trail was much nicer than sidewalks and asphalt and traffic, but Louise was fully aware of the trade off: greater opportunity, or all this natural beauty. She'd just be sure to enjoy it while she was here.

Maddie's kitchen always smelled like home cooking. It had become one of Louise's safe places and Maddie seemed happy to share.

"It's going to get busy, so I wanted to have you over now. Next week is Sarah's Christmas pageant at school and then Jenny comes home from college."

Carrying a pot of herbal tea scented with sweet spices, Maddie led them into the living room and they settled on the soft couches facing the decorated Christmas tree.

"Lovely tree," Louise said, holding back a laugh.

Maddie smiled fondly. "It may be a Charlie Brown tree, but Jake and Sean and the girls went out and cut two trees in the forest the other day. Amber was thrilled— apparently Christmas had been kind of hit or miss with her grandparents. So yes, it may not be as perfect as a farmed Christmas tree, but it was harvested and decorated with love."

Louise suddenly wondered what the plan was with her

dad and Brandy's tree. If Belinda would get it together. *Doubtful.*

"This domestic scene really seems to agree with you," Louise said.

Maddie's face glowed, beaming her happiness out to the room. "I love it."

Louise looked at her carefully, trying to decode her secret. How she managed it all so well. "You have a career. Was it worth giving it all up for the kids?"

"I didn't give up much to marry Jake, in fact I *found* my career when I moved to Fortune Bay. Before this I just had a job, a job I didn't love."

Maddie selected a gingerbread snowman and thoughtfully bit off his head. "I did give up my career when I had Jen, though. I was fresh out of art school and had only had a few photography jobs when I got pregnant. My then-husband was a bit of a control freak and didn't think I should work. But our problems weren't entirely his fault—I was young. I let him make the decision for me."

"It must have been hard when you were a working single-mom, though."

"It was, but parenting is always a challenge. Having Jen was wonderful. I'd do it again in a heartbeat."

"And leaving the city?"

"That was no hardship for me. Besides, my work and my family are here, now."

"Brandy and Amber talked me into taking a table at the Artisan's show at the resort next week, so we've gone into production."

"Wow, that's great," Maddie said. "It sounds like it's going to be a lot of fun. I'm pumping out framed black and white prints for the bedrooms at the resort. Max is single-handedly keeping us all employed.

"Nice of you to include Amber in your baking for the booth," Frankie said. "She seems so excited."

"I shudder to think of the life she's led," Maddie said. "The things she's seen. I know the hair and piercings don't really mean anything on their own, but she has a look that says she's seen too much for a sixteen-year-old."

Louise said to Frankie, "You're at the high school. Have you noticed who she hangs out with? Does she have many friends?"

"I am trying to keep an eye on her. So far, she's kept pretty much to herself, as far as I can tell."

As Maddie poured the tea, Louise said, "I saw Blue the other night. He seems kind of different these days."

Maddie shot her a look. "What do you mean?"

"Well, kind of ...hot."

Frankie snorted a laugh. "Blue has always been hot."

Louise looked at her in surprise. "Really?"

Frankie gave her the *daah* look. "Totally."

Louise turned at Maddie for confirmation. "Really?"

Maddie nodded, her lips curving up in a smile. "You've only just noticed?"

Louise took a sip of her tea and thought for a moment. "I haven't *just* noticed. And he hasn't always been hot."

"Really?" Frankie asked.

"Not in junior high." Louise blushed. That sounded so lame.

Maddie laughed. "Who among us was hot in junior high?"

"I know, but Blue was big, kind of clumsy and, well, excessively chubby. He was like that right through high school. A really nice guy—he's been my best friend forever—but I would never have called him hot."

"Well, he is now," Frankie said, sharing a smile with Maddie. "Funny you missed that. In fact, I kind of wondered, at the wedding last summer, if there was something between you two. And then he seemed so broken up at your going away party."

Louise's stomach twisted uncomfortably. "I didn't notice. I thought it was just game on as usual."

"He's such a great guy, quiet, but so helpful and...hot." Maddie laughed. "With those big brawny muscles."

"And that scruffy woodsy look," Frankie added.

"I didn't think scruffy and woodsy were your thing," Louise said, thinking of Sean's clean-cut style.

"It's not," Frankie agreed. "But if you were into that kind of thing, he'd be the one."

Louise thought about how lately she'd wanted to wrap her arms around his strong torso, both over and under his soft flannel shirt. "I don't know why it's hit me so suddenly..." Louise said as she took a sip of her tea.

"Hormones," Maddie said flatly.

Louise looked at her askance.

"I get so horny when I'm pregnant." Maddie said. Frankie sputtered her sip of tea in a laugh. "It's true. One of the perks of being pregnant. And Jake's certainly not complaining."

"You mean it's not all puking and back aches?" Frankie asked.

"Except for the puking, I love being pregnant," Maddie said. A soft smile settled on her face. "I feel so, I don't know, content."

"I've never really thought I was the motherly type," Louise said, then held her breath as she awaited their response. She didn't have to wait long.

"That's not true," Maddie protested. "Sarah adores you, and you are great with Brandy."

"Amber thinks you're the best. And look how you are with Scrawny."

Louise laughed. "I call him Brawny now—and he's not a kid."

"No," Frankie said. "But I've always thought that people transfer their maternal instincts onto their pets. You can tell what kind of parents they'll be—and when they're ready—by watching how they treat their pets."

Not a comforting idea, Louise thought, as she remembered Marco literally throwing Brawny out of the apartment.

Maddie reached over and patted Louise's hand. "You'll make a great mother. Fierce, like a mama lion."

Louise nodded, tears springing to her eyes. She would be fierce. She would protect this child from everything.

* * *

The following morning, Louise went to her dad's house for their daily walk. When she got there, he was standing in the middle of the living room, swinging his arms energetically, playing with the Wii she'd picked up on her shopping trip a few days before.

She grinned. "Hey, Dad."

"Just a sec." He swung his arm at the bowling pins lined up on the TV screen and they flew in all directions. "Yeah, strike. I haven't lost it."

He turned to her with a smile the likes of which she hadn't seen since before his heart attack. Her chest expanded, part pain, part joy, with a dash of hope. "Good job. Ready for our walk?"

They walked to the stream, as they always did, but now most of the salmon had spawned and died and were rotting corpses on the stream bed or fished out by the eagles and lying on the shore.

Louise covered her nose with the cuff of her heavy sweater. "It's starting to stink. Might be time to go somewhere else."

"Maybe we could drive to the end of Dugan's Road," her dad said. "See if we can get back to the marsh—look for swans."

Flocks of Trumpeter swans spent the winter in the marshlands that fed into the lake. Her dad had never been a hunter, but he loved to search out wildlife and knew every spot you were liable to find it at any given time of year.

"I think the Jeep could get in there."

She reached out to take his arm on the slippery slope up from the creek, where the fallen maple leaves formed a slick mat, but saw he was managing just fine with his cane.

They walked out into the yard and Louise took a good look around. The signs of her father's weakened condition were everywhere. The grass was long and scruffy —too late in the season to do anything about that now—and lawn furniture still sat out in the yard.

"Let me put these chairs away for you, Dad."

"I can help."

He could not. "I've got it. Just unlock the workshop for me."

She brushed the fallen maple leaves off the aluminum and mesh lawn chairs, stacked them in twos and carried them to the back shed that her dad used for a workshop and storage. Leaving the first pair by the door, she went back for the others as he fumbled with the key.

When she got back, he was inside, had turned on the lights and was holding a table leg.

"I was working on this when I had my attack," he said, not looking up. Suddenly she remembered this was where he had been when it happened.

"See here? It's split." His finger moved along a crack in the wood where the bolt would have held the leg to the tabletop. "Not a big job. I could probably manage it now."

"If you feel up to it," Louise said carefully, her heart pounding. Surely this was a good sign—as long as he paced himself.

"I think I could handle a little job like this. Maybe Blue would help me get this place back in shape. Wouldn't take much."

"I bet he would."

The front of the building, the part that he'd used as his workshop, had a general air of abandonment. Tools lay where he'd left them the day of the heart attack, the power tools and workbench covered in a light film of sawdust.

Louise made her way around the workbenches to the rows of shelves in the back half of the building. They were lined with things they never used but couldn't part with. "Spare parts," her father called the boxes filled with pieces of wood, metal springs and chain, things he was sure he would need for some future project.

"Do you still have the old Christmas decorations we used to use?"

They never said, *when mom was alive*, but when she was here, she felt the loss of her mother and her childhood as an ache in her heart. At first, she hadn't wanted to talk about her mother, could hardly bear to think about her. Over the years they had stopped mentioning her and in her own mind, Louise had skirted that time whenever memories threatened to surface. Now, as she probed those old scars, she found the pain had softened and the memories were melancholy, but sweet.

After years of pushing the memories away, she suddenly wanted to talk about her mother and wondered if maybe her dad did too. She doubted he and Belinda ever spoke of her.

"Mom's old decorations."

The words hung on the frosty air and she waited for the world to stop turning. Nothing happened, in fact, she felt a definite sense of relief. Glancing at her dad, she noted that he didn't show any strong reaction one way or another.

"I think they're back there." He pointed generally toward the dim back of the building.

At the end of the last row were a pile of boxes marked,

"Christmas." Christmas had virtually stopped in their house when her mother died and Louise spent the next few Christmases, and part of every Christmas since, with the Murphy's. Her throat tightened with emotion as she thought of how Stephanie had seamlessly folded her into her own family.

She pulled a couple of the boxes down off the shelf and found plastic greenery crushed into one, hidden wire holding the fake pine needles together. Another box held strings of old outdoor Christmas lights, white and blue incandescent bulbs, faded with time. Her mom's favorite. "You think these lights still work?"

"They might, but they cost a fortune to run. Hard to get the bulbs anymore, too."

Louise dragged the box out into the light and pulled out a tangled nest of lights. "Surely we can get one set to work." Finding an end, she plugged it into the wall and the whole knotted ball sprang to life.

"I loved these soft colors Mom always used."

"Yeah. I'm not crazy about the bright colors Belinda picked, but it makes her happy."

Louise busied herself untangling the lights. "Does she make you happy, Dad?"

Henrik picked up a bench brush, leaned his cane against the wall and brushed the sawdust off the bed of the band saw. "She does, Louisie. I was a terrible mess when your mom died, and I've always wanted to apologize to you for that. I let Stephanie pick up the pieces when I should have been taking care of my girl." He lowered himself onto a stool. "I'm really sorry."

Louise looked up and gave him a soft smile. "It's okay, Dad. I got through it."

"You did, and turned out good, too."

Tears prickled behind her lids, but she kept her hands busy pulling out the long end of the string of lights.

"Then I met Belinda, and I remembered there was more to life than sitting in the house staring into a bottle. She was a breath of springtime."

Belinda? Springtime?

"You were already grown up, working at the café, out with your boyfriends, but Brandy was still a young girl. She brightened up the place."

"I loved the little runt. It was great to have a sister."

"I was so happy you took to Brandy the way you did. She hadn't had it easy either."

"She loves you too, Dad."

He smiled, then his brows pulled together. "I know you and Belinda have never seen eye to eye, but I wish you'd try to get to know her."

The last knot in the string of lights came free and Louise could see there were actually three strings, one plugged into the next.

"I think one string will be enough," she said, unplugging it from the others. "And there are plenty of bulbs that still work."

She began to unscrew bulbs from further down the line to replace those burnt in the first string.

"Belinda won't be happy if you try to hang those on the house."

"Don't worry. I want them for the porch at the cabin. It's so dark these days, it'll be nice to have them to welcome me home. They'll remind me of Mom. Just like old times."

Her dad's eyes misted over. "Just like old times."

Chapter 18

A few days later, Louise stepped out of the Jeep in the resort parking lot, her rubber boots cracking the frozen crust on the puddles. The day was crisp and clear, the sun almost blinding after days of misty rain. She buttoned her jacket around her neck as the wind off the lake dug in its icy claws.

When she'd signed up for the show a week ago, the parking lot had been full of workman's vans and it had been hard to believe the resort would be ready. But today, with four days to go, only one furniture delivery truck was backed up to the open front door.

Brandy pulled into the parking space next to her in their dad's car, with Amber riding shotgun.

"You're just in time to help me unload." Louise's car was full of supplies, bags of flour and sugar, bottles of spices and vanilla, and the frozen cookies and Stollen that had been clogging the small freezer at the cabin.

She was sure she'd forgotten something, her mind was a sieve lately, but home was just a few minutes away and the general store was right across the road, so she figured she'd be okay. At least the resort kitchen had plenty of bowls and pans and utensils. She couldn't wait to try out the new ovens and range, but it was too soon to do too much more baking if they wanted everything fresh for the show.

Busy people criss-crossed the lobby, each set on a mission of their own. Max was at his post at the front desk, writing on a stack of papers, phone to his ear, so Louise hurried through to the dining room and the swinging kitchen doors with Brandy and Amber in tow.

When she pushed her way through into a quiet, pristine

kitchen, behind her, Amber said, "Wow."

Louise had forgotten that the girls had never seen a commercial kitchen before.

"I know, it's beautiful. Max is so sweet to let us use the ovens. We'll have to be sure to leave it just like this when we're done."

She walked over and set the heavy bags of flour down on the counter of the pastry station. "Why don't you unload the car?"

While the girls went back to get another load from the car, Louise loaded the Stollen and frozen fruit breads into the industrial refrigerator. Thawed and tied with big red bows, she hoped they'd be a hit.

Too bad she hadn't known about the sale sooner, in time to make traditional Christmas fruit cake. Her mother's recipe added a cup of strawberry jam that kept the loaves moist, but they needed to cure for more than a month. Maybe next year.

But who knew where she'd be next year? Her mind habitually flew to an image of herself in a restaurant or, even better, a hotel kitchen somewhere in Seattle. But then she felt a small hand tugging at her apron and—no, wait, she couldn't have a baby in a hotel kitchen. So, where was she working in this dream? Out of her own kitchen? Could she make enough to live on doing that? Would she be living alone? With Marco? That seemed less likely every day.

She pushed her hands to her chest to stop the palpitations and brushed the thoughts away. *Concentrate on what you have to do right now.* It was how she was getting through the days.

One thing they could do right now was make a small batch of cookies to test the ovens. The kitchen was stocked with measuring cups, bowls and an industrial mixer, so she set the girls to making a batch of gingerbread cookies to try it out. The day of the sale, she planned to have pans of gingerbread cookies baking, letting the aroma lure people over to the booth.

While they worked, she went back out to the dining room where, through the wall of windows, the lake sparkled cobalt blue against the mountains beyond. Max had chosen a wonderful location.

The small square tables Blue had made were lined up in rows down the centre of the dining room, and she dragged two of them over next to the kitchen doors to use for her booth.

Stephanie was lending her some white linen cloths, and she had bought boxes and paper plates decorated with holly leaves and berries, but she'd need more decorations to draw people in. Maybe some flowers—no, better, a bouquet of wild holly and berries from the edge of the forest by the cabin. She'd also need something bright to draw attention to the goods on display. Then she remembered her mother's decorations, still in the Jeep.

As she walked back through the lobby, two men were wrestling a queen size mattress onto the freight elevator. Max was at the reception desk with a sheaf of paper spread in front of him.

He looked up as she approached. "So many details. The rooms in this building are all booked for the weekends before and after Christmas. Just a trial run. No dining room, just breakfast served in the bar."

He shook his head. "That's this weekend already. Running the Artisan's Fair ensured a full house. Sean is a genius."

"And I haven't forgotten your Christmas brunch." Louise smiled as Max's brow furrowed again at this reminder.

She followed the delivery men back out to the parking lot where two people were stringing Christmas lights, dripping like white icicles from the young trees planted in the central flowerbed. It would be lovely when darkness fell, as it did so early at this time of year. She couldn't wait to get her own lights up.

Sean's pickup truck turned into the lot.

"Mom's paintings," he said, hopping out and pulling a tarp off the load in the back where the four-by-six-foot canvases were held in place by cardboard boxes and rope.

"Let me help," Louise said, taking the first one out of his hands. They weren't heavy, wood stretchers and canvas with a thin, modern frame that seemed to float around each one.

The painting she held consisted of energetic swirls of greens and blues that, when seen from a distance, became windblown fir trees around the lake. "I swear, your mom must be a witch to paint something like this."

Sean took the next one out of the back of the truck. "Maybe not a witch, but charmed for sure."

Max held open the lobby door for them. "Wonderful. I've dreamt of how fabulous they'd look in here. Even though I hadn't met your mother yet, I built this space with these paintings in mind."

They leaned the first two against the glowing wood walls where they seemed to jump and dance.

When all the paintings were inside, Louise took the decorative greenery from her car back to the kitchen where the girls were ready to roll out the cookies. She let them go at it while she figured out how to work the controls on the industrial ovens. Oh, the joy of having two ovens! She could set one for cookies and one at a lower temperature to toast the almonds for the mince.

While the ovens preheated, Louise worked on the mince pies, grating the half-and-half mixture of lard and butter for the pastry. Soon the pastry was cut in circles and pressed into the tart pans and she was chopping the dried fruit and roasted almonds. As they worked, the girls chattered about boys and clothes, and boys and makeup, and boys and the environment (she was glad to hear one serious note) and boys.

Louise didn't think about *the problem* for hours, as they adjusted the ovens and made notes on their recipes. In fact, she was in heaven.

In a couple of days, they'd seriously get to work for the show and then she'd have the pastries for the brunch to think about—right now she was leaning toward chocolate croissants and sweet loaves—and then...

And then, back to reality.

Before she knew it, the sky had darkened and the girls were packing up.

"You did a wonderful job on the cookies," Louise told them. "Great idea to sprinkle some with colored sugar."

Amber smiled, slightly abashed but obviously happy. "Need us tomorrow?"

"We could probably do a few hours, then, in a couple of days, we'll really get started."

After the girls left, she cleaned the sinks and wiped the gleaming counters and stove. Admiring the pies one last time, she covered them with cloths and moved them into the refrigerator.

The bite sized, star-shaped gingerbread cookies had turned out crispy and buttery thin. The air was rich with the smell of sugar and spice.

She dragged an empty chrome baker's rack out of the kitchen and into the dining hall and lay her mother's fake greenery out on the tables. Twisting the wires holding it together into something resembling a fir bough, she spread the needles in a natural way. She decided to take the greenery back to the cabin and vacuum it before attaching it to the baker's rack. Maybe with red ribbons.

As she packed the greenery back into the box, Blue came into the dining hall, a life-size carving of an eagle cradled in his arms.

"Wow, gorgeous," she said, then grinned when he blushed. "I meant the bird."

He grinned and flipped her a middle finger.

She held up a star in her hand. "Cookie?"

He put the sculpture down on her table and eyed the cookie. Then he eyed her.

Her lips curled at the corners. *Come and get it.*

He walked toward her, stopping right in front of her and tugging the cookie she held tight between her fingers. Her teasing backfired when he gave her a look that shorted her entire internal electrical system, and she let the cookie go. His smile made her circuits crackle again as, still holding her gaze, he took a bite.

Energy raced between them, pulsing stronger as he stepped an inch closer.

He had cookie crumbs scattered on his beard and Louise reached up and brushed them away, gently running a finger over his lips. So soft. What would it feel like to kiss those lips? Feeling the brush of that beard on her cheek?

Something shimmered in the air between them. His lips opened slightly and for a split second she was tempted to slip her finger into his mouth...then Blue stepped away.

He picked up the eagle and set it on his table across the aisle. "Come and see the tree I brought for Max. A big Noble fir for the lobby."

Giving her head a shake to bring her back to earth, she followed him out to where Sean and Max were struggling to keep the giant tree upright while two of the work crew, up on tall ladders, screwed thin guy wires to the wall to keep it steady. The ceiling in the lobby was at least twenty feet high and the tree swept within a foot of the peak.

"Wow," she said. "That's enormous."

"I had to take my truck to Bremerton to get it." Blue stretched out his arms around the tree and pushed his chest against it to help hold it still.

"Do you have enough decorations?" Louise asked Max.

He eased away from the tree as Blue took over, and pointed to a stack of boxes piled against the wall. "I ordered them after the fire in October. It was a leap of faith, hoping we'd be able to open for Christmas, but we made it." He beamed with satisfaction.

Blue turned to Louise. "I got a tree for your dad. I dropped it off at his place already."

In the last few years, Louise's dad and Brandy had taken care of getting the tree, but she remembered how when she was a child, she went with both her parents to pick one out. That had stopped after her mother died, and after Belinda and Brandy arrived, Louise had kept her distance during holiday preparations.

To be honest, she felt kind of pushed out by the new family unit that emerged. But this year she wanted to help her dad and connect with Brandy. Belinda could be the one to step out of the way.

"That was nice of you."

"Well, I was getting one for myself and knew our dad wasn't doing too well, so I offered. No big deal."

But it was a big deal. Louise remembered her vow to stop taking Blue for granted. "Well, thank you. And thank you for chopping and stacking their firewood."

"Like I said, no big deal. I could have got you a tree too for the cabin, but I thought you'd be spending Christmas with your dad."

"I will be. I don't need a tree there, but I am going to put up some lights. I got a string of our old Christmas lights from Dad's shed and thought they'd be nice on the porch at the cabin. Remind me of my mom."

Blue frowned. "You shouldn't be climbing around putting up lights."

"I'll be fine. I've done it a hundred times."

"I'll help you."

Louise smiled. "You're on."

Dusk was falling when they pulled up to the cabin. Louise could have hung the lights herself, but it was nice to have Blue's help. He was tall enough to hammer the nails into the eaves of the slightly rickety porch without a ladder while she untangled the string and fed him the lights.

"I remember your mom. She was great."

Louise sighed. "Yeah, she was. I've been thinking about her a lot lately."

When the lights were up, Louise plugged them in and the white and blue bulbs glowed in the misty dusk.

"Thanks, Big Guy." She gave him a hug, and this time he hugged her back. The new reserve was gone and it was just like old times...but not. The hug was a little longer, a little warmer, with a little more full-body contact.

She pulled away. "Hungry?" She didn't want this feel-good moment to end.

He took a long Blue-like pause as he thought over his answer. "Yes. Let's have dinner. We can watch the game."

She smiled. "If you have food in the fridge, I'll cook." She unplugged the lights, not trusting the old wiring while she was away.

As they walked toward the vehicles, she said," Actually, I've been on my feet all day. Let's order pizza instead."

Chapter 19

Blue headed home, the Jeep's headlights bouncing behind him in the rear-view mirror. Pizza sounded great, but spending the evening curled up on the sofa with Louise sounded like sweet torture.

Why did he do this to himself, snatch at any crumbs she offered when her new boyfriend could show up any day? And where was this guy, anyway? Had he detected a hesitation in her voice when she talked about Marco, or was that just wishful thinking?

Maybe Sean was right. Maybe he should make a move, declare himself in the race before this guy showed up. How well could she know him, anyway? They could only have been dating for two months and according to Louise's time-honored pattern, it would be just about time for her to break up with him.

Except now she was pregnant, so all bets were off.

Why had he invited her for dinner? Stupid, *stupid* move.

It had been raining all day and was still coming down so hard that his wipers were scarcely up to the job. When he got to his house, he swung the steering wheel hard and fishtailed the truck into the dry parking spot behind the house. Louise's Jeep barreled in behind him and pulled up by the front door where he planned to dump a load of gravel one day soon, but right now was a small lake.

Jumping out of the truck, Blue waded through the water in his rubber boots to the driver's side of the Jeep where Louise was looking down at the ankle-deep ooze.

"I dressed for the resort," she said. "Not for this."

He grinned. "Wimp."

Reaching into the Jeep, he slid one arm under her legs and the other across her back and lifted her out. When he gave her a bounce to get a better grip, she shrieked and grabbed tightly to his neck. Louise was no featherweight, but he was used to hauling carving logs in and out of the shop so carrying her up the stairs would be no hardship.

No hardship having her eye to eye either, to smell the scent of vanilla and spice that clung to her clothing. And probably to her skin. If he took off those clothes, she'd probably smell like gingerbread cookies.

Pay attention. He didn't want to drop her in the mud. Not in her present condition.

He whacked the Jeep door closed with his hip and she laughed into his neck, deep and throaty. His quads felt the strain of her weight as he climbed the steps, but he would have kept on climbing right up to the bedroom on the second floor if he thought it was the right thing to do.

But it wasn't.

Sean's voice rang in his head. *This is your chance.* She wasn't engaged to this guy, Marco.

This might be his only chance.

"You can put me down now," she said, and he realized he was standing on the porch in the rain, still holding her in his arms.

He stepped up to the door so she was under the overhang. The runoff from the roof was running down his back but he didn't feel it. Pressing her gently against the door, he slowly let her slide into a standing position, wedged between him and the door.

She kept her arms around his neck, stared right into his eyes. The awareness he saw in her gaze was new, as if, for the first time, she was seeing him not just as a friend but as a man.

Damn right he was. "When's this boyfriend coming?"

She pressed her lips together and her eyes swiveled

away. Then she blew out a long breath and looked back at him. "I don't think he's coming."

That was all he needed to hear. All bets were off. He put his hands on either side of her face and leaned in an inch closer. Then stopped.

Like in a dream—the dream he'd had over and over ever since he was fifteen—she lifted her face to his. He bent down and kissed her. Gently. Hardly a touch. Just a whisper of his lips on hers.

He could hardly believe she didn't smack him on the head, laugh and pull away. Instead, she kissed him back, equally tentative, and when he pulled away, her eyes stayed closed. He ran his tongue around his lips and stood for a moment with the icy rain dripping into his jacket collar, soaking him to the skin. Then he reached down and opened the door.

Louise opened her eyes as the wall—no, the door— behind her gave way. She felt like her knees were going to give way next, so she grabbed Blue's shoulders for support.

His deep brown eyes were just inches from hers, and he smiled. Not the shy, distracted smile she was used to, but a warm, sexy smile she could swear she had never seen on his face before. Had other women seen this smile? That look in his eyes? Where had she been all these years?

She cleared her throat. "Okay then. Didn't know you were a mistletoe kind o' guy."

"No mistletoe, Louise. Now step inside before I drown out here." He put his hands on her shoulders and gently pushed her into the house.

Just like that, one tiny kiss—hardly even a kiss, just a brush of the lips—and he rocks her world. A wave of anxiety rushed by her, just for a second, then it was gone.

On the one hand, she didn't want anything to change between them because she had a feeling she needed him as a friend more than ever now.

On the other hand, ever since she found him waiting at the cabin when she arrived back in Fortune Bay, she'd been having these thoughts, these fantasies about him that made him hard to resist.

He closed the door and leaned on the wall, wedging off his muddy boots. "Order the pizza why don't you while I get changed. I'm soaked. The game's almost starting."

"Okay." *Why not? Let's pretend that my life has not just irrevocably changed. Again.*

He dug the brochure for Majestic Pizza out of a kitchen drawer, set it on the counter and headed for the stairs. "One double hot sausage and one whatever you want."

Double hot sausage. No, nothing had changed. But it had, and whatever had happened had flipped the switch igniting a fire in her belly—no, be honest, in her *loins*—that left her aching for more.

She eyed the stairs to the second floor where Blue had just disappeared, no doubt to the bedroom where he was probably stripping down, taking off his wet shirt at the very least.

She could imagine his chest, toned and broad because, now that she thought about it, she hadn't seen him without a shirt on for years. Maybe a decade. Maybe ever.

As a pudgy kid he hadn't stripped down like the other boys, and they hadn't been swimming together since they *were* kids. From his dense beard, she'd bet he had some hair on his chest, although his arms were only lightly sprinkled so she doubted he was a hairy monster.

But right at the moment she didn't care. It might be kind of hot. She just wanted him to press her up against the wall again and...

Oh my god. Louise pressed her hands to her burning cheeks. *Hormones, hormones.* Wasn't that what Maddie had said? And why, for heaven's sake, did he kiss her now when she was pregnant. Maddie said Jake loved her spiked interest in sex. Maybe guys knew. Maybe they liked pregnant women. Maybe they thought *that* was hot.

Who knows?

She grabbed the pizza flier off the counter. *Double hot sausage.* Suddenly everything sounded suggestive.

She heard his footsteps on the stairs and grabbed the phone out of her jacket pocket—she hadn't even taken her coat off yet—and dialed the number on the flier.

Blue turned on the TV on his way through the living room and came into the kitchen just as the pizza guy answered.

"I'd like to order two pizzas," she said quickly, feigning intense interest in the descriptions on the flier, although nothing registered in her brain.

Her eyes flicked up to Blue who mouthed, "double hot sausage," with those full, soft lips.

She blinked. "One double hot sausage," she said. And what? She didn't think she could eat. "The Majestic Special."

A safe choice. Unlike spending the evening with the new Blue. New and improved. The new and improved, double hot Blue. Although, right about now, dangerous sounded like a fabulous idea.

Heart racing, she disconnected the call and put the phone on the counter. She licked her lips. "They'll be here in half an hour."

"Doubtful," he said, opening the fridge and pulling out a bottle of beer. He stopped. "I guess you're not..." he indicated the frosty bottle.

She shook her head.

"Soda?"

"Sure."

While he got her a glass, she kicked off her shoes and hung up her jacket. Was he not going to acknowledge the kiss? That things—*everything*—had changed? Was he going to drive her *insane*?

He handed her a tall glass, then took her hand and towed her to the couch. "Game's started."

They both sat on the couch, her in the middle and him at the end farthest from the TV. She tried angling her body away from him to watch the game, but she felt awkward, her back and shoulders stiff and unbending. She pulled up her feet and tucked them under her but unlike the previous visit when she'd turned into a virtual puddle of emotional angst in his arms, she couldn't get comfortable.

She shifted again.

"Settle down," he said and pulled her back so she was leaning against him. Her body immediately responded and she relaxed.

The arm he'd lain along the back of the sofa dropped down to massage her shoulder. She angled her head away to give him access. His other arm came around her body, his hand landing on her belly.

And suddenly she wasn't relaxed anymore. A tingle radiated from every point of contact, and now that he was wrapped right around her, that seemed to be almost everywhere.

His hand moved down from her shoulder and rubbed, feather light, over her sweater, down the side of her breast. She blew out a breath and arched into his hand. He gently continued the slow circular rub.

The other hand came up and palmed the other breast. She was so sensitive, not sore any longer, just sensitive. Extremely sensitive. She leaned back against him to give him better access. She wanted him under her sweater, under her bra, she wanted to see his face, his eyes.

Then his lips found the soft spot on her neck and she sighed again. He nuzzled and kissed and rubbed his thumbs over the sensitive points, until she was a puddle again, a seething puddle of lust.

Her skin was as silky as Blue had imagined. Her breasts had grown in the past few weeks, torturing him with every glance as he longed to feel them under his hands. Now he could feel her vibrating, like a volcano about to erupt.

He was pretty volcano-like himself, but he wanted, needed in a way that was part of him, had always been part of him, to feel her soft skin beneath his hands. Run his lips along every part of her, discovering the places he'd imagined a thousand times.

Suddenly she put her hands firmly on his, stopping his train of thought, pulling him out of the dream. Then she spun around and straddled him on the couch, grabbing his hands in her own.

She was breathing hard. "You want to do this Blue?"

His eyes widened in surprise.

"Do you really want to do this?"

He nodded, choking on a breath.

"Because you should know better than to fool with a pregnant woman."

She leaned in to kiss him and he put his hands on the back of her head. This time he wanted a real kiss. A meaty kiss.

He thrust his tongue into her mouth and tilted his head to increase the contact. When he realized he didn't have to hold her in place, that she wasn't going to change her mind, he moved his hands down to her ass, kneading.

She responded in rhythm and soon was rubbing her hot, sweet core on his hard ridge. So damn good.

She put her hands on his head and rolled them over so they were lying on the couch. This wasn't going to work. Blue could hardly fit on the couch by himself but before he could finish the thought, the doorbell rang.

She broke the kiss, breathing hard, and he laughed,

groaned, not sure which exactly, and pushed himself up to his hands and knees over her. "Don't go anywhere."

She rolled onto her back on the cushions and shook her head. He held up a finger to emphasize the point and pushed off the couch.

He ran his hands through his hair and adjusted his pants, grabbed his wallet from his coat pocket and opened the door.

The pizza guy looked like a drowned rat standing in the rain so Blue gave him an extra ten for his trouble.

As Blue closed the door, he heard footsteps run up the stairs.

Blood on fire, he threw the pizza boxes on the counter and raced up the stairs after her.

Chapter 20

Louise woke the next morning with a heavy weight on her ribcage. Blue's arm lay over her. She gave him a shove but he didn't respond, so she pushed him again. "Move over, you big lug."

His hand curled around her waist and pulled her back so her butt nestled in the warm, safe curve of his body. Her eyes drifted shut and as he kissed her neck, she felt him harden against her.

Her eyes flew open as the realization hit her—she'd slept with Blue.

A chill washed over her as the enormity of her mistake became clear. Had sex, not just sex but intimate, fantastic sex. How had she not known it would be like that? He was so strong, so firm, yet so gentle. True Blue. She could surrender to him like to no one else because no one else knew her, knew all her secrets, the way he did.

She knew a lot about him too, though. That he'd only had a few girlfriends and didn't go to bed with someone lightly. He was much too honorable for that.

Of course she didn't either, but their parameters were different. So different.

She would never knowingly do anything to hurt him— and yet she just had. This would change everything. And if it weren't for the mess she'd gotten herself into with Marco and the baby, she might be thinking very differently about what had happened last night, and where it might lead. But how, in good conscience, could she go there now?

Blue nibbled on her ear and his hands crept up until they brushed the underside of her breasts. She stopped his hands with her own.

"Blue."

His arms stiffened around her. She rolled over so she was facing him and—*oh, no.* Instead of the warm, open expression she'd seen on his face the night before, the face of her oldest and dearest friend had closed into the mask that she suddenly realized he'd been wearing around her for—cripes, how long?

Now that she thought about it, for a long time.

But he wasn't distant last night. Last night he had opened his soul to her and his love had come pouring out like honey because, cripes on a donkey, she saw it now. He loved her. Not as a best friend or good buddy, but *loved* her. And she was going to hurt him.

If she promised him too much—and by sleeping with him she may have—she would break his heart.

"Blue." Even she could hear the sickening pleading in her voice. "You know what's going on. I have to give him a chance."

"When are you going to give me a chance?"

Her face went stiff and cold as if all the blood had been sucked out of it. "The timing's all wrong."

"The timing's always wrong. There's always a reason you can't get close. To me or to anyone."

His words stung. She put her hands on his chest and pushed herself back to get a better look at his face. "That's not true. You have to see how the circumstances right now—"

"Jeeze, Louise, when are you going to stop running? How long do you expect me to wait? You know what? I'm finished waiting for you to get your shit together. I have to start taking care of myself."

He swung around and put his feet on the floor. "Have a good life. See you around."

He grabbed his clothes and strode out of the room.

Louise lay on the bed in shock, dry eyes staring at the

ceiling. A moment later she heard the growl of his truck as the tires threw up gravel and he sped down the drive.

* * *

Blue roared into town, his whole body vibrating. She was damaged, he knew that, but somehow he'd hoped that if he ever had a chance to show her how much she meant to him, how much he *loved* her, they could get past her instinctive defences and he could help her heal. Help her regain her trust in life, in love.

Who was he kidding? This wasn't like when they were kids. He couldn't kiss this and make it go away.

Well, he'd never make that mistake again. He couldn't take it anymore. He was finished waiting for her. He was not one of her easy-going guys. He was hurt and confused and *mad* to even be lumped in with them.

He shook his head. After all these years, he should have known better. She couldn't love, she'd proven that time and again. Why did he think it would any different with him?

And he just bet she wouldn't stay with Marco, either. Anyway, that was not his problem. He wasn't sticking around to pick up the pieces. Not this time.

He swung into the parking lot at the shop and ground to a halt. Sleet splattered the windshield but he sat in the cab as the truck grew cold. He was an idiot to think it would ever be any different.

He stared out the front window at the apartment attached to the shop and after a few moments, realized Star was staring back. Waving. She must think he was crazy, sitting in the rapidly freezing truck.

He opened the door and stepped out, ankle deep into a puddle of slush that found the leak in his rubber boots. "Christ!"

He sloshed into the shop and Star came running out to

take his coat. "It looks nasty out there. Were you trying to wait out the rain in the truck? You could have frozen to death. Come in and sit by the stove."

Now that was the kind of greeting a guy deserved. Blue went into the station, sat in the chair by the fire and pulled off his soggy boot. When he turned it upside down, water dripped out.

"I'll take that," she said and turned his wet boot upside down on a stump beside the oil-burning heater to dry. "Want some coffee? I just made fresh."

"Sure." Star made damn good coffee.

She put a cup in his hand. Concern puckered her forehead. "Everything okay?"

As Blue drank his coffee, he took a good look at the woman who'd been living at his shop for the past two months. Tiny, cute, kind of like a fairy in the colorful knit clothes she made for herself. Bright sparkly eyes, bright red hair, bright smile. Every damn thing about her was bright. Not like dark, moody Louise, who was one problem right after another.

Why hadn't he noticed this great woman who was right here under his nose? Well he was noticing her now.

She sat on a stool and picked up her knitting, some new striped thing. Bright.

"What's up for today?" she asked.

He thought about that for a moment, his brow tightening fiercely. Not the day he'd imagined when he woke up this morning. *Get over it. That's finished.*

"I told Sean I'd give him a hand at the resort."

"That's nice." She looked up from her knitting and gave him a sweet smile, then went back to her work. No questions. No complications. No tying him up in knots.

"Want to go out to dinner tonight?" He was surprised to hear the words come out of his mouth, but damn it, he was glad they did.

Her knitting needles stopped and she looked at him in surprise. "I'd love to. Where?"

"Into Majestic. There's a new sushi place I've been wanting to try." *Not.* But it was the first thing that came into his mind, some place Sean had mentioned the other day.

Her face brightened. "Sure."

He wasn't ready to make a date at his place or hers, but dinner in public—it was a start.

* * *

Blue shifted the heavy, tarp-covered package onto the dolly and wheeled it up the ramp and into the lobby. The package was as tall as he was and probably outweighed him, so when Sean came over and offered a hand, Blue accepted the help.

They wheeled the sculpture into the dining room and over to his booth which was, *Christ Almighty,* directly across from Louise's bakery table. He shot it an angry glance that could have lit the tablecloth on fire. Thank God she wasn't here yet. Maybe he could get in and out before she arrived. But he couldn't avoid her forever. The stony look settled back into place.

Sean smirked at him. Sean never seemed to have problems with women and now that he and Frankie were together, he was damn near insufferable.

"What put a bug up your ass?"

Blue growled and whipped the tarp off the statue, a full-size black bear, as tall as a man, up on its hind legs.

"Cool," Sean said. But he wasn't distracted for long and was back in Blue's face, in his business, in a minute. "What happened?"

Blue cocked a head to the kitchen. "She here yet?"

Sean shook his head. "Why."

Blue just frowned. He couldn't tell Sean. But he didn't

have to.

Sean looked puzzled for a moment, then his face cleared. "Ohhh, you told her."

Blue shook his head. "Worse."

Again the puzzlement, but only for a second. Sean's eyes widened and he dropped his voice. "You kissed her?"

Blue looked away, looked back. "Worse."

"Christ, Blue, did you go to bed with her?"

Blue glanced over his shoulder. "Keep your voice down, would you? Yes, I did, but it's not going to happen again."

"Why not? Wasn't it good?"

Blue growled. "It was friggin' great."

"Then what's the matter?"

"She's waiting for her boyfriend to arrive. And I'm not waiting anymore."

"She's still waiting for him? You couldn't change her mind?"

"It's not just that. It's...Well..." It was not his secret to tell. When Louise wanted people to know she was pregnant, she'd tell them herself. "No. I couldn't."

Sean blew out a breath. "That's tough man." He slapped Blue on the shoulder. "He won't last long. They never do. Maybe after—"

"Not this time. I'm not waiting around anymore just to have it thrown in my face. I have a date tonight."

Sean whistled a toneless note. "Right back on the horse, eh? Who with?"

"Star. It's just dinner."

Sean grinned. "Your place or hers?"

Blue frowned. "It's just dinner. In town. That sushi place."

Sean laughed. "Sushi? You?"

"First place I could think of," Blue muttered.

They were silent for a moment and then Sean said, his voice serious, "Louise is one of my oldest friends, but I have never thought she was fair to you. Now more than ever."

Blue gave him a long look. "She has her reasons this time."

And he headed back out to his truck.

* * *

The white and blue Christmas lights glowed on the porch when Louise got back to the cabin. She hadn't left them on, so there were only two possibilities: Augusta or Blue. And considering the way Blue had stormed out of his place half an hour ago, she'd bet it wasn't him.

The lights were a comforting greeting on a sleet-grey morning so she left them on and let herself into the cabin.

Brawny slipped in from wherever he'd spent the night before she closed the door. Possibly he'd slept under the couch on the porch. He complained loudly, though, and demanded his breakfast before Louise did anything else.

"You're getting soft," she grumbled back.

Her feet were so cold that she hardly had any feeling left in them. Icy water had soaked through her shoes—no Blue to carry her over the puddles this time—and she was chilled to the bone.

The cabin was cold, too. The fire in the stove had gone out hours ago, but she had lit one a thousand times before and could start another in her sleep, which was lucky because she was having trouble thinking about anything but Blue. The hurt in his eyes and the anger she'd felt emanating from him when he stormed away left her cringing in shame.

He'd never been this angry with her before, but this time he had every right. She'd planned to wait for Marco to get here—*if he ever came*—and convince him he wanted to have this baby with her, so she should have kept right away from Blue until she'd straightened that out.

But these days Blue was like catnip and she was the cat. Hanging out together had never been like this before.

Taking one of the last two matches from the tin, she lit the woodstove. Kneeling before the open door, arms wrapped around her ribs, she watched the flames leap from paper to kindling. Her body ached with loneliness as the black fog that had followed her for half her life threatened to swallow her up again. Ever since the night she'd woken up on the side of the road, the night her future had crumbled, it had been there, hovering in the background, sometimes swooping in and swallowing her up for weeks at a time.

She'd thought she had lost her chance to have a family that night. Eventually she had come to terms with that and had been able to get on with her life. But every so often, the loneliness settled over her and she would look around for a new man, someone to remind her that she was alive.

But Blue was right. It was an endless circle. She could never be that vulnerable again so she never let them get close. Which was why she had never been with Blue. He was different than the other guys. If she let herself love him, it could destroy her in the end.

So she remained alone, and never let herself consider being with him—until now. Making love to him had opened a floodgate of feelings that she realized had been locked up for years. Her feelings for Blue shimmered in the danger zone. He'd been a best friend, a brother, although she had to admit that in the last couple of years, things had changed between them.

And since she'd returned from Seattle, her feelings for him had leapt to a whole new level. But recognizing the change and letting herself feel it were two different things. Once she admitted she loved him, it could never be the same between them again.

And she had to give Marco a chance. She just hoped she

hadn't blown her friendship with Blue by sleeping with him. He'd been mad, but surely they could get past it and he'd go back to being her old friend again.

Leaving the stove door open to get the fire burning, she went into the bedroom and pulled on dry clothes. When she went back to check, the flames burned brightly. She pulled up a chair, rested her cold feet on the metal fender and stared into the dancing flames.

Outside, a storm was building, the light level more like dusk than mid-morning, but she didn't turn on the light. The fire's soft illumination left the corners of the cabin mercifully dim.

Her eyes burned hot with unshed tears and she just wanted to sit and stare at the flames. She should probably eat, but nothing appealed. She should go to the resort and get the girls busy wrapping the baked goods for the show, but seeing anyone—especially Blue, who could easily be there—was the last thing she wanted to do.

Maybe a shower. Yes, a shower sounded good. By the time she was finished, the cabin would be warm. Then she'd have something to eat and figure out what to do next.

After a half hour massage by the warm jets, Louise did feel marginally better—still like she'd been hit by a logging truck, but better. She didn't know what to do about Blue, how to get their friendship back to the way it had been before without risking both their hearts, but she couldn't hide in the cabin forever.

Rubbing a towel briskly over her hair, she stepped from the bathroom into the old laundry room. Her mind was still firmly on Blue, so it took her a moment to realize that Marco was standing on the porch.

Chapter 21

Marco knocked on the cabin door. He looked almost dream-like, an illusion in the misty air, with the rain running off the porch roof behind him diffusing the world outside.

Louise stepped back into the shadows of the laundry room. He hadn't seen her yet. *I could step back into the bathroom and close the door. He probably wouldn't look for me there.*

But that would be crazy. Hadn't she been wishing he would come? Calling and leaving increasingly desperate messages? Now that he was there though, the thought of telling him her news, their news, sent nauseating shockwaves through her body and she felt like throwing up.

How would she tell him? What would he say when she did? Would he ask her to come and live with him? Be a family? Her stomach rolled like a boat on an angry sea. Wasn't that what she ultimately wanted? To have a family *and* go back to the city?

She blew out a long breath. She didn't know anymore. Regardless, she had to tell him.

She stepped out through the doorway onto the porch. "Hi."

He started, then turned in her direction. A sultry smile settled on his face. "Hi, Babe."

She pulled her old robe tighter around her waist and briskly rubbed her hair with the towel.

Marco drifted toward her across the porch. He never moved quickly, except in the kitchen. Putting his arms around her, he kissed her on the lips.

Not much passion, she observed, oddly detached. More of a hello kiss. A claiming kiss.

Her arms didn't reach for him, stayed in the air at her hair and although she did return his kiss, she pulled away first. "You should have called."

She led him into the cabin, continuing to towel her almost-dry hair, mostly to keep her hands busy as her mind raced. He had a small satchel with him. Didn't look like he was planning to stay very long. A wave of relief rolled through her at the thought.

"Yeah, well, I woke up this morning and thought, *I'll just go. Surprise her.*"

She forced a smile. "I'm surprised all right. Want some coffee?"

Her body was begging for it now. She put on the kettle to make a pressed pot and headed to the bedroom. "Just give me a minute to get dressed."

Brawny stepped out from behind the stove as she passed and gave a ratchet-ty meow of greeting to Marco. Was his fur a little on end or was she imagining it?

"Did you bring that stupid animal? I would have thought you'd have left it where you found it."

"Yes, I brought him."

Marco reached down to pick him up, no doubt to throw him out.

"Just leave him alone. He lives here." *And you don't.*

Marco shrugged and followed her to the bedroom doorway, catching her from behind when she turned away and wrapping his arms around her waist. He nuzzled her neck. "Mmm, you smell good. Maybe there's time right now..."

He kissed the vulnerable spot beneath her ear as his hands slipped up to cup her breasts. Her sensitive breasts. She used to love it when he caught her from behind like this, like he couldn't wait to get her attention. Now her shoulders curved in to protect her chest, and she lifted his hands and moved away.

"I have to get dressed, Marco. I'm already late."

He did that little boy pout she used to think was cute. "It's been so long, Babe, I thought you'd be glad to see me."

"I am, but I have work to do."

"What work?"

Heart racing, she rooted through her dresser drawer, rejecting the thong, going for full coverage instead. "I've got a booth at a local artisan fair. It's this weekend and I have to go into the resort and do some baking."

"Really? Why?"

His obvious lack of enthusiasm sucked all the fun out of it. "I'm working with my sister and her friend." Should she explain about Amber? Sean? Everything?

"It's at the lodge that's opening in town. They're letting me use the new kitchen."

She tugged on the underwear under the robe, along with a pair of leggings. Keeping her back to him, she shrugged off the dressing gown, pulled a turtleneck over her head and grabbed a heavy black sweater.

When she turned, he was perched on the arm of the sofa, waiting. "Why are you doing this thing? What is it, a country bazaar?"

"It's a big community event. The resort is a big deal for the town, for the whole valley, and the owner is a friend. This is their grand opening and I want to be part of it. Besides, like I told you, I'm working with my sister and her friend. Family, you know?"

"Yeah, I guess. My family was never that close."

She stopped fussing at the kitchen and turned to look at him. He'd never mentioned his family before.

"That's too bad."

"My parents divorced when I was a kid. My mom's in San Francisco, my dad's in L.A. I mostly lived with my mom. When I was sixteen, I started working in a kitchen and moved out on my own a year later."

"Are you going to spend Christmas with your mother?" She hadn't thought of that before, but it made sense that he'd want to spend Christmas with his own parents.

He didn't answer right away, just looked at her, his lips pressed together in a thin line. She had never noticed before what thin lips he had.

Then he said, "I haven't spent a Christmas with my mom in ten years. There are always so many jobs at this time of year, I hate to pass them up. But this year I might."

She set two cups of coffee on the table. "She'd probably love to see you."

He didn't reply.

After an awkward moment, she asked, "Hungry?" Her voice sounded too bright.

"Sure. I'd eat."

She took the eggs and cheese from the refrigerator and set her omelet pan on the turquoise stove. As she put a dab of butter in the pan to melt, it occurred to her that they had never had breakfast together before. The occasional midnight snack, but never breakfast. Or lunch, or dinner.

She cracked an egg into a bowl and whisked it vigorously. "I have to go to the resort. I promised I'd meet my sister for a couple of hours. Did you see it when you drove through?"

"Big kitschy carved sign? Yeah, I saw it."

She opened her mouth to defend Blue's beautiful sign, but then held her tongue and put bread in the toaster.

"You could come with me, meet my sister. I'd like you to meet my dad, too."

"Yeah, sure. If we have time."

"How long can you stay?"

"I'm not sure. I'm looking at some jobs in Seattle. I really should get back."

She kept her back to him while she buttered the toast. "You could come with me today." She held her breath, waiting for him to answer.

"If it's okay with you, I'll just stay here. I didn't get much sleep last night. I'll grab a nap, work on my computer."

She let the breath out slowly, trying not to let the surprising wave of relief show as she set the two plates on the table. Just as well. She had work to do. He'd just be in the way.

"There's no wifi here. Well, sometimes it leaks over from Frankie's place next door. She's a good friend too. I'd like you to meet all of my friends."

He smiled. "Sure, Babe."

Although it had never bothered her before, she wished he'd stop calling her Babe.

* * *

Half an hour later, Louise rushed into the resort dining room. She glanced at Blue's tables across the aisle. He wasn't there, but he had obviously been in. A life-sized bear stood in his place. Hopefully he had already left. She didn't feel strong enough to deal with him again today.

He'd also added a carving of two otters running along a log to his display and some small carvings of bears and eagles that she knew had been sketches for the larger carvings, like the standing bear and the diving eagle he'd brought in yesterday.

The attention to detail in his work was amazing, and the way he allowed the natural grain of the wood to enhance the composition brought his animals to life. She could almost see the otters running and playing on the log.

"Hi, Louise."

She jumped. Put a hand to her chest. Sean was standing behind her. "Cripes, you scared me."

"How are things." He looked unusually serious, not Sean-like at all.

Her eyes narrowed. Something was up. "Fine."

"I hear your boyfriend's coming. Will he make it to the show?"

He was fishing. "As a matter of fact, he arrived this morning." She tried to infuse her voice with the appropriate amount of enthusiasm.

"Really? Interesting timing."

Her eyebrows jacked up, then she glanced away. What did he know? What had Blue told him? She rubbed a hand over her belly. Did he know about the baby?

"Yes. I won't have as much time to spend with him as I'd hoped, but I'm sure you'll get to meet him."

Sean gave her a long look. "I'm looking forward to it." Then he turned on his heel and left.

He knew something. That was one of the things she hated about living in a small town—it was almost impossible to keep a secret in Fortune Bay.

Louise's cheeks burned with guilt when she thought about how she'd treated Blue. Ripples of shame spread through her body, leaving an icy feeling in her stomach at the thought that Blue may have been serious. He might really be ready to move on with his life and leave her behind.

When the girls arrived, ready to work, Louise tried to focus her attention on pricing packages with them, wrapping loaves and putting them in the freezer. But her mind was on Marco, waiting at the cabin. What would she say to him when she got back? She'd have to tell him—and the sooner the better. They had to start making plans.

Now that he was here though, she had trouble picturing what life with Marco would be like. They'd never spent a whole day together, never gone out in public, never had breakfast together until today. What did that say about their relationship?

It sounded like he was considering going to California for Christmas. She couldn't imagine not having been home for Christmas in ten years. Is that what her life would be like if they were together? Would she have to fight to visit her family and friends in Fortune Bay?

He had always been sweet to her though, and they had a lot in common: they were both passionate about food, listened to the same music, would be in the same industry and could understand the demands of each other's jobs. They were compatible in bed and most importantly, he was the baby's father. Was that enough to build a life on? She didn't know, but that was their starting point. There was nowhere to go but forward.

She forced herself to stop thinking about Marco and to focus on the work she had to do. By mid-afternoon, she let the girls go home, put the last of the packaged bake goods in the refrigerator and went into the lobby. Max stood at the front counter, talking to a man she didn't recognize. He called her over.

"Louise. I'd like you to meet a new member of the team. Nick is the new bartender. He's starting tonight."

Louise smiled and shook his hand. His warm brown eyes and lanky build promised an easy, friendly manner. Good traits in a bartender.

"New in town?" she asked.

"Pretty new. I came to the valley last summer. This place is paradise if you're into outdoor sports. I'm from Montana. When summer was over, I just couldn't face the thought of another Missoula winter."

Louise laughed. "We do get a bit of a break here near the coast, but we'll get some winter before we're through."

Nick grinned. "I can handle it."

"We're lucky that Nick is free for the next couple of months," Max said. "He's not sure if he can stay on for the summer, he had a job at the kayak rental in Majestic but was laid off at the end of October. He's free for the next few months though and that's what I need right now. You know the bar is opening tonight? Are you coming?"

"Are you serving food?"

"Bar food," Nick said. "Hot wings and tapas."

Louise grinned. "I'm in." The opening would be a good way to introduce Marco to all her friends without having to go door to door. Somehow, she couldn't see him sitting in Stephanie or Maddie's kitchen.

And it would get them out of the house for the evening. Their first time out in public. A test of their relationship. If Marco saw how beautiful the resort was inside, maybe he'd form a different impression of the village.

As she walked out to the Jeep, she remembered that Max was looking for a chef. Marco was looking for work. Wouldn't *that* be perfect.

Chapter 22

When Louise pulled the Jeep up to the cabin, the sky was almost dark. She dreaded going inside. Her life seemed like a snarl of yarn that she was too tired to untangle.

Her mother's white and blue lights sent a reassuring message that everything would be fine. It was what she'd always said when Louise was a child, *everything will work out fine.* And she was usually right. With enough time, they usually did.

I'm trying, Mom. Heaving a soul-shuddering sigh, Louise dragged herself out of the car and went inside.

Marco sat at the kitchen table, typing furiously on his laptop. He glanced up and smiled. "Hi Babe. I'll be done in a minute." His fingers jabbed at a few more keys, then closed his computer. "So, how was the bazaar?"

"It's not a bazaar. And it wasn't today—it's Saturday."

He shook his head. "I didn't realize you'd be so busy. I was hoping we could, you know, hang out."

He meant have sex. "You should have called." But he was here now, and she should try to enjoy his visit. "The bar at the resort is opening tonight. Everyone will be there. I thought we could go."

He drifted over and wrapped his arms around her. *Took possession* was how it felt. But didn't she want him to feel a strong connection to her and, by extension, to their child? She wrapped her arms around his neck.

He pulled her close. Although their bodies fit together like a jigsaw puzzle, hitting all the right pressure points, she felt twitchy to escape.

"I was hoping we could spend some time together. Right here," he whispered, his breath tickling her ear as he backed her into the bedroom.

His lips firmly captured hers and she let herself be persuaded onto the bed. He lay down beside her, enfolded her in his arms and kissed her again, tongue probing every corner of her mouth.

She should want this, she thought as she responded automatically. She had always been eager for sex with Marco before. And what about those randy pregnancy hormones? Where were they now when she needed them?

The kiss was slow and thorough, but all she could think was, *He's going to drag this out.* Hopefully not too much foreplay—she was not in the mood.

She reached down to undo the snap on his pants. He brought his hands down to stop her. "Slow down, Babe."

She stopped, but her arms tensed. Her whole body was tense. She tried to concentrate on the slow perusal of his mouth on her neck as he worked his hands under her sweater to undo her bra. This was his method, undo the bra then pull everything off in one go. Like a stripper's tear-away pants. A moment later he stopped kissing her neck and pulled the sweater over her head and her bra fell away.

A chill shot through her and she shivered involuntarily. He pulled back to looked at her.

"Cold? That damn stove gave me trouble. How can there be no electric heat in this dump?"

A cast iron frying pan fell from its hook on the kitchen wall and clattered to the floor.

His head swung towards the sound. "What's that?"

"Nothing. Come here." She didn't want to explain.

She pulled the soft quilt over them both and retreated into the cocoon-like warmth. Her hand reached for his waistband again, but again he stopped her and nibbled on her ear. "I haven't seen you in weeks. Don't be in such a hurry."

Why wasn't *he* in more of a hurry? She noticed he didn't

say *he* hadn't had sex in weeks. She'd always suspected he was seeing someone else while he was sleeping with her. Maybe that was why they had gone to such lengths to keep their relationship secret.

He pulled off her jeans and underwear and crouched between her legs. She stiffened, holding herself still, waiting for the uninhibited heat she'd felt last night with Blue to wash over her again. She'd had no trouble getting turned on then. She'd been boiling over with randy hormones.

Don't think about Blue! Waves of shame washed through her at having slept with him when she was supposed to be with Marco. She never slept with two guys at once. She was always careful to break it off cleanly with one before starting anything with someone new. That way no one got hurt.

Strangely, though, she felt surprisingly little shame at having deceived Marco, the detached voice in her head pointed out. No, the shame was for having led Blue on, given in to her feelings, her need to have a caring body holding her, have *him* hold her. Shame for having given in when she knew it would mean everything to him—and she could promise nothing.

She reached down and grabbed Marco's head and pulled him up from between her legs until he was lying on top of her. "Come on. I can't wait."

He chuckled and reached for a condom he'd obviously left on the bedside table. He'd been expecting to have sex—and why not? She had always been happy to participate before.

The old bed sagged under their weight. She made all the right moves and noises—she knew he wouldn't take his own release until he was sure she was satisfied. Outside the window, the light from her mother's white and blue Christmas lights shimmered through the tears that brimmed in her eyes.

Finally, he groaned and stiffened above her, then slumped on top of her. Without moving, he turned his head and kissed her cheek. "Great, Babe."

His expectations obviously weren't very high.

She waited a beat and then pushed him off her. He rolled until his head was on the other pillow, but he kept a firm arm around her waist.

She wiped the moisture from her eyes. *This is crazy. It's not like we haven't done this before.* But this time felt different. This time she felt ashamed and faintly violated.

She pulled away. "What time is it? I'm starving. It must be time to eat. Let's go and check out the new bar."

"Couldn't we just eat here?"

Louise rolled out of bed, laughing self-consciously when Marco made an unsuccessful grab to hold her back. "No. Come on. I want to go."

Maybe if she got out into the company of her friends, if they met Marco and liked him, she'd get over this feeling that their affair was a sleazy secret.

Quickly, she pulled on her clothes.

"Tonight is the grand opening of the bar at the resort. Max and Sean have kept the glass doors covered with paper. I can't wait to see what they've done in there."

"Probably decorated with antlers and mounted moose heads," Marco said, sitting in his briefs on the edge of the bed. "But okay, I'm game."

Her phone chimed and she dug it out of her jacket pocket. *Biltmore H* showed in the caller I.D. She felt like a cotton ball suddenly lodged in her throat. "Hello?"

"Louise Ingstrom?"

"Yes." Her voice squeaked. She cleared her throat. "Speaking."

"This is Elvard Motherwell of the Biltmore Hotel in Seattle. You applied for a job as a pastry chef?"

Her eyes swung across the room to Marco. He must

have heard the excitement in her voice because his eyes were focused on her.

"As it turns out, we have an opening and are taking interviews tomorrow. Can you possibly come in at two?"

Her pulse raced. "Certainly. Thank you for calling. I'll see you at two."

After the click, she stared at the phone, letting the news sink in. Then she let out a happy shriek. "It's the Biltmore. I have an interview tomorrow."

Marco smiled, a genuine smile. "That's great, Babe." He really looked happy for her. She pulled her coat off the hook by the door and tugged it on. She wanted to tell everyone the news. "Let's go. I'm starving."

They drove into town in Marco's silver BMW. In the resort parking lot, the low, sleek two-door stood out among the pickup trucks and SUV's. Louise grabbed him by the arm and towed him up the resort steps and into the lobby. She was so excited about the hotel interview that she almost skipped across the slate floor. This was a real job. The elusive job all the graduates were hoping to land.

The doors of the bar were flung open and she could see neon lights reflected on a succession of chrome and glass tabletops in the long narrow room. Opposite them, tall stools lined Blue's artfully rustic, wooden bar. Thankfully, there wasn't a moose head in sight.

At the end of the room, a space opened up for a small band, although there wasn't one playing tonight, with room for a few couples to dance. Beyond that was a bank of vertical windows that in summer would showcase a view of the lake glinting through the trees, but on this dark winter night, revealed the sparkle of white Christmas lights hung on the branches outside.

Sean and Frankie stood by the bar. Sean was obviously the greeter tonight, but Louise's good mood fizzled when his face went uncharacteristically blank as she walked in.

He was still pissed. The only reason Louise could think of was that Blue had told him they'd slept together. Sean was the only one Blue might have told. The only one who could have gotten it out of him. Louise's stomach lurched with nerves—or morning sickness, she wasn't sure which. She just hoped she made it through dinner without throwing up.

Sean turned and said something to Frankie. She peeked around him and waved to Louise. Hopefully Sean had kept the news to himself. Getting out in public with Marco wasn't making her feel better about their relationship. If anything, so soon after spending the night with Blue, it made her ashamed of how she was treating her old friend.

But there was no turning back now. Nerves rolling like ball bearings around her stomach, she took Marco's hand and led him over to where her friends stood at the bar.

"Marco, these are my friends, Sean and Frankie." She turned to them. "This is Marco—"

She ground to a halt. What should she call him? *The father of my child?* Absolutely not. *A friend from the Academy?* Kind of understating the facts.

Marco held out his hand and said smoothly to Frankie, "From Seattle."

He took her hand, holding it in both of his. "Always delighted to meet Louise's friends."

Always so charming with the ladies.

Marco released Frankie's hand and turned to Sean, whose eyes narrowed suspiciously, although you'd have to know him well to tell. Behind the men's backs, Frankie's eyes were wide and her brows raised behind her long taffy-colored bangs as she sent Louise a questioning look: *Does he know? Have you told him?*

Louise gave her head a slow shake. *Not talking about it.* The big IT. The elephantine IT in the room.

Sean's look held no welcome, but he held out his hand

to Marco. "Welcome to The Cedars. So glad you could make it for opening night. Please, help yourself to a complimentary glass of Champaign and some appetizers." He indicated the trays of glasses on the bar.

Marco glanced at the silver platter of attractively displayed appies beside the tray of sparkling flutes. Louise cringed when critical creases formed at the corner of his eyes as he took in the platter of smoked salmon tartines topped with capers, and mushroom caps stuffed with fresh crab. Since the kitchen wasn't open yet, Louise assumed Sean had prepared them himself. They were bound to be delicious, he was a fabulous cook, but she was afraid that Marco, food snob that he was, wouldn't even try them. On principle alone.

But that might be for the best. *Please, don't say anything negative.*

Desperately attempting to deflect attention, she beamed at Sean. "The bar looks fantastic. And these look delicious."

Taking a small plate from the pile on the bar, she loaded it with appetizers, popped one in her mouth and moaned in appreciation. Marco glanced dismissively at the platter, but deigned to take a glass of Champaign.

Frankie caught Louise's eye and tilted her head questioningly.

Louise looked away. What could she say? Marco was acting like a jerk, but Sean wasn't much better.

A hand fell on her shoulder and she turned to see Max at her side. He wore a striped shirt under his suit jacket, open at the collar, no tie. Casual for Max. Stephanie must have coached him.

"Glad you could come," he said, kissing her cheek.

"It looks amazing Max. And these appetizers are fantastic." She shoved another salmon tartine into her mouth. Max was smiling expectantly at Marco, so she struggled to swallow quickly.

"I'd like you meet Marco Roselli, an instructor from the Academy. Marco, Max Finster is the owner and manager of the resort."

Max blustered. "Part owner. So, you're from the school. A teacher of Louise's?"

Marco shook his hand. "I was never Louise's instructor. I wasn't in pastry." His tone was so patronizing, it was Louise's turn to narrow her eyes, but if he noticed, he didn't show any sign.

"Marco is a culinary chef," she explained. "Specializing in charcuterie."

"And actually, I'm not instructing at the Academy anymore."

"Marco's on the open market now, looking for work."

Max's eyes lit up. "Really? We're looking for a chef here, starting in the spring. You wouldn't be interested, would you?"

A simple "no" would have sufficed, but Marco looked around the bar with a slight sneer on his lips—lips that, once again Louise couldn't help but notice looked thin and almost mean. He shook his head. "I don't think it's my style."

Max's expression slammed shut. He pulled himself up and squared his shoulders.

Desperate to change the subject, Louise thrust the plate of appetizers at Marco. He glanced down with just his eyes and shook his head.

Max smiled tightly. "Maybe not. A lodge would not be everyone's choice, but we are proud of it."

"And so you should be," Stephanie said as she sailed in through the open doors. Her long, elegant silk jacket, obviously one of her own designs, hung over a slinky silver tank and black trousers. She took one look at the scene and came over to give Louise a hug.

"Hang in there," she whispered.

Louise hung on to her for a moment, bolstered by Stephanie's strength. Then Steph pulled away, giving her shoulder a squeeze.

"This must be Marco," she said, holding out her hand to shake. "Louise told me you were coming. I hope everyone has made you feel welcome?" Louise didn't miss the hard look she shot at Sean.

As Marco turned to Stephanie, the smile he reserved for women fell over his face like a silken mask. Louise suddenly realized it happened every bloody time he spoke to a woman. Sean was charming too and had a way with women, but you always felt he was sincere. Not like Marco.

Stephanie smiled, but Louise was mortified to realize that Steph saw it too.

"Nice to meet you," Stephanie said briskly, then lightly shook herself free of his hand and turned to the bar. "Nick. A club soda please. With lime."

"You got it."

Stephanie diffused the situation with comments about the room and a moment later, casually set the soda in front of Louise. Louise did a quick scan of the room. Frankie noticed, but none of the men seemed to catch the switch.

Louise could feel two streams of energy racing around her: the fiery red, testosterone-fueled male stream between Marco, Max and Sean, and the cool green, supportive energy flowing to her from the women. Not that Sean, and probably Max too, weren't supportive, they just had a different way of showing it.

Louise was fading under the tension. Trying to capture her former elation, she said, "I got an exciting phone call just before we left the cabin. I have a job interview tomorrow at a lovely boutique hotel in Seattle."

Sean's eyes narrowed in disapproval.

Bite me Sean. She was getting tired of his silent reproach. Stephanie and Frankie exchanged a quick look and although they made excited murmurs, Louise sensed they were concerned.

Suddenly Louise noticed a shift in the energy in the room. Her friends' eyes flash to the doorway behind her, widened, then they all focused back on her.

It had to be Blue.

Chapter 23

Louise put a hand on her stomach to stop from hurling the hor d'oeuvres right there, onto the bar floor. Everyone was so tense. Did they all know she had slept with Blue?

She'd known he would be there but short of hiding in the cabin with Marco for the next few days, sooner or later they would have to meet.

Marco picked up on the undercurrent and looked over his shoulder at the door. Louise pulled herself upright on the bar stool and swung around.

It was Blue all right. With Star clinging to his arm, looking more like an elf than ever tonight in green sequined tights and a thigh-length, filmy green tunic.

"Hi, everybody," she said in her fairy-like voice. On her head, she wore a strange headpiece of sparkly colored rhinestones that looked like part of a Christmas table decoration gone wrong.

Louise cringed as Star homed in on her.

"I heard you're catering the Christmas Eve brunch. You just let me know if you need any help, you hear?"

Marco raised his eyebrows and smirked at her. "Really? You're catering brunch? Here?"

Louise stiffened her back. She didn't need to defend her decisions to him. "Yes. For family and friends."

Blue stood in the doorway, the look on his face so black she was surprised smoke wasn't puffing out of his ears.

Star held out her hand to Marco. "Hi, I'm Star. Starlight actually, but everybody calls me Star."

"A lovely name for a lovely lady."

Louise could hardly stop her eyes from rolling back in their sockets, but Star giggled, so apparently that stale old line still worked.

Blue shook himself out of his funk and stalked over.

Louise closed her eyes. *Don't make a scene.*

Her eyes popped open as she realized she had just had the same thought about Marco moments ago. This was exhausting.

Blue stopped right in front of her. He took a hard look at her drink, then took her by the arm. "I want a word with you. In private."

Louise pulled her cheeks back in what she hoped was a reassuring smile and said, "I'll be back in a minute," over her shoulder as Blue dragged her past Marco and out the door.

Marco didn't seem to notice anything was amiss. His attention was already focussed on Star.

Louise's heart was thumping so hard she felt sure it would bruise her chest. Shaking off Blue's hand, she stalked through the lobby and right out the front door.

Outside, the air was crisp and cold. White Christmas lights had transformed the parking lot into a fairyland. Louise's breath came in white pants in the frosty air but she wasn't cold, she was steamed. She wrapped her arms around her ribs to hold herself together.

"Seattle, Louise?"

So he'd heard what she'd said. In a *whoosh*, her chest deflated and the previously exciting news became a poisoned dart aimed right at her old friend's heart.

"It's just an interview," she said softly.

Blue looked at Marco's silver Beamer parked under the Christmas lights by the opposite curb and his eyes narrowed.

"Have you told him?" he asked. His voice was harsh.

Louise hugged herself tighter and looked out at the twinkling lights reflecting in the wet pavement. "He knows about the interview."

"Jeeze, Louise. You know what I mean."

"No, I haven't." She spat out the words. "And it's none of your business."

"You are my business. The guy's a creep."

"And you know this how? On two minutes' observation?"

"Guys know guys and this one's a sleaze."

Louise wanted to defend Marco but couldn't find the words. Blue's eyes held hers for a long moment, and suddenly she felt tears well up. She couldn't cry now. She blew out a breath that hung white on the frosty air between them.

Then she pressed her lips together and stared at him, unflinching. "I will tell him. I have to tell him."

Blue broke eye contact and abruptly looked away.

She shook her head. "I just haven't had a chance, yet. I was here all day. I'll tell him soon. Tonight."

Blue looked back at her and his eyes were warm and pleading. Her heart crumbled.

"You don't need him. We'll take care of you." He took a step closer until she could feel the heat radiating off his body. "I'll take care of you."

Okay. Now her heart was really breaking. She'd give anything at this moment to be able to say, *yes.* To wrap her cold arms around him and drop her head onto his warm, broad chest like she'd done so many times before. But she had lost that privilege when she'd gotten pregnant with another man's child. The kindest thing she could do for him now was to set him free.

"I can take care of myself Blue. I don't need your help— or your pity."

He stared at her hard for another moment, then wrapped his big warm hand around her arm again and pulled her back to the door. "Get inside before you catch your death of cold."

He opened the door and she wrenched her arm away. It wasn't hard, his hold wasn't tight. Then, shoulders back, she marched inside. When she heard the door close behind her, she glanced back and saw him standing on the deck in the icy mist, arms folded over his brawny chest, steam rising from his shoulders, his thick curly hair backlit like a halo by the fairy lights as he stared out into the night.

She turned and raced for the bathroom—and lost all of Sean's hors d'oeuvres in the toilette. After a couple of minutes, she hoisted herself up and splashed water on her face, pressing her fingers against her eyelids.

He still cared. Of course he cared. Maybe, when the dust cleared, she'd have a chance to win back his friendship.

But first, she had to tell Marco.

Back in the bar, Marco and Star were sitting on adjoining bar stools, knee to knee, heads together, laughing. They both looked up and smiled at Louise when she walked in. If only friendships were that easy for her. She knew she came across as easy-going and off-the-cuff, but that was a colossal bluff.

There was no hiding this time. She had to step up.

Suddenly, eating in the bar seemed like a bad idea. Marco was sure to say something negative about the food, and better to get out before Blue came back. Let him have a shot with Star without their baggage in the way.

Louise smiled faintly at Marco and touched her hand to her forehead. "Do you mind if we go?"

He stood up immediately. "No. Of course not."

Louise said her goodbyes quickly, avoiding the enquiring looks from Frankie and Steph, and the daggers from Sean.

Outside, Louise quickly scanned the parking lot. Thankfully, Blue was nowhere in sight. They climbed into Marco's sports car, a little less shiny now after being sprayed with backroads slush and mud and a few minutes later, her footsteps heavy, she climbed the stairs to the cabin. Once again, the Christmas lights were on, but she didn't have the energy to think about how.

As she opened the door, Brawny streaked out, almost tripping Marco. "Stupid animal."

Louise flipped on the kitchen light. As her disclosure drew closer, time slowed to a crawl. She hung her coat on the hooks behind the door. Sat on a kitchen chair to tug off her boots. Every action seemed deliberate and heavy, sapping what little remaining energy she had.

Marco seemed oblivious to her distress.

"I was glad to get out of there," he said, hanging his hat on a hook and loosening his scarf. "I know they're your old friends, but even so. How can you stand it?"

He looked so smug and self-assured. She felt that tonight, for the first time, she was seeing him clearly. He walked over and took her hands and pulled her up. "You're better than that, Babe. You don't belong here anymore."

She looked at him for a long moment, then he angled his head and came in for a kiss.

She put a hand on his chest, holding him away. "How do you know?"

"How do I know what?" He nuzzled her ear.

"How do you know where I belong? I mean, what do we really know about each other?"

He pulled back and looked at her with a grin. Smarmy, she thought. A smarmy grin. An I-just-want-to-get-you-in-bed grin. "Seriously? Now? You want to have the talk now?"

The lights flickered then flared and Louise felt the surge of energy she so desperately needed. "Yes. Now."

She pulled away and he let her go without a fight. At the sink, she banged around, filling the kettle, putting it on the stove, mostly to give herself a chance to settle. She turned on the burner, then turned to face him.

The condescending smile was still on his face, as if

whatever she had to say wouldn't matter, that he could calm her down, humor her into bed.

She wanted to smack him. How could she have been so blind?

"I'm pregnant."

The smile dropped from his face like the mask it was and he took a step back as if he had been slapped. *Good.*

His eyes darted around the room and she could almost see the panic surround him like a white fog. "It can't be mine."

She gave a humorless laugh. "Oh, it's definitely yours."

He thought for a minute, and although his eyes were on her, she felt he didn't really see her.

Finally, his face cleared and he shrugged. "How far along could you be? Not far. Not three months yet. That's the cutoff, isn't it? There's still time."

The temperature in the room dropped and goose bumps crawled up her arms. "Time for what?"

He shrugged one shoulder. "You know. To take care of it."

She couldn't think, felt like an emotionless lump of concrete, watching herself from somewhere outside.

"What if I want to keep it?"

He smiled. *Smiled!* "Come on Babe. You know it's not what we planned."

She had her answer. He wouldn't stand by her.

She stood up. "I'm going to bed. We'll talk in the morning."

"Okay. But do you have anything to drink?"

Her feet felt so heavy she could hardly drag herself over to the cupboard to get the half-bottle of scotch she'd bought for him in the city, and set it on the table.

He got two glasses, poured a healthy shot and held out the glass to her. "Why don't you join me?" His eyebrows rose, the question hanging between them.

His intimation was clear. If she wasn't going to go through with it, if she was going to abort the pregnancy, she could get shit-faced drunk. It wouldn't matter.

He didn't get it. She wasn't just pregnant—she was having a baby.

His smile turned seductive as he held the glass out to her.

Not a chance.

She shook her head. The smile slid from his face and she caught a glimpse of the self-centered man behind. He thought for a moment, then looked at his watch, downed the shot and smacked the glass on the table.

"You know, I think I'll pass. Just hit the road. You have to get out of here early tomorrow morning for your interview and if I leave now, I'll just make the last ferry."

No mention of them going together, that unemotional voice in her head observed.

At this point, she wouldn't have gone if he'd asked.

Five minutes later, he'd packed up his laptop and was putting his hat back on. "Listen, let's meet for lunch tomorrow. To talk. Noon at Le Fab?"

She nodded and smiled wearily. This wasn't the time to burn any bridges.

He kissed her on the cheek, taking a moment to look in her eyes. "Don't worry. We'll work something out."

And then he was gone.

She closed the door behind him and turned the lock.

When she turned to the room, a movement by the attic stairs caught her eye. A wooden cradle, handmade by the look of it, sat low on the ground, rocking gently from side to side. She'd have sworn it hadn't been there before. Who could have left it?

As she walked toward it, it kept on rocking, as if moved by an invisible hand.

For the baby.

The words came from nowhere, were just there in her mind. Marco's words came back to her. *Take care of it.* As if it was an annoying little problem that she should 'take care of".

She firmed her lips. "Thank you, Augusta. We will take care of it—our way."

Chapter 24

The following morning, in honor of her job interview and her lunch date with Marco, Louise put on her all-black city uniform: black stockings, black pencil skirt, and a dressy black silk blouse.

She'd called Brandy the evening before and told her she'd be gone for the day, but that they would start preparing for the show in earnest the following morning. Then, with only one day to go, it would be time to fire up the ovens and bake.

Under a leaden sky, Louise started the long trek to the city. The old Jeep was designed as more of a summer vehicle and, even with the heat on full, drafts crept in around the doors. She drove along the lake, through Majestic and down the river valley. The valley had been logged and replanted years ago and now a respectable growth of mature evergreen trees lined the road and blanketed the mountain slopes.

It was all so familiar, but today, she didn't feel the excitement she usually experienced when she left the valley for the city. A feeling of dread, which she attributed to with her lunch date with Marco, weighted her shoulders.

She decided to think about her interview at the Biltmore instead, how wonderful it would be to work in the kitchen of the prestigious, historic hotel. She hadn't decided if she should tell them she was pregnant. It was early enough she could probably get away with pretending she didn't know yet, but that was dicey, not to mention dishonest. Seven months of work was scarcely enough time to expect maternity leave, if the hotel offered leave at all. Pastry was an extremely competitive business and she knew they could replace her at a day's notice.

When she reached the road that ran along the coast, the landscape changed from forest to fast food outlets lining the highway, then she was driving through Bremerton to the ferry terminal. As the ferry chugged through the fog across Puget Sound, she tried to read, but her mind was churning over the possible ways she could make this situation work.

And it had to work. She had just escaped from Fortune Bay, finishing the course with the friggin' *Pretzel*, for cripes sake. What was the universe trying to tell her by making her pregnant now?

When she was sixteen, at the hospital after the accident and the miscarriage, they'd told her that she probably wouldn't have children, that unless she adopted, she'd never have a family of her own, so it was pretty darn clear what the universe was telling her. Inside her, a tiny flame burned brighter every day. She'd been given another chance.

So she'd give Marco another chance, too. After all, she'd sprung the pregnancy on him last night. Look how long it had taken her to come to grips with the idea of a baby. It had probably been a good thing that he'd left when he did last night, before they'd both said things they regretted. Things they couldn't have taken back. Maybe, by today, he'd have gotten used to the idea and they would be able to work it out. He may even be excited.

She would put his intimation that they *deal with it* aside and try to make it work.

When she arrived at the restaurant, Marco was already seated. La Fab was a trendy loft with soaring ceilings, glass and chrome tables and big bright artwork hanging on painted concrete walls. He sat at a table halfway down the room. Instead of watching for her, he was facing away from the door, looking instead at the tiled wall at the end of the room with the pass-through window to the kitchen.

Louise smiled, trying to radiate positive energy as she

came up beside him, but the smile stiffened on her cheeks at his surprised expression, as if he'd been so involved with the kitchen scene that he'd forgotten she was coming. But he jumped up and gave her a peck on the cheek, his hand on her shoulder directing her to the chair facing him.

In a low voice, he said, "This is one of the places I want to work. I heard the chef is leaving and I've been talking to the owner." Marco was a great schmoozer; he knew half the restaurateurs in town. Taking an agitated sip of his water, his eyes stayed on the pass-through in the wall behind her through which he could see the kitchen staff at work.

His eyes flickered to her and then back to the wall. "You know, a baby will just complicate things if you want that job at the hotel."

Louise stared hard at him, willing him to look directly at her, but failing. "I know, but surely we can work it out."

"Childcare is expensive; we are both just starting new jobs. I'll have to be on the job twenty-four seven for the first few years."

He would be. She would be too, if she wanted to get ahead. If she wanted to work her way up, maybe save enough money to open her own café. They'd be living in an apartment, if they were even living together. He hadn't said anything about that yet and she wasn't about to suggest it. If he wanted to live with her, surely he would have mentioned it by now.

So, she'd have an even smaller apartment. Like the one she'd had with Jess. Her mind recoiled at the thought of trying to childproof a deathtrap like that, but she might just have to.

Thousands of women do it.

"I know. We'll be busy," she said.

Did she really have to choose? A baby or a career? She glanced at her watch. Her stomach felt too unsettled to eat.

She stood up and gathered her things, finally getting his

full attention.

"Are you leaving?"

"I think I should go. I want to be sure to get to the interview on time."

That was a lie, she still had plenty of time, but this conversation was going nowhere. She hated competing for his attention with the kitchen but, the truth was, she would always come second.

His eyes were back on the action in the kitchen. "Will I see you before you leave the city?"

That was the definitive answer to all of her questions. He wasn't going to ask her to move in with him. *Tiny, rat infested apartment it is.*

"I don't think so. I have to get back to prepare for the Christmas show at the resort."

"Well, good luck at the interview. Let me know how it turns out." He jumped to his feet, as if he realized he should say a proper goodbye, gave her another light kiss on the cheek and a pat on the shoulder. "We'll figure something out."

What happened to the passion? Her lips smiled, but she knew what he thought the best solution was. Terminate the pregnancy.

Absolutely not.

Once outside, Louise decided to walk to the hotel. It was only six blocks. Breathing the sharp, cold air calmed her stomach and she wrapped her scarf around her neck against the raw wind.

Arriving at the hotel on Queen Anne Avenue with half an hour to spare, she ducked into a coffee shop across the road, ordered mint tea for the butterflies in her stomach, and studied the hotel façade.

The Biltmore was one of the art deco remnants of a more gentile time in the city's past. Eight stories of cream-colored brick and black iron grillwork rose above a fan-shaped glass roof over the entrance. A uniformed doorman rushed out to greet taxis and airport limos as they pulled up in front, chatting with the guests and helping them with their luggage, offering umbrellas to visitors foolish enough to visit Seattle in December without one.

She could see herself greeting the friendly doorman each morning as he welcomed her. It would be a lovely place to work.

Her meeting with Marco hadn't been encouraging, but it was still early days and even if they didn't live together, surely he would chip in to support the baby. Maybe she could work here at least until the baby came. Get something on her resume besides the Fortune Bay Café.

She could work it out. Women did every day. Like Monica, who had been in her class. She was a single mom who was managing on her own. Louise did seem to remember something about family helping care for the child, and Monica had always had dark circles under her eyes, but they had all been exhausted during the course. She'd just have to work something out. And a job was step one.

Five minutes before the appointed time, she paid her bill and crossed the road. The doorman, a friendly young guy, opened the door with a smile. When she asked where she would find Mr. Motherwell, he took her arm and gently pulled her back out onto the street, closing the door behind her.

"Staff enter off Harrison Street," he said pleasantly.

Of course they did. Staff wouldn't enter through the lobby. Too bad. The glimpse of it she'd gotten was so elegant and classy.

She found the staff entrance, a plain steel door marked with a discreet sign. Mr. Motherwell's office was just inside. She knocked tentatively, then, deciding that was not the image she wanted to portray, pulled herself up and knocked again, more firmly this time.

The door opened abruptly and a short, dark haired man in crisp white shirt and dark suit and tie ushered her in. Max had worn three-piece suits when he first moved to Fortune Bay but Stephanie soon shook him out of that. Now Max didn't even wear a tie to the resort every day.

The man introduced himself as Motherwell and glanced at his watch.

"Glad to see you're on time. We run a tight ship here." He smiled through taut lips. "Let me show you the kitchen."

He led her down a long, unadorned hallway. "Usually, we want someone with hotel experience for this job, but since you won the Pretzel and do have kitchen experience, I am willing to give you a try. You would be on probation for the first three months, then we could discuss a contract."

Three months. By then they would have figured out she was pregnant.

A cacophony of sound like an airplane preparing for takeoff grew as they walked towards the double swinging doors at the end of the hall. As they pushed through, it mushroomed into the clanging and shouting that was the hotel kitchen.

"We'd expect you to be here at four a.m.," Motherwell shouted over the din. "To start the bread, morning pastries and evening deserts."

Louise smiled and raised her voice, too. "I expect it will be quieter here at four a.m." Pastry chefs always started before dawn, but she preferred that to working in this commotion.

Motherwell didn't return her smile. "The whole morning crew begins at four. The lunch crew comes in at ten thirty and the evening crew starts at four. Of course, everything is made fresh in-house every day."

"Perfect." She had ideas for tarts and pastries, cheesecakes and sweet buns, things she'd worked on at the

Academy and was dying to try.

Motherwell reached into a cubby hole and brought out a slim binder. On the front was an index, a list of common pastries.

"These are the pastries we have on the menu. Tried and true. The Biltmore not interested in innovation."

Louise studied the list. Four kinds of Danish. Pecan tarts. Chocolate cake. She opened the booklet and read through the list of ingredients. Excellent ingredients could turn a run-of-the-mill chocolate cake into something sublime, but...

"It says here," she pointed to the page. "'Prepared mix.' What exactly does that mean?"

"We get most of our prepared ingredients, the fillings, the puff pastry, the cake mixes, from the standard suppliers."

A harried woman whose hair had turned to frizz in the steamy kitchen walked by and Motherwell introduced her as the woman Louise would be answering to. Louise didn't catch her name since someone clanged a soup pot lid right at that moment, but the woman gave her a brief nod and a quick, visual once-over before turning to the latest crisis at hand.

"We would need you to start right away," Motherwell said as he ushered Louise out of the kitchen. "Before Christmas, if possible."

Overwhelmed by the noise and the smells—simmering beef and something that smelled like asparagus—the now familiar feeling that she was about to up-chuck swept over her.

"Where is the washroom?" she asked urgently, then unceremoniously hurried down the hallway in the direction of Motherwell's pointing finger, hoping she'd make it in time.

She did make it, but just barely. Throwing up in the staff

washroom, while memorable, did nothing to make the experience more positive. In the end, she told Motherwell she'd get back to him soon.

It was a good job—a great job for someone right out of school. Sure, it seemed tight-laced with not much room for individual creativity, but she would probably be able to incorporate some new recipes into the rotation once she was in and had proven herself. Once they tasted her deserts.

The pay wasn't bad—wasn't great, but wasn't minimum wage either. Anyone from the course would jump at that job.

Louise sat in the car and stared out the window.

Who was she kidding? It was a nightmare.

Start before Christmas? What about her Christmas plans? What about the show at the resort? The girls were looking forward to it so much. Louise sensed that having something like that to do might prevent Amber from falling into her old partying ways, and dragging Brandy along with her.

And what about her dad? She was starting to see some improvement from their daily walks. He was getting some color back in his cheeks and was walking better, looking stronger, losing the geriatric shuffle. A few more weeks and she was sure he would really turn a corner.

And how could she raise a baby in the city with those hours? What kind of day care opened at four o'clock in the morning?

But this job was her chance. The door The Pretzel had swung open for her.

Sleet splatted against the windshield as she headed for the ferry, no clearer about what she was going to do.

Chapter 25

By the time Louise drove off the ferry, the weather had changed for the worse and the drive back to Fortune Bay was horrendous. The temperature hovered at zero and the precipitation changed from rain to sleet and back to rain making the roads unexpectedly icy in spots.

Coming down a long hill into the river valley, Louise braked lightly sending the Jeep into a skid, the rear end fishtailing first one way then the other. Years of winter driving experience kicked in and she took her foot off the break and steered gently into the skid. But her heart was in her throat and once she got the car under control, she pulled over to the side of the road and sat clutching the wheel with clammy hands until she stopped shaking.

She'd driven in bad weather other years with no problem, but now that she was pregnant, memories came flooding back of that other snowy drive years ago, heightening her worries about what lay ahead.

She didn't know how she'd survive losing another baby.

Finally arriving at the cabin, Louise sat for a moment in the car, staring sightlessly at the gray waves on the lake rolling into the shore. What would she do when she was stuck in a tiny apartment in the city, so far away from her friends? Oh sure, she'd make new friends eventually, but it would be different with a baby. Her new friends would probably be other single mothers. They'd help each other out, but with those hours, when would she have time to reciprocate?

And would Mr. Motherwell even give her the job if she told him she was pregnant? Or worse, fire her once he found out.

The Christmas lights on the porch blinked on, a clear *Welcome Home.*

She gave a short, rough laugh, unwrapped her stiff fingers from around the steering wheel and climbed out of the car.

Once inside, the cabin was ...quiet. *What did you expect?* She put on the kettle.

Brawny stretched on his cushion behind the stove and yawned, his eyes squeezing shut, the leonine yawn showing his pearly whites.

"I'll have to call you Paunchy soon if you don't get out and get some exercise."

He answered with his signature, creaky-gate, *mer-oww.* He didn't seem to notice that she'd been gone. Someone had been in—there were hot coals in the woodstove and food in his dish. She turned off the kettle, added some logs to the coals in the stove and, setting the damper on low, headed back out the door.

She needed some company tonight. Not necessarily to talk about the job, or Marco, or what her future might hold, just people to block out the voices in her head.

Moments later, she raced through the rain up Stephanie's back stairs. Shaking the droplets out of her hair, she knocked on the kitchen door.

"Enter," Stephanie's voice issued from within.

Louise stepped inside and inhaled the distinctive aroma of Earl Grey Tea. Stephanie sat at her jumbled kitchen table with a cup of the tea, glasses perched on her nose, reading the back of a box.

"What's that?" Louise asked.

"Hair dye." Stephanie laughed, squinting one eye closed. "Dumb idea?"

"I don't know. You have such great hair. Perfect salt and pepper. What color are you thinking?"

"Purple."

"Purple?" Louise hooted. "What brought this on?"

"The show. I feel so dowdy—"

"You?" Louise asked in surprise. "I always think you look so cool and trendy."

Stephanie laughed. "I have never been trendy."

"Well, artsy, then. And that haircut you got last fall looks amazing."

"Maybe so, but now that I'm starting to sell my work I want to feel like an artist. I thought a purple streak would give me some oomph."

"I say do it. It would look great with your color of grey. I'll help."

Amber shuffled into the kitchen. "Help with what?"

Brandy was right behind her. Both girls wore pajama pants, slippers and heavy sweaters. Obviously a sleepover.

"*Ohmygod!*" Brandy exclaimed when she saw the box in Stephanie's hand. "You're dying your hair *purple*?"

"Just a streak."

"Cool," Amber said, with an obvious lack of excitement. "It'll look good. My hair is probably too dark to put in a streak." Behind the tangled black hair, Amber's face, always pale, looked so young without the harsh shield of makeup she so usually wore.

Louise stood behind her and pulled her crow-black hair into a ponytail. "You have such great hair. Nice body and so long." She flipped up the ends. "It could use a trim though, and the roots need touching up. The blonde growing in on top of your head kind of looks like a bald spot."

Brandy giggled. "That's what I told her."

Amber blushed. "I am tired of having to dye it every few weeks. And I heard it isn't too good for you."

"You would kill as a blonde," Brandy told her. "I don't see why you dyed it black to begin with."

Amber shrugged. "To piss off my Grandpa."

Louise had heard about Amber's grandfather, Jasper. Apparently, he was a nasty piece of work and had made Amber's life a nightmare. Louise was pleased to think Amber had fought back, anyway she could.

Stephanie put her arm around the girl. "Those days are over."

"You'd drive the boys crazy as a blonde," Brandy said.

"And isn't that the point?" Louise asked.

Brandy giggled. "Trevor?" Amber blushed to her blonde roots.

Brandy took the box from Louise. "I'd *love* to get some streaks in my hair. Would Mom go ballistic?"

"Probably," Louise said. When Brandy's face fell, she smiled. "It's temporary though."

Then she had an idea. "What if we all did it? Then what could she say?"

"Let's do it," Brandy shrieked, her bright blue eyes pulsing with excitement.

Louise smiled conspiratorially at Amber. She'd love to see Amber go back to blonde. "What do you say? I could call my friend Charlene, she's a stylist in town, and see if she could fit us in tomorrow. She could bring you back to blonde and put in a temporary streak."

Amber looked at her hopefully. "Maybe aqua?"

"That would look great with your coloring," Louise said. "We could all show up at the Christmas show with our colored streaks and really make a statement."

"Please," Brandy beseeched. "A united front. My mom couldn't be mad if we all did it."

Amber grinned, the first real smile Louise had seen from her. "Let's do it."

Stephanie's hair turned out great, the purple stripe adding to her artist's mystique. But she wouldn't let them use the remaining color on Brandy without Belinda's consent.

"Bad enough I'm such a bad example for you girls without actually doing the deed myself," she said. "Us mothers have to stick together. No, if you want a streak, you'll have to get Charlene to do it."

So Louise made the appointment. With the girl's excited squeals filling the kitchen, Louise smiled as she punched in Charlene's number. *This is my family.* She'd miss them when she went back to the city. The girls would have made great babysitters. And Stephanie, too. She could think of a slew of people here who would probably have stepped in to help.

Too bad you can't have it all.

Charlene was busy, it being so close to Christmas, and the only time she could squeeze them in was early the next morning before her regular clients.

The sun was barely up when Louise pulled up at Stephanie's house. Brandy and Amber were waiting and scrambled out the door before she had even rolled to a stop.

They talked non-stop all the way to the salon in Majestic where Charlene unlocked the door to let them in. "Coffee's on."

Louise made a bee line for the pot. "You're a dream."

Charlene zeroed right in on Amber, running her hands through her long hair, flipping up the brittle black ends to have a look.

"What are we going to do for you? Please say you're going back to blonde."

"Blond with an aqua streak," Amber said. Then giggled. Louise stopped, coffee pot in hand. She had never heard Amber giggle before. Such a lovely, girlish sound.

"Okay then," Charlene said, whisking out an apron and leading Amber to one of the stylist's chairs. "Let's get started."

Charlene dealt with Louise and Brandy while Amber was processing. Brandy was quick, one off-center, iridescent purple streak that made a punchy contrast to Brandy's still youthful face. She was thrilled with the result.

Belinda would go ballistic.

Louise's cut had grown significantly and wasn't exactly a pixie cut any more. Charlene gave her a trim and toned down the color, bringing it closer to her own blonde roots, adding purple pops of color on top that contrasted nicely with the pale blonde.

But Amber was the showstopper. Although younger than Brandy, with her black rimmed eyes—or maybe it was what those eyes had seen—she had always looked older. But now, with her shoulder length hair a healthy, bouncing blonde with one wide aqua stripe on the side, she looked softer and more girlish. More true to her age.

"Wow," Brandy said when Charlene spun Amber around.

"Stunning," Louise said. "You'll have those boys on their knees. Both of you."

They arrived at the resort a little later than planned. Louise dropped the boxes she was carrying on the central kitchen island. Brandy and Amber followed her in, each equally laden.

"Okay girls. Last day. Let's get at it."

"Yes, boss," Amber said.

Louise pre-heated one of the ovens, then checked herself out in the shiny, stainless steel refrigerator door. She gave her hair a shake, pleased with the result. Just the pick-me-up she needed.

"I'm going to get the rest of the ingredients from the car."

The girls nodded, Brandy's one, daring, purple stripe shimmering in the light. Yes, Belinda would freak out, but it was only hair. And Amber! The transformation was remarkable. She'd gone from Goth girl to a blonde princess.

Now if they could just get rid of that black eye makeup...

But, Louise reminded herself, baby steps.

By the time she had retrieved the last boxes from the car, the girls had one cookie sheet of leaping reindeer ready to go into the oven and were working on the next.

Louise grinned as she pulled on a pair of oven mitts. "Let's see what this baby can do." Opening the wide oven door, she slid the first cookie sheet onto the rack.

They worked as a team and an hour later, one hundred cookies were cooling on the counter. Reindeer, Christmas trees and simple stocking shapes.

Louise started another batch herself. "These will all be stars, my favorites. So small and special, we can give them away to everyone who stops at the booth. A tasty morsel to encourage them to buy."

When the stars were done, she piled them in a wide-mouthed glass bowl, careful not to break off any tender tips. Covering the bowl with plastic wrap, she put them in the refrigerator.

Their sales table stood right outside the kitchen door where it would be easy to access the extra baking. All day she vacillated between hoping she had enough stock and praying they wouldn't be swamped by reindeer cookies. Finally, she ordered herself to stop obsessing.

People she didn't know started to trickle in. Sean stood at the door with a floor plan in his hand, directing the other artisans to their booths.

"Hey, Sean," she said, ruffling her hair as she walked up to him.

He grinned. "Cool, Lou. Did you do that with Mom?"

"No. Charlene did it." She smirked. "She was asking about you."

Sean blanched.

Louise gave a satisfied laugh. "Gotcha."

Last year he'd had a thing going with Charlene that had caused nothing but trouble when he and Frankie were first getting together and Louise had to razz him about it when she had the chance.

"So, how many artisans are there?" she asked, waving to Stephanie who was arranging some smaller paintings on a corner table.

"Almost forty."

"Wow. Perfect. I still have all my Christmas shopping to do. No time at school and there's not much choice here at the General Store."

"I don't know. A new pair of gum boots never goes amiss."

"Okay. If that's what you want..."

"Gee, thanks. You can look for a pair from me under your tree, too."

She did a quick tour of the tables as the other artisan's set up. There was everything from rain hats crocheted out of recycled plastic grocery bags to soapstone sculpture carved by a local recluse who turned out to be an internationally renowned sculptor. Louise hadn't realized there were so many talented people hidden in these hills.

Baby clothes knitted by the Presbyterian Ladies stopped her in her tracks. So small. So soft. She bought a tiny blue sweater with pearly buttons and guiltily tucked it away.

As she worked her way around the room, she bought some Christmas presents as well: a maple bread board for Sean and a knit scarf from Star in a shade of purple that would match Brandy's streak.

When she got back to their table, Brandy and Amber were arranging the freshly cleaned, fake greenery on the baker's rack, incorporating tiny sparkly lights Brandy had brought from home. Louise went into the kitchen and was washing some bowls when she heard Sean, outside the door, say, "Brandy, have you seen Amb—"

Louise rushed out, wiping her wet hands on her apron. She couldn't miss Amber's reveal.

Amber turned slowly toward her dad, grimacing as if waiting for the axe to fall.

Sean was speechless, his eyes glued to his blonde daughter. "How...? When...?" He walked up to her and ran his hand lightly down her hair. "You're beautiful."

Amber's smile was still tentative. "You think?"

Sean wrapped his arms around her in a hug. "I think."

He didn't hold her for long, Louise could see they weren't quite there yet in their relationship, but when he pulled away she was happy to see that his eyes were suspiciously moist.

"You too Brandy. You look great. Has Belinda seen it yet?"

Brandy groaned. "Not yet."

Sean gave her a pat on the shoulder. "Well, I think it's awesome."

Before he left, he hugged Louise, too.

She cleared her throat. "Looking good, girls. I like the lights."

Using safety pins attached from the back, they swagged red tinsel to the lower drape of the white tablecloth. All that was left for the decorations was to gather holly and ivy from the forest around the cabin for the table bouquet. She'd do that right before she left for the show tomorrow morning.

The girls made royal icing to pipe stripes on the stockings, and sprinkled sparkling sugar on the reindeer, giving each Rudolph a red cherry nose.

When Louise finally pulled the last cookie sheet out of the oven, she realized the girls had ground to a halt. "What?"

Brandy glanced at the door. "It's dark outside. Dinner time."

Louise glanced at the dark windows, mortified to realize the girls had eaten nothing but cookies since she'd picked them up at dawn.

"Well, good job today. Let me look." Like a parade marshal, she inspected the rows of prancing reindeer, plucked up a stocking and bit off the toe. "Perfect. And you're right. It's time to go."

Brandy hesitated. "I'm afraid to go home alone. You said we'd all do this together."

"Okay. Let's pack up and I'll go with you."

Amber stepped up. "I'll come too. You know, for solidarity."

Brandy nodded solemnly.

By the time they had finished packing the cookies, the rest of the artisans had left, and the dining hall was quiet. The immense Christmas tree in the lobby twinkled with sparkly lights that reflected off the hundreds of red and gold balls. Louise pulled on her coat as she passed the check-in desk where Max was staring at the computer screen.

"Bye Max."

He looked up and smiled. "I'm surrounded by beautiful women."

"Do you like it?" Louise asked, running a hand through her tousled hair.

"Love it! Which one of you talked Stephanie into it?"

"She talked *us* into it."

Brandy giggled. "It didn't take much talking."

Max laughed. "Have a good night. And Louise," he said. "Changed your mind yet?"

"No, I haven't," she said, automatically. "Very nice kitchen though."

He flashed her a grin. "Thanks. I'll interpret that as, 'There's still a chance I'll take the job.'"

She laughed. "You interpret that any way you want, but I had an offer for a real job."

His head snapped up and he looked her squarely in the eye. "This is a 'real job'."

She hadn't meant to hurt his feelings. "I know it is. It's a great job. For someone else. I just had my heart set on going back to the city. That's the plan. That's why I took the course in the first place. I've had an offer from The Biltmore."

Max's eyebrows went up. "Really? I know Motherwell. He's tough."

"That was the impression I got. It would be a good place to start, though."

He grunted noncommittally and looked back at the screen.

"I guess you're heading over to Stephanie's," Louise said. She was sorry to have hurt his feelings but really, he should give it up and hire someone else.

"Not tonight. A few guests are arriving tonight and the others first thing tomorrow morning. I may just sleep in my office." His eyes sparkled at the prospect.

"Exciting," she said. "I might be in really early tomorrow morning. I'd like to have some fresh baking ready when the show opens."

"I'll be here."

A few minutes later, Louise and the girls pulled up to her dad's house. She had missed her morning walk with her father, had phoned to tell him she wouldn't be there, but still felt she owed him a visit. This might not be the visit he was expecting, though.

For the first time, she realized how far over the line with Belinda she had stepped by making the appointment for Brandy. Stephanie was right. It was one thing for two teenage girls to sneak away and do something like this themselves, but entirely another for an adult—that would be Louise—to organize it for them. She'd been driven by the urge to help Amber go back to blonde and hadn't considered the impact of Brandy's streaks.

Sean had loved it because Amber's change was a big step up, but while Brandy's hair wasn't nearly as dramatic, it still hadn't been Louise's place to aid and abet.

As she mounted the porch steps, she prepared to grovel. Apologize to Belinda? That would be a first.

Chapter 26

Brandy stopped on the porch. Louise came up behind her and put her hands on her sister's shoulders.

"It's now or never," she said, trying to inject an optimistic note into her voice.

"Well, it's got to be now," Amber said. "What else can you do? Run away?"

"Go live with you and Stephanie?" Brandy said hopefully.

Louise laughed. "Stephanie's turning into Fortune Bay's own Guardian of Wayward Souls." She shot Amber a grin. "Sorry Amb. No offence."

Amber grinned back. "None taken."

"Stop joking," Brandy said.

"It'll be okay." Louise opened the screen door. "Let's just do it."

They filed into Belinda's kitchen. She glanced up from the sink. "There you are. And you too, Louise. Good. Are you here for super? Your father was just asking—"

She turned around and stopped cold. "What on earth?"

"Do you like it Mom?" Brandy's voice sounded unusually high pitched. "We all did it together. Stephanie too."

Belinda's face was expressionless. "Stephanie did this?"

"No," Louise hastened to explain. "Stephanie did her own hair. Well, we helped her. It looks really cool. But she wouldn't have anything to do with the girls getting streaks. We went to the salon in Majestic..."

As they stood nervously in the middle of the kitchen, she felt like she was fourteen again. Belinda walked around them, studying them from all sides. Her blank expression didn't give Louise any clues to her reaction and she steeled herself for the explosion.

Belinda stopped in front of Amber. "Is that your natural color, dear?"

"Pretty much. Hard to know when it's black to start with."

"It looks lovely."

Not what Louise was expecting, but Amber did look great. What else could Belinda say? Brandy was a different story.

She moved on and stood in front of her daughter. "I would have appreciated it if you'd told me first."

"I know," Louise burst in. "I should have made sure Brandy cleared it with you first. We were caught up in the heat of—"

"I might have gotten mine done too." Belinda fingered her thin, non-descript brown-going-grey hair. It always looked, well, pretty bad, but it had never occurred to Louise that Belinda might have wanted to *do* something about it.

"I could probably get you in next week if you want."

"Possibly." Belinda studied the streak in Brandy's hair. "Purple? Is it permanent?"

"Oh no," Brandy sputtered. "It'll wash out by the time school starts."

"I wouldn't have chosen purple with your coloring, but it's your hair so you'll have to live with it."

Brandy threw her arms around her mother's neck. Belinda smiled. A sweet smile that somehow Louise had missed before.

Was Belinda really *not* an ogre? Had the world truly shifted on its axis?

Henrik shuffled into the kitchen. "What's going on out here? I thought I heard my girls come home. Hi, Amber."

Louise gave her dad a hug. "Sorry I missed our walk."

He ruffled her hair. "I survived. Can you stay for dinner? Afterwards, we're going to decorate the tree."

Louise glanced at Belinda who nodded her assent.

"I'd love to."

It was only eight o'clock when the party wound down. Henrik was obviously tired, so Louise decided it was time to go.

When she got home, the cabin was silent and dark. Without the lights and activity that had kept her busy all day, she finally had to acknowledge the sick feeling, like a rock in her stomach, that had been there for days.

She had lost Blue, her best friend. Somehow, she had to get him back.

Running into the cabin, she grabbed a loaf of Blue's favorite Challah bread from the box of loaves ready for tomorrow's sale—that man inhaled fresh bread like oxygen. She was back on the road in a matter of minutes, the Jeep racing to the log house on the point.

Sure, they had argued at the opening of the bar, but she could tell he still cared. She'd bet he'd been the one who kept her fire going while she had been in the city. Surely they were still friends.

Friends with benefits?

No. Definitely no more benefits. Not with Blue. He was off limits.

Things had changed between them lately—and not just the sex, although that was... words failed her. Like nothing she had ever experienced before. Sex had always been fun, a go-to when she felt alone, but there had never been much *feeling* involved. At least not on her end.

But sex with Blue had left her dazed and weak and...afraid. Afraid of how deep they could go, of how easily she could lose herself in feelings she could not control.

She'd always felt safe with him, even in bed. That was dangerous, of course, because she wasn't safe. Not ever. Not really. Not when her heart was involved.

She'd gone down that road with Tony and swore, never again. When she'd lost Tony and the baby, she'd almost lost herself, and if anything like that ever happened with Blue...well, she might never make it back.

And anyway, she couldn't think about being with Blue now, not with Marco's baby in the picture. But she could make sure they were still friends. Make sure he knew how much he meant to her.

As she navigated the dark, wet road, she wrestled with the problem of how to keep Blue as a friend. Although none of her lovers lasted, she was almost always the one who pulled the plug. She'd managed to keep most of them as friends. Good friends.

But deep inside, she'd always known that it wouldn't be that way with Blue. If they became a couple, then sooner or later when the split came—and it always did—Blue wouldn't remain her friend.

Hopefully it wasn't too late to make things right.

She pulled into his driveway, the living room lights shining through the trees. His truck was parked off to the side and she stopped beside it. He was home. Her breathing became tight. She hadn't planned a speech.

With the loaf of Challah clutched to her chest, she ran through the rain to the porch and knocked on the heavy wooden door. When it opened, she forced her cheeks into a smile, but when she saw him, her shoulders fell.

Suddenly, it seemed like too much weight to carry alone. The baby, Marco's noncommittal response, her dad's illness, her own uncertain future. She needed a friend.

"Merry Christmas," she said brightly, holding out the bag with the loaf of bread. "Can I come in?"

He closed his eyes, sighed deeply, then stepped aside.

She stepped into the house and he closed the door. "What are you doing here, Louise?"

She couldn't keep up the pretense any longer. Her

shoulders sagged and she tried, not very successfully, to keep the pleading out of her voice. "I just need a friend."

Blue sighed again, as if anticipating trouble, and motioned her into the living room. A bottle of beer sat on the end table and she automatically plunked herself down in the middle of the sofa. He grabbed his beer and took a seat in the armchair.

All right. Message received.

"Did you get the job?"

Blue was never one to mince words but even so, his question took her by surprise. "Yes, at a hotel in the city."

He nodded. "Just what you wanted."

"I guess. They want me. It's not my dream job and the pay's not that good, but it's a great start."

"Better than the resort?"

No. "Well, it's what I wanted and, you know, I'd be near Marco."

His expression hardened and he looked more like an angry bear than ever.

Now that she was here, she didn't know what to say. Her eyes dropped to the floor. Hmm. Tiny white bits littered the carpet. Looked like popcorn.

"*Near* Marco? Aren't you going to move in with him?"

Her head jerked up, meeting his eyes for a brief second before resuming their search of the floor. "Maybe. We haven't decided."

"He's not Tony, you know. When are you going to get over that guy? He wasn't worth it."

"We were young. He was good to me, but I came to terms with his death a long time ago." She looked up. His dark eyes pulsed a message to her like life blood to her veins. "It wasn't true love."

Overcome, she glanced away. "It was the miscarriage that destroyed me. I'd lost my mother, and pretty well lost my father too, and I thought Tony and the baby would be my new family. It might not have worked out with Tony, but that baby would have been mine.

"When I lost it, they told me I probably couldn't have another, so that dream of a family of my own died that night too."

Blue looked stricken. "I never knew that was what it was about." She knew he meant the months of depression, the years of adjustment.

"I didn't really know either, at the time. Certainly couldn't verbalize it. But you were there for me. You're my rock. Without you, I'm floundering—then and now. I just want you to know how much that means to me, how much I still need you in my life."

Blue was silent for long enough that she was pretty sure she'd rounded up all the stray kernels on the floor. Then he said, "You don't have to stay with him, you know."

Her eyes flashed to his face. She needed to make him understand. "I have to try. He's the baby's father."

"He's not a father, he's a sperm donor. If he was a father he'd be here now."

"He has things to do..." That was weak. Blue was right.

"What does he think about the baby."

He thinks I should get an abortion. "He's happy."

"Is he coming back?"

"I don't know. Eventually. He might visit his mother in San Francisco for Christmas."

This was not going well. Not at all. He was barraging her with questions she didn't want to answer. Didn't even want to think about.

She wasn't sure what she'd expected. Was a hug too much to ask?

Blue crossed his arms over his chest.

Apparently it was.

"You know, I think I'd better go."

She stood up and hurried to the door because yes, she

was running away.

There was one beat, then he was on his feet and after her, long strides eating up the distance. She opened her mouth, but Blue held up a hand to stop her.

"I've loved you forever Louise. I tried to tell you after Tony died, but that *was* the wrong time. You couldn't hear me then.

"I should have told you again, a hundred times, but I was a coward. I thought being your friend would have to be enough. Was all I could expect. All I deserved.

"I was afraid if I told you, you'd reject me, dismiss me again, and maybe you will." He laughed harshly. "God knows I wouldn't be surprised. But I had to make sure you knew."

Tears pricked her eyes and she covered her mouth with her hand. "I've never dismissed you."

She opened the door and took one step out into the rain on the porch. Her voice sunk to a whisper. "But I have to give him a chance."

"When are you going to give me a chance?"

Louise looked back at him. "Maybe—"

Before she could finish her sentence, he stepped onto the porch, took her by the shoulders and pulled her into a devouring kiss. He lifted her up until her feet barely touched the ground. Probably just as well because her knees had gone soft and she would have collapsed. Preferably against the soft flannel of his chest.

But his hands kept her upright, one on her back and one on the back of her head, where he used it to hold her while he deepened the kiss and—*Oh my god*—it was like falling into a vat of warm, melted chocolate. So rich, she just wanted to rub it all over her body, immerse herself in it because she couldn't think about anything else.

His tongue probed her mouth fiercely, then suddenly softened. Caressing.

Okay, she took it all back, he could have all the benefits he wanted. Her arms went around his neck. She wanted to climb him, have him pick her up and carry her inside—he'd done it before.

Then he set her firmly onto the porch and pulled away.

She stared at him, pressing the back of her hand to her lips. Was she panting? She was panting.

So was he. Staring back at her and breathing hard.

"Has he ever kissed you like that, Louise?"

She couldn't respond, but of course the answer was *no*. No one had ever kissed her like that.

He tipped his head to the side, raised one sardonic brow, stepped back into the house and closed the door.

Louise stood on the porch with her mouth open, rain dripping off the roof onto her head.

No, Marco had never kissed her like that. His lovemaking was smooth and methodical. Pleasant, but he had *never* rocked her world. Not like that. Not like Blue.

She shook her head, then ran for the car. Hands on the steering wheel, she sat for a minute, knees bouncing. So, what was the verdict? Friends? Hardly!

Swinging the Jeep through the giant puddle, spray flying in all directions, she peeled down the drive.

* * *

Okay, so he couldn't walk away from her. In that case, he'd have to take a stand. Fight for her. Fight *with* her. *Whatever it takes.*

He grabbed the scissors from the kitchen drawer and went into the bathroom. Turing on the light, he studied his beard. Big and bushy, it was at least two handfuls.

He'd never want to be as slick, as slimy as Marco, but maybe it was time to step up his game. Time for a change.

Time to see the man behind the beard.

Chapter 27

"And then he said," Louise deepened her voice. "'Has he ever kissed you like that, Louise?' And closed the door in my face, leaving me standing in the rain."

Maddie said, "No!" Frankie sucked in a scandalized breath.

"Yes." Louise emphasized the word by taking a gulp of her Perrier.

"Well, has he?" Frankie asked, a grin tugging the corners of her mouth.

"Of course not. This was a heart-stopping, mind-boggling kiss."

"Anything else?" Frankie asked, wiggling her eyebrows suggestively.

"Oh." Louise blushed and rubbed her forehead with her hand. "I skipped the part where we, uh, slept together the other night."

"What?" her friends shrieked in unison.

"I know, I know."

"What are you doing?" Frankie asked.

"And when did you have time?" Maddie added.

"I'm not proud of it. In fact, I feel terrible about being with Marco so soon after Blue. And I wouldn't have, but I didn't know Marco was coming, and I would have sent him on his way when he got here if I didn't have to tell him about the baby."

Maddie shook her head in disbelief. "It's like a soap opera."

"And what did Marco say, about the baby," Frankie asked.

"He wasn't thrilled," Louise admitted. "I can't believe it.

For once, when I actually want a show of commitment from a man, I'm not getting it. Marco is the baby's father and I feel like I have to give it a chance to work out with him. But he doesn't seem interested in having a child."

She couldn't bring herself to tell them he'd suggested she get an abortion. "He doesn't seem interested in living together, either. He just said, we'd 'work it out.' Whatever that means."

"And what are you going to do about Blue?" Frankie asked.

Louise blew out a shuddery breath. "I don't know. Things have, well, heated up to an incendiary degree in the past few days—like a friggin' blast furnace and..." she trailed off, shaking her head, not wanting to think about it.

Frankie finished for her. "And it puts you at risk."

"How so?" Maddie asked. "It is kind of like jumping in at the deep end, but Blue's a great guy."

"Too great," Louise said.

Maddie shook her head. "You've lost me."

"You may not have noticed," Frankie explained in her best schoolteacher voice. "But Louise always picks, shall we say, men unsuitable for serious relationships. Men with commitment issues. Men she won't fall for. Men who are fun for now and won't be hurt when she kicks them to the curb."

Louise straightened up. "Hey!"

Frankie waved a hand. "Just a figure of speech."

"But why?" Maddie asked. "Isn't that kind of self-defeating?"

"No," Frankie said, more gently. "It's self-protecting."

"Well that may have been true in the past," Louise said. "But I'm finished with short-term relationships. You can't do that with a kid. But it can't be Blue."

"Hmmm," Maddie said. "Lost me again. Because Blue's too—what? Great?"

"He is great. But I know if we get together, I'll just end up hurting him. But, if we don't get together, I might lose him as a friend, anyway."

"To say nothing of missing out on all that mind-blowing sex," Frankie said.

Louise's eyebrows arched in surprise. Frankie had certainly changed while Louise had been away. It seemed like everything had changed.

"Is that all you want him as? A friend?" Maddie asked softly.

"That's all we are. All we can be. He's fantasizing about the me, but it's not the new me. Not the one who's about to balloon out and then have a kid."

"That could be true," Maddie said. "But he knows you're pregnant. Surely he knows what that means."

"I guess." Louise blew out a long breath and her shoulders slumped. "But bottom line? He's not the baby's father. I really feel like I have to give Marco a chance." Even as she said it, she realized the old argument had lost its punch since her meeting with Marco in the city.

"Sounds like he's not interested," Frankie said, "And Blue is."

"If only it were that easy."

"Sometimes we make things more difficult than they need to be," Frankie said. "We don't see the prize that's staring us in the face."

"Well, you can't have it all."

Maddie straightened in her chair. "I disagree. I think sometimes you can. It's all a matter of perceptions. Of knowing what "it all" is, what you really want, then letting your guard down and taking a chance."

"But I won the freakin' pretzel. I feel I owe it to myself to try to make a go of it in the city. I have a job offer at a good hotel. My dream job," she said morosely. This no longer felt like a prize-winning argument either.

"You don't sound very excited," Frankie said.

"I thought it would be my dream job but it didn't turn out to be as good as I thought it would be."

Then she said more firmly, "It would be a good first job though. A rung in the ladder. I just got away from Fortune Bay. I can't come crawling back."

"I don't get why you think you'd be crawling," Frankie insisted. "You are coming back in triumph, waving the Golden Pretzel over your head."

Louise gave a sad smiled. "That's one way to look at it. Max did offer me a job at the resort."

"That would be perfect. You know he'd be flexible when the baby comes."

Louise pressed her lips together and bobbed her head. Not quite a nod of agreement, mostly to end the discussion. She didn't know what she wanted anymore.

Later that night when she got back to the cabin, Louise lay on the couch in her darkened living room, staring into the fire through the open door of the stove. Brawny was curled up beside her under a blanket, purring loudly. Louise stroked his short, silky fur. "What do you think, pal? Here or there? Him or—him?"

Beneath the covers, Brawny stilled, then stuck out his head, whiskers bristling.

Louise heard a clicking sound like Star's knitting needles and her eyes flashed around the room searching for the source. On first glance, nothing presented itself, but then the cradle in the corner started rocking.

You are lucky to be having this baby.

Louise pulled herself up into a sitting position on the couch. Who said that? Was the voice in the room? In her head? Was she completely losing her mind?

I only had one chance and I lost it, the voice continued. *My husband made me this cradle but I never had a chance to use it. We were trying to have another child when he died, lost on the river with the log run. So much loss.*

Louise hitched herself up and swung her feet to the floor. Goosebumps ran down her arms, but she couldn't tear her eyes away from the rocking cradle. Brawny jumped to the floor and hissed, fur standing on end, his back arched, looking twice his size.

I never got a second chance, the voice continued. *Take this chance and make the most of it. This is your life.*

The cradle stopped rocking just as suddenly as it had started. The clicking sound faded and everything returned to normal. Except for the goosebumps on Louise's arms.

She laughed nervously. "Thanks for the advice, Augusta." Then she glanced around the empty room. Was she talking to herself, or to a ghost? And which was crazier?

Scuttling back onto the couch, she pulled Brawny under the blanket with her. He only objected for a moment, then pushed his warm body against her, better than any hot water bottle, and started his purr-machine again.

She *was* going to take this chance. At her age, it might be her last chance.

But her choices were like the proverbial fork in the road. The hard way, but maybe the right way, with Marco, the father. Struggling through what was now an emotionally distant relationship— had it ever been anything else? She couldn't remember— and a tough slog at a job she'd thought she wanted, that her fellow students would *kill* for, but that now seemed more and more unlikely.

She stopped when she heard how she'd just phrased that: *The job she'd thought she'd wanted.* Past tense. File that one away for future thought.

Or the easy way, which in some ways was riskier. Raising her baby alone in Fortune Bay, with family and friends, people she loved who loved her in return, and who would give her the help she would need. And a job, a good job, to boot. A job that a few years ago she would have thought was a gift from heaven.

Unfortunately, she'd lost her faith in *happily ever after* on that snowy road fifteen years ago. Maybe this pregnancy was a sign that life was giving her a second chance. Maybe her relationship with Marco was the best she could hope for.

The cradle started rocking again. This time, Brawny didn't stop purring and Louise was too tired to react.

Plan "B" sounded perfect. So why was she so afraid to stay?

Frankie had nailed it. Because she was afraid to risk loving Blue. Because she could, so easily, love him.

And, if she was being perfectly honest, she already did.

Chapter 28

Louise awoke on the couch with a stiff back and a kink in her neck. It was still dark outside, the room dimly lit by the glow of the coals in the woodstove.

A beam of moonlight fell on the cradle. Had that been a dream? Her own unconscious whispering in her ear? She could accept Augusta as a roommate as long as she stayed silent, but Louise wasn't too sure about the arrangement if Augusta was going to start talking to her.

One thing she did know, she desperately had to pee and was glad she was still dressed as she raced outside in bare feet, across the icy porch floor to the bathroom. The temperature had dropped overnight. A white haze hung over the lake and made a ring around the almost-full moon.

She hadn't checked the time, but since she was awake and the Christmas show was today, it was never too early to start baking. If she got to the resort early enough, she could get some currant loaves in the oven before the event started and have them fresh and warm when the first customers arrived.

She had decided to spend the whole day baking in the kitchen and leave the sales to the girls. She was not in the mood to talk to the everyone in the village, and baking would be a whole lot easier than confronting Blue every time she glanced across the aisle.

She showered, made a quick press pot of coffee and dressed in her best blacks. Her bright white chef's jacket with the traditional stand-up collar and double row of buttons down the front was freshly laundered. She didn't know how much longer it would fit, but she would wear it today. She'd be in and out of the kitchen and wanted to look professional. At this point, she had no idea what her future held, but you never knew who would be there and when an opportunity might present itself.

It was four thirty when she arrived at the resort. The lights in the parking lot and over the front entrance doors shone like bright fuzzy orbs through the night mist. Her breath puffed little white clouds as she crunched across the thin film of ice covering the parking lot with her chef's jacket over her arm.

Tapping on the glass door, she peered inside. The lobby was in shadow, but a minute later Max emerged from his office, hair rumpled, one hand rubbing his eyes.

When he opened the door, she thrust a thermos of coffee into his hands. "Sorry to wake you."

"It's okay. We are on light staffing and I'm on the desk. We do have guests tonight, you know." She could hear the pride in his voice.

"That's great. How's it going?"

"Really well. I sponsored a couple of rooms for the press and retained a suite for myself this weekend. If you could just listen for the desk, I think I'll dash up to my room, have a quick shower and change. I don't think anyone else will be arriving yet though, and Sean should be here in half an hour. Just dial 999 if there's a problem."

"Sure. You might want to sprinkle salt on the parking lot and steps. It's pretty icy out there."

"Will do."

Louise crossed the dimly lit dining hall. Most of the booths were ready to go, just waiting for their people to bring them to life.

Walking through the swinging doors into the kitchen, she flipped the switch and the room burst into readiness, all bright white tile, shiny steel and warm butcher block.

It was a good kitchen to work in and during the past week she'd started to feel at home in the space. She had appropriated one refrigerator and, opening it now, was gratified to see it filled with neatly packaged and labeled loaves of Christmas fruit bread and Stollen, boxes of cookies and coffee cakes, cheesecakes and minced tarts, all ready to go.

Peeking at their first attempts at Royal Icing, she was gratified to see how far they had come in their technique. Amber seemed to have a knack. Working with the girls had been a wonderful experience. She'd miss them when she left.

If she left. Truth was, she was wondering if she could, in good conscience, take *any* job, knowing she'd have to take a break so soon. Assuming they even had maternity leave at the Biltmore, it was probably not for someone who had been with them for less than six months. And then what would she do if she was alone in the city? She breathed in deeply and shook her head. She couldn't think about that now, but she would have to decide soon.

The first-attempt cookies went in a big mixing bowl to give away to children during the show.

Half an hour later, she was kneading the currant loaf dough when Sean stuck his head through the doorway.

"You're here early," he said.

She smiled and washed her hands. "It's a baker's life."

Pulling a cranberry sweet bread out of a bag, she sliced it and arranged the pieces on a plate.

Then she turned around and held it out to Sean. "I'm pregnant."

She hadn't meant to tell him today, but it just came out. Sean took the plate, set it on the counter and pulled her into a warm hug.

"I kind of figured. I'm so happy for you."

The bright lights of the kitchen turned starry as tears pricked her eyes. She buried her head in his shoulder for a moment, wiping her eyes on his shirt, then pulled away. "I am too. Not sure what I'm going to do, but happy."

"And the father is...?"

"Marco." It came out with a little huff of breath that she realized spoke volumes.

"To tell the truth," Sean said, "I wasn't too taken with him that night at the bar. He seemed kind of—slick. Shouldn't he be here now?"

"He has things..." She shook her head, waved a hand. *Why was she making excuses for his sorry ass?*

Sean frowned. "*This* is his thing. This should be his most important thing. You're giving the guy too much credit."

His eyes were hard on her, forcing her to maintain eye contact.

"Do you love him?"

Now she did look away.

"Does he love you?"

She could only shrug and helplessly shake her head.

"Christ, Louise. You can't stay with this jerk if he doesn't love you, or you him. And why would you bother when there is someone who does?" He lowered his voice. "Who always has."

"Blue and I aren't like that."

Sean raised his brows meaningfully. She huffed a laugh and shook her head. *Who's slick?* He had got her to admit there was something between them.

"Anyway, Marco's the father. He has some rights."

"He's only a father if he acts like a father. What he has are some obligations."

"Look, I know what you went through with Amber."

"Turning my back was the wrong thing to do, but I was a kid. This guy's no kid, he must be forty."

"Forty-two."

A silence followed while they both thought that over, and finally Sean said, "If he's not ready to step up now, he never will be."

Tears filled Louise's eyes and her throat became hoarse. "But I don't know if I can do this alone."

Sean's eyes softened. "You wouldn't have to be alone."

She grabbed a tissue and wiped her eyes. "That's what Augusta said."

Sean's eyes went wide. "She spoke to you?"

"I think so. It was kind of hard to tell. But the cradle started rocking and I heard these words..."

"What did she say?"

"She told me her husband made the cradle—have you seen it? It's beautiful. It showed up in the cabin a few days ago."

Sean nodded. "It was in the attic."

"She said her husband was killed on the river."

Sean nodded again.

"That she'd never had another chance to have a child and I should make the most of this chance." She laughed nervously. "Whatever that means."

"Augusta can't help butting in. But she's usually right."

"I'm sure something will work out. But now," she turned to the counter and lifted the currant studded dough from the bowl, "I have loaves to bake."

"You look pretty comfortable in this kitchen," Sean observed.

She plopped the mound of dough on the counter. "It's a great space to work in."

After a moment's silence, Sean said, "Just think about what you'd be giving up, Louise."

Then he picked up the plate of cranberry loaf and walked out the door.

It wasn't long before the artisans began arriving *en masse*, the last-minute stragglers rushing to set up their tables, the others carting in more stock, standing in the aisle chatting and assessing their booths.

The girls hustled in at eight.

"You've been busy," Amber said, eyeing the two dozen small loaves cooling on the counter.

"Bakers start early," Louise said mildly.

"I would have been here sooner but Brandy wouldn't get out of bed."

"This *is* early," Brandy objected.

"It's fine," Louise said. "I'm just going to keep baking so we have fresh buns and bread and cookies all day. Why don't you two get the box of breads out of my car and then set up the table."

She needed to keep busy to stop the arguing voices in her head. She'd make cinnamon buns—they had always been a hit at the café.

With her head down in the kitchen, she didn't notice the patrons streaming in until she walked out through the kitchen doors at eleven o'clock with a tray of warm sticky buns.

The place was packed.

Across the aisle, Blue stood beside his life-size carving of the standing bear. With his arms crossed over his chest, he looked hilariously like the bear beside him, except— *Ohmygod!* —he'd shaved off his beard. Left just that sexy stubble all the movie stars wore and he looked good enough to eat.

He was talking to a trim woman with long dark hair who, despite her L.L. Bean jeans and pullover and vest—or maybe *because* of her obviously new outfit—was clearly not local.

The pad and paper in her hands suggested she was possibly a reporter, one of the media Sean had invited. She wasn't writing though, was just staring up at Blue. Then she tossed her head, throwing her dark mane back over her shoulder and said, "May I?"

Being only ten feet away, Louise could hear every word they said, even over the noise of the crowd.

Blue nodded and the woman set the pad on the table and rubbed a hand over the back of one of the sleek, carved otters-playing-on-a-log in a clearly sensual way. Louise's eyes narrowed. The woman smiled up at Blue and, *cr-ipes*, he smiled back.

Louise was still standing beside the table with the tray of hot cinnamon buns in her hands when she noticed Brandy looking at her strangely. She'd obviously said something that Louise had missed. Fiona was coming toward her, too, so she wrenched her attention away from the table across the aisle.

"Cinnamon buns," Fiona exclaimed. "We've missed them at the café."

She lowered her voice. "Star tries, bless her heart, but her baking is like sawdust. She's good with the short orders, but isn't really a baker. Could I talk you into bringing a tray of these by the café, say, twice a week to start? How many did you used to sell?"

"About six dozen a week," Louise said, as Brandy took the tray out of her hands and started packaging them up for the crowd of people who'd suddenly materialized in front of their booth.

The baking was a hit. Brandy handed Louise the empty bowl that had held the reject, giveaway cookies and she went back into the kitchen to refill it with the buttery, crispy stars she had just taken out of the oven. She grabbed a few loaves of the cranberry bread to fill the empty spaces on the baker's rack and headed back into the fray.

Brandy and Amber had the sales-end well covered, and Louise stayed busy forming another batch of cinnamon buns, pulling pans of gingerbread stars out of the oven, and keeping the outer shelves stocked.

Over the past weeks she'd been a virtual baking machine, hiding away in the kitchen from the problems in the real world. There'd been times when she'd been sure she had way too much stock for the show, that they'd be eating reindeer cookies until Easter, but now she was glad she had so much tucked away.

The crowd was mostly composed of adults. Some were local but from conversations she overheard, she knew others were from as far away as Port Townsend and Seattle.

As the only thing going on in town, by afternoon, a bunch of teenagers had descended on the resort. They were curious and, for the most part, respectful. She suspected Max, ever watchful in the lobby, may have had something to do with that, as did Blue, whose presence alone was enough to keep the boys in line.

Louise tried to keep her eyes off him, but it was next to impossible with him watching her with laser-sharp focus from ten feet away.

Star had a table on the far wall and even from that distance Louise could see her brightly colored knitting. At one o'clock she dropped off a sandwich for Blue, which he ate, staring at Louise.

Around three, the crowd thinned out. There was nothing more to do in the kitchen and she realized Brandy and Amber had been living on cookies again all day, so she sent them off for the last two hours with a promise they'd come back at five to help her pack up.

The girls didn't go home. Instead, they stayed and looked around the show, and were immediately surrounded by a group of teenage boys who'd been hovering on the periphery of the booth all afternoon, cruising by to snafu free cookies every few minutes. Ever since the party-gone-wrong, when Blue had brought the girls to the cabin, Louise had been watching out for them.

Most of the guys were typically gawky and shy. Amber was strangely shy too, but she knew how to use her long blonde hair, flipping it over her shoulder to flirt. Then a big teenage bruiser with tats on his neck and giant holes in his ears, who must have been eighteen if he was a day, stalked in and walked right over to the crowd of kids.

Brandy whispered something to Amber and stepped out of the way as the guy sauntered up to Amber. She batted her heavily kohled eyes back at him, and it was at that moment that Louise realized that her work here with the girls was far from done.

She was filling a need and for once she felt she could be a role model. She might be single and pregnant, but she'd do her best to keep them in line.

Then her dad and Belinda walked through the salmon arch. He was using his cane and seemed to be leaning on it heavily. He nodded in her direction and conferred with Belinda who had his other arm. She looked at Louise and made a circle with her hand in the air, indicating they'd look at the other aisle first and end at Louise's booth.

Louise watched them slowly navigate the booths.

"Hey, Louise."

Behind her, a stocky man in a checked jacket, with a knit hat pulled low over his forehead, was standing next to her booth. He had a baby in a snuggly attached to his chest and was pushing a sleeping toddler in a stroller.

She smiled. "Hi, Felix."

She and Felix had been in high school together and a few years ago, for a couple of fun filled summer months, he'd been her friend-with-bennies. As usual, they'd stayed friends when it was over.

"So," she said, eyeing the babies with a smile. "This is new."

Felix smiled, both sheepish and proud, an endearing combination in such a tough guy. She'd always known he'd had a good heart, though, or she never would have gone out with him.

Suddenly curious to see more, she rounded the table and peeked in the snuggly at the sleeping baby. She felt herself go soft and mushy inside at the sight of the sleeping newborn.

"So cute. Boy or girl?"

"Girl. Emma. And this big guy," he indicated the sleeping toddler sprawled in the stroller, "is Howey."

Louise nodded. "After your dad."

"You got it."

Louise couldn't tear her eyes off the cherub sleeping in the snuggly, a reddish-blond kewpie-doll curl on top of her head, perfect rosebud lips, eyelashes splayed on her soft pink cheeks. Her arms ached to hold her. Louise sighed, overcome by a warm and fuzzy feeling she'd never experienced before. Baby envy.

Just then, a woman walked up and slipped her arm through Felix's. "Hi, Louise."

Her greeting wasn't quite as warm as Felix's had been. The women in town tended not to be as forgiving.

"Hi, Sheila. Nice family. That was fast, wasn't it?" No, wrong, that sounded harsh.

"Well, time is marching on, you know."

She knew. *Make nice.* She smiled. "Are you still working at the library?"

Sheila shook her head. "Only a few hours a week." She laughed. "Mostly to get out of the house. Felix has a good job at the mill these days and we thought I should stay home with the kids for a few years. We're having another."

A look passed between them, a warm little bubble that clearly, Louise was not part of.

Then Sheila laughed again. "But this is the last one. I swear!"

Louise bit her lip. "Well, congratulations."

She wished she could tell people about her own pregnancy with such obvious happiness, knowing the baby would have a father who would help look after them both in those early years. But that was just foolish. There were no guarantees in life.

"You take care, Louise," Sheila said in a kindlier voice as they walked away.

She seemed nice. Really nice. Louise hadn't had many girlfriends growing up. Just Colleen, and she was quite a bit older. And once Colleen met Alex, she had moved to the other side of the lake and started a family. They rarely saw each other after that.

It had been great to see her at Maddie's, though. Louise wished she had spent more time cultivating women friends. She sensed she was heading into a stage of her life where their support would be invaluable. Well, she had a few friends and they were good ones, and it was never too late to make more.

The reporter was back, across the way, talking to Blue. Although the room was quieter now, Louise couldn't hear what they were saying, just saw the woman put a hand on Blue's arm and lean in to say something privately to him. She angled her head toward the lobby and he nodded in response. She smiled. He smiled. She walked away.

Louise's eyes widened. If that wasn't a hookup, she was Betty Boop.

A few minutes later, Blue left too, heading out to the lobby. There was only an hour left until closing and only a few shoppers cruising the aisles. Some of the crafts people had abandoned their booths and were standing together in clusters, talking.

Louise gripped the table, trying hard not to follow Blue out into the lobby, to see if he was meeting up with the reporter.

Hooking up with the writer would be good for his career, so, good for him. How could Louise be jealous? Did she think if she couldn't have him, no one could?

Pretty much.

But she had to pee. That was a legitimate reason to

follow him out into the lobby. Stashing the cash box under the table, she headed for the door.

At the check-in desk, Sean glanced up and smiled when he saw her, but the smile froze on his face as his eyes flicked to the entrance to the bar. So did hers.

Blue was sitting at the bar with his back to the door, facing the reporter. Louise figured they must have been pretty well knee to knee. The reporter said something and batted her eyelashes. Then she leaned in to hear what he said in return, threw back her head and laughed.

Oh, come on! Blue had a subtle sense of humor, but was rarely laugh-out-loud funny.

As Louise made her way past the front desk to the washrooms, Sean gave her a sympathetic purse-of-the-lips and shake-of-the-head, which she did not acknowledge.

"Almost finished for the day," she said brightly.

When she emerged, Sean didn't look up from his papers and although she tried not to let her gaze drift into the bar, she couldn't help flicking a glance. Blue and the reporter were gone.

What did *that* mean? Had she gotten what she wanted for the story, or was she getting what she wanted upstairs in her room right now?

Having fired up a good head of steam up, Louise headed back into the dining hall.

Chapter 29

Blue was back at his table, beside the bear, and he glowered at her as if he could read her mind. Louise's cheeks burned at what she'd been thinking. Hooking-up was so not his style. And anyway, she had no right to even wonder about what he was up to. That wasn't the way she had left things between them. He was a free agent. Not her Blue anymore.

Louise watched her father slowly shuffle up the aisle toward her, leaning on his cane with one hand and heavily on Belinda's arm with the other. As they approached, Louise noted again the new wrinkles lining Belinda's forehead.

Her dad's face was much too pale, his breathing labored. Louise took a chair from behind the table and put it in the aisle for him. He sank heavily into it.

"Hi, honey."

"What are you doing here, Dad?" She glared at Belinda. What was the woman thinking, allowing him to come?

"What do you think?" he said wearily. "I'm tired of being cooped up in the house like an old man."

"Yes, of course, but—"

She didn't get the sentence out before Marco walked into the room. The tension that always seemed to hover over her these days solidified into a cold lump in her stomach.

Time slowed to a crawl, like a spotlight had isolated a triangle of players on a stage with her at the center.

Across the aisle, Blue stood on guard, his arms crossed on his chest like the bear at his side, now glowering at Marco instead of Louise. This time, though, the comparison didn't strike her as nearly as funny.

Her dad sat in the chair, but he had leaned on his cane when Marco walked in and was watching the unfolding scene with interest.

Marco stopped just inside the door. He looked at Blue. His gaze slid to Louise. "Can I talk to you outside?"

She could almost hear the screech as time warped back to normal speed. Louise touched her dad's shoulder lightly as she walked by. "I'll be right back."

As she passed Blue, she hesitated. Something she couldn't deny shimmered between them.

He said in a low voice, "You don't have to go with him, Lou."

"I know."

But she walked out the door anyway.

In the parking lot, Marco was leaning against his silver BMW, arms crossed on his chest, legs crossed at the ankles. "How did the job interview go?"

"Fine. They said the job was mine if I want it."

"Great, great." He nodded, obviously relieved.

He thought she was going to take it, and for the first time she realized without a doubt that she wasn't. She couldn't do that to her child, bring it up alone in the city, with her away working ten hours a day.

Because suddenly she was certain she would be alone. She had yet to hear a promise or offer or declaration of support from Marco, let alone hear him asking her to move in with him.

A weight lifted from her shoulders.

She was on her own, and you know what? It felt okay.

At the sound of a commotion behind her, Louise turned and saw Blue conferring with Max in the lobby.

Brandy ran past them, out the entrance door, pale and frantic. Her gaze swept the parking lot until she found Louise, but she seemed to be frozen to the steps.

Louise ran over to her, sliding on a patch of the ice that was reforming in the shade. "What?"

"It's Dad. He's collapsed."

"Call 911," Louise called as she raced into the lobby.

Behind the desk, Max had the phone to his ear. "They're on their way."

In the dining hall, the tableau had changed. Blue and Belinda knelt on the floor by her father. Louise skidded to a stop, unable to move, torn by the desire to help and the desire to run. Helpless, all she could do was wait for the paramedics to arrive.

Max hustled in with a glass of water and something cupped in the palm of his hand.

"Aspirin," he said, giving it to Belinda.

Blue lifted Henrik's shoulders—her big brave father looked shrunken in his arms.

"Come on, Henrik," Belinda coaxed. "Chew it slowly. I know it tastes bad but chewing makes it work faster."

Henrik kept his eyes fastened on Belinda's and chewed. When he tried to swallow, she gave him a sip of water. Then he sank back in Blue's arms and closed his eyes.

His complexion was a sickly gray like used wash water, and a slick of perspiration covered his forehead. Louise stood frozen in panic, her heart scarcely beating in her chest. She couldn't lose him too. Not now. Not when they were finally rebuilding their family.

Henrik's hand clutched his shirt over his heart and his breathing was shallow, as if every breath hurt.

Max hurried back in with a pillow and blanket and Blue lowered Henrik's head onto the pillow while Belinda gently lay the blanket over him, tucking it around his shoulders.

Amber was speaking quietly into her phone, her eyes wide. Brandy came back into the dining hall and stood wringing her hands. Amber put an arm around her.

A small crowd had gathered. Now that Henrik was as

comfortable as they could make him, Max and Blue tried to disperse the people to clear the way for the arrival of the paramedics.

Louise had never felt so helpless in her life. Helpless and useless. And where were the paramedics? How much time had passed? Surely every minute counted.

She turned and walked out to the front entrance where— *Thank God!*—the ambulance was pulling up, colored lights flashing in the descending dusk.

The paramedics, a man and a woman, were out of the cab in seconds and opening the rear doors. They pulled out the stretcher and Louise held the resort's big front door open for them as they rushed inside.

She was still at the door when, moments later, they hurried back out with her dad strapped to the gurney. Belinda followed, her hand brushing Louise's on her way by. The women exchanged a brief look—numbness mixed with horror at the possibility of...

Louise firmly shook her head. She wouldn't go there. Not yet.

Belinda climbed into the back of the ambulance with Henrik and one of the paramedics, and the last thing Louise saw before they closed the doors was Belinda taking her father's hand.

Siren howling, the ambulance pulled away, exposing the silver sports car behind it.

Marco. Louise had forgotten all about him. She raced down the steps and over to the car, pulling open the passenger door. "I need a ride."

"You got it."

The Beamer peeled out of the parking lot after the wailing ambulance, hugging the twists and turns of the road to Majestic.

Louise clutched the handle over the door as they were thrown first one way then the other. It was dusk, the road was slushy, but her mind was on the ambulance up ahead.

"Louise, we have to talk."

"Now, Marco?"

"Yes, now. I was only stopping in to tell you—I'm moving to San Francisco."

Her head jerked back and she turned to look at him. "Seriously? You're telling me this now?"

"I have to leave right away. They want me before Christmas. The job starts the day after tomorrow."

The job. It was always the job.

"Fine. Go. I hope it works out for you." *I don't want you in my life, or my baby's life, anyway.*

"I'll keep in touch."

Really? That's your response to this chance to be a father?

He frowned at the road. "Will you...?"

She tried to hide her scorn. "Don't worry, Marco. I'll take care of it."

He puffed out a short breath of relief. "Thank you. The timing's just all wrong. I'll send you some money."

"Don't bother. I'll handle it."

The timing might be wrong for him, but she'd take this chance and be happy for it. She'd already written him out of the script, so whether Marco stayed or went was of little consequence. What mattered was her family and, right now, her father.

Marco put the pedal to the floor as if eager to be gone and flew around a corner. The car started to slide and he cranked the wheel as they hit the next curve.

Bile rose in her throat. *Please God. Not again.* She couldn't die now, on this road. Too many people were counting on her. Her dad, the baby. She couldn't lose this baby.

Louise pressed both hands against the dashboard as Marco pulled the car out of the skid.

"Wow," he said. "That was close."

She was breathing hard, her heart pounding as if she'd run a marathon.

"Slow down, you idiot," she said, as they roared into town.

The ambulance was standing at the ready in front of the outreach clinic in Majestic. Not quite a hospital, it was the first stop in a situation like this. The doctors there would quickly assess Henrik's condition and decide whether to send him on to Bremerton for further treatment.

Louise jumped out of the car and held the door open. "Are you coming in?"

"No. There's nothing I can do."

Except hold my hand.

But that clearly wasn't his job anymore.

Chapter 30

Louise rushed into the hospital as Marco roared away. When the odor of pine cleaner and antiseptic chemicals assailed her, she stopped, frozen to the spot.

She hated this place. She'd spent too much time here, first during her mother's final days, while she watched her mother fade away and her father fall apart, and then the night of the accident and in the days that followed.

Her lungs closed like a trap door swinging shut, but she forced the breath through. After a minute, her pulse slowed enough that she could walk down the corridor.

Same peach colored walls—she'd heard peach was supposed to be soothing—and those awful green, plastic chairs.

The nurse at the desk called out to her as she walked past, but she went directly to Belinda, who was standing like a statue at the end of the hall, staring at the closed double doors to the examining room. The bustle at the nursing station in the corner only accentuated her stillness.

She looked so small and alone that Louise pulled her into a hug. Belinda's head barely came up to her shoulder, but she hugged her back, hanging on tightly.

Despite their differences—and truly, at this moment Louise couldn't remember what they were—this woman obviously loved her father, and that was what he needed right now. To be surrounded by people who loved him and would stick with him no matter what. That's what family did. They put aside their differences when times were tough. And this was about as tough as it got.

Louise pulled away. "What did they say?"

"Not sure. We have to wait."

Louise pulled the other woman into the waiting room and nudged her into a chair. That seemed to break her trance.

"I knew he wasn't feeling well all day, but I couldn't stop him. He was determined to go to the show. He wanted to see everything, but he really wanted to support you."

Belinda's tears spilled over and streamed down her face. Louise sat beside her and put an arm around her shoulders as the little woman cried quietly. Why hadn't she seen how much this woman loved her dad?

"He's stubborn," Louise said. "If he wanted to go, there was probably nothing you could have done."

Then Brandy raced into the waiting room.

Louise stood up. *Brandy!* She had forgotten all about her when she and Marco had chased the ambulance out of the resort parking lot. Of course Brandy would want to come too.

"We brought your jacket," Brandy said, handing it to Louise.

She gave her sister a hug. "Thank you."

Shrugging out of her wet Chef's jacket, she pulled on her warm, dry winter coat, only then realizing that she was shaking, chilled to the bone. She didn't think she'd feel warm again until her father was out of danger.

Then Brandy saw Belinda and ran to her mother's side. "Mom."

Belinda pressed her lips together and blinked, then she reached up to give her daughter a hug. "How did you get here?"

"Blue brought me."

Louise turned toward the entrance and saw Blue standing just outside the glass doors, looking in. He was solid, the tower of strength she needed right now. She lifted her chin, beckoning him in.

He got her message, but silently shook his head. Then

he turned and left, and Louise felt her hope for a reconciliation crumble inside her.

"How is Dad?" Brandy asked, drawing her attention back to the waiting room drama.

"We don't know anything yet," Belinda told her.

They sat together for another hour before a young woman doctor emerged from the examination room. Her serious expression hit Louise like a blow to the chest. She reached for Belinda's hand, making a strong family chain as they waited for the doctor to speak.

"He's stable," the doctor said. The clamp on Louise's chest eased and she could breathe again. She slumped back in the chair.

"He had a second, minor heart attack. He might need bypass surgery, but as long as he's quiet, he can go home in a couple of days. No big Christmas celebrations this year though. Quiet." She looked at them sternly and they nodded as one. Louise felt like crying in relief, but managed to hold it inside.

"We'll set up an appointment for right after New Year's with his specialist," the doctor said, then hurried away.

"It was all my fault," Louise said.

Belinda frowned. "How do you figure that?"

"I forced him to walk everyday when he obviously wasn't ready."

"That was what his doctor had prescribed. I would have done it myself but he wouldn't listen to me. Maybe if I'd been able to get him out sooner..."

Louise took Belinda's hand in one hand and Brandy's in the other. "We can pull him through."

Stephanie's voice echoed down the corridor and she rushed around the corner and into the waiting room with Sean close behind.

She bent down and hugged Belinda. "How is he?"

Belinda nodded, tears in her eyes. She was obviously

unable to answer so Louise stood up and filled in the newcomers.

Now that her anxiety about her father's life had subsided, exhaustion rolled over her in a dizzying wave. She grabbed the back of a chair.

Stephanie looked at her with concern and pushed her gently into the chair. "Sit down, dear. You've had a long day. We came in two cars. Brought the Jeep."

"My keys," Louise said, patting her pockets.

"You left your keys and your purse at the resort." For the first time, Louise noticed her purse hanging over Stephanie's shoulder. She really was losing it.

"You don't look very well," Sean said. "Everything is under control here. Let me drive you home."

The doctor was still standing nearby. "You won't be able to see him for another hour, and then only one of you for a few minutes. Tomorrow you can visit for longer."

Suddenly home sounded like a great idea, and Louise nodded to Sean.

Stephanie said, "I'll stay with Belinda."

Brandy chimed in. "I'll stay too."

Louise smiled wanly at her sister. Brandy was growing up.

Pushing to her feet, Louise took the purse Stephanie held out to her. Sean held out the keys but she shook her head.

"Take me home, Sean. Please."

"You bet." He held out an elbow and she took it willingly.

Louise collapsed into the passenger seat of the Jeep, glad Sean was at the wheel because her mind was totally on her dad. She had to be here for him, helping Belinda and Brandy. They had to work as a team until he was back to his old self. She knew they could do it if they worked together. She couldn't lose him now that they were finally starting to talk, finally starting to feel like a family again.

So, she was staying. At least for a while. Having this baby, without Marco, here in Fortune Bay. One strain had lifted but had been replaced by another.

She closed her eyes in exhaustion. She needed a break. When she had more energy, she'd rethink her position on her relationship with Blue, too. It was the easier road, but it might be the right one.

As they drove, the windshield wipers could hardly keep the fat, wet snowflakes off the windscreen. Louise glanced at Sean. He was intent on the road, both hands firmly on the wheel.

"He'll be okay, Louise."

She put her head back on the seat and closed her eyes, totally drained. "I know."

After a few minutes, she opened her eyes and watched the swirling flakes in the headlights, flakes that were rapidly turning to rain. It was pitch dark, and other than the odd dirt road running off into the trees, it was solid forest on both sides of the road. There were no houses or streetlights for the whole ten miles from Majestic to Fortune Bay.

When they hit a long, straight stretch of road, she began to make out a light at the end. This road was as familiar as an old friend's face but Louise didn't recognize the light where the road made a sharp turn to the left.

"Did they put in a light at the corner?" she asked, coming out of her daze.

"No." Sean's voice was raw. "Someone's gone off the road."

The road was lightly travelled so odds were good it was someone they knew. And because so few people lived at the end of the paved road to Fortune Bay, this was always the last stretch the county salted and sanded. Sean switched to four-wheel drive and gently applied the brakes, barely keeping the Jeep under control on the greasy surface as they slid to a stop.

Louise leaned forward to peer into the storm, her seatbelt tight across her chest.

A truck was nose down in the ditch, its headlights illuminating the bank of trees ahead and the falling snow. An old green truck with low wooden sides. Louise gasped. Blue's truck.

"Blue," she shrieked, and was out of the Jeep before Sean had brought it to a full stop.

He was right behind her. "Be careful. The truck might slide."

She could see Blue's face, lit by the headlights' reflection bouncing off the snow. He was sitting, head back, eyes closed, not moving. A trickle of blood ran down from his nose.

Louise struggled with the door, crying and cursing when it wouldn't open.

Sean pushed her aside, took the handle in both hands and, bracing a foot on the frame, yanked it open. Blue turned his head and opened his eyes.

Louise pushed past Sean and climbed up on the running board, touching Blue's shoulder, his face, afraid to move him. "You're hurt. Don't move."

Blue groaned and blinked. "What happened."

"You drove off the road," Sean said, wrestling Louise out of the way to turn off the ignition and undo the seatbelt.

Blue rubbed his forehead. "The brakes..."

Sean stepped back and pulled out his phone.

Louise took Blue's head in her hands to focus his attention on her. "Are you hurt?"

He thought for a moment. "No. Just my head." He reached up and rubbed his sternum. "And my ribs ache something fierce."

"Let's get him out," Sean said. "I don't like the look of that truck. The ambulance is on its way."

By the time they helped him out of the truck and over to the Jeep, Louise could hear the shriek of sirens and see colored lights approaching down the straight stretch of road from town.

The ambulance approached slowly. The same paramedics they'd seen earlier climbed out.

"Hey Sean. Busy night. Better get your car off the road. This is a bad spot to park."

As the paramedics helped Blue into the ambulance, Sean put his arm around Louise's shoulder. He called to the medics, "We'll meet you there."

He tried to pull her toward the Jeep, but she couldn't move until the ambulance doors closed.

Then, as the ambulance pulled away, the black fog rolled in around her. She was shaking uncontrollably as Sean helped her into the Jeep.

"It almost happened again."

"But it didn't," he said firmly. "He's all right."

Maybe. This time. But she'd never be safe as long as she cared.

Sean helped her out of the car and, inside the hospital, they found Stephanie standing in the waiting room.

"Was that Blue? What on earth's going on?"

Louise sank into a plastic chair and let Sean fill his mother in.

Then Louise asked, "Where are Belinda and Brandy?"

"In with your father."

At that moment, they emerged through the double swinging door.

"How is he?" Louise asked.

"Groggy but seems okay. He asked about you. I said you'd come in the morning. I thought you'd left."

"We found Blue's truck in a ditch," Sean said. He glanced at Louise. "I think he's going to be okay."

A tiny woman doctor came around the corner into the

waiting room. "He'll be fine. His nose isn't even broken, although it'll be bruised and sore for a while. He might have cracked a couple of ribs when he hit the steering wheel. We'll take an x-ray, and if they are cracked, we'll tape them up. He'll be good to go."

Good to go. Good news. But it didn't dispel the fear in her heart.

Stephanie was gathering up Belinda and Brandy's belongings. "I think we'll go, then. It's been quite a day. Sounds like they're both going to be okay. Give the big guy a hug from me and we'll see you all tomorrow."

"Drive carefully. The roads are a mess," Sean said as he walked the women out, leaving Louise alone in the waiting room.

Overhead, the oppressive fluorescent light crackled and hissed. She stared at a Safe Sex poster tacked to the wall. Blinking was an effort. It was easier to stare.

The smell of hospital—disinfectant, overcooked food and that overriding smell of illness and despair—made her stomach roil. She'd been here before, shoulders tight, hands rubbing together, hour after hour, waiting for news.

Now she had almost lost him—and maybe next time she would. If not in an accident on the road, then to something else. She couldn't spend her life waiting for that to happen.

She couldn't fall apart, not this time. She had to gather her reserves and pull herself together. Protect herself because she couldn't afford to sink into that black hole. Not anymore. Not with a baby to take care of. And she couldn't go looking for random guys to sooth her pain. Those days were over, too.

She'd raise this baby on her own, with the help of her family, but it would be just her and the child from now on. She didn't know if she could even afford to have Blue as a friend. It was just too dangerous.

Sean walked back in carrying two cups of coffee. "How

are you?"

She took the paper cup in her icy hands. The smell turned her stomach—they must have brewed it hours ago—but at least it was warm. "I'm fine."

"It wasn't too bad. Just a cracked rib."

"I know," she said. "He'll be fine."

Her face felt frozen in an expressionless mask. She'd stopped shaking and was dry eyed. Wide-eyed, in fact.

Sean picked up a tattered magazine, but Louise just continued to stare at the wall until the cup in her hand turned cold.

An hour later, Blue wobbled out into the waiting room, a giant on the arm of the tiny doctor.

"He's had a few painkillers, but he should be okay. Two ribs are cracked, but not broken. No concussion. Take him home and put him to bed."

Sean helped Blue out to the Jeep and Louise followed behind.

"I'll drive," she said.

Sean shot her a look. "You sure?"

She reached for the keys, pleased to see her hand didn't shake. "I'm fine."

Her nerves were solid now that she knew what she had to do. She'd been wrong to keep Blue dangling while she decided what to do about Marco. Tomorrow she'd apologise and explain to him that this really was the end. That she was staying in Fortune Bay but it would be better if they didn't see much of each other. That he had to find someone else and give up this dream of them together. It would be hard, but cutting him loose was the right thing to do.

She drove straight to Blue's house and pulled up beside the porch.

"Would you stay with him tonight, Sean? Please."

He frowned. "I thought you would want to."

"Please," she whispered.

He looked at her for a moment, disappointment clear on his face, then he climbed out of the Jeep and opened the door to the back seat.

"Okay, Big Guy. Let's get you inside."

Louise stayed in the driver's seat, hands clutching the wheel. When the men were safely up on the porch, she turned the Jeep around and headed for home.

The cabin was dark. No twinkly lights to greet her tonight. Wearily, she trudged up the steps. The day had begun at four in the morning and it was now somewhere near midnight. She'd been on her feet all day at the show, done all that baking, gone through the scene with Marco, the tension with Blue, her father's attack, two trips to the hospital—no wonder she felt like she'd been through the grinder.

Opening the screen door, she turned the knob on the front door and pushed. The door stuck shut. She tried again, putting her weight behind it, but still nothing.

She closed her eyes, her shoulders sank. "Come on Augusta, I've had a long day. I'll deal with him. I promise. Tomorrow, when we've both had some sleep."

A breeze brushed her cheek and she opened her eyes. The door had swung open.

Louise stumbled into the cabin and fell gratefully into bed, sure she would be asleep in seconds. Instead, she tossed and turned into the night. The wind rattled branches against the cabin walls as questions swirled in her brain, the same questions she'd been asking ever since she discovered she was having a baby.

At the hospital, she'd thought she'd been clear in her mind about what she had to do about Blue. But now, lying alone in the dark, she wondered if Sean had been right. If she should have stayed with Blue tonight.

Chapter 31

Blue sat at a table in the bar, slumped in a chair, feeling like he'd been run over by his truck last night instead of in it when it slid off the road.

His sunglasses blocked the most searing of the sun's rays—who'd ever heard of this much sunshine in December for Christ sake? He ached all over despite the painkillers he'd taken again that morning. The first ones hadn't work so he'd taken a few more. No wonder he couldn't think straight.

He'd come in half an hour ago with Sean. He had to find out what happened to his truck.

Max had laid out a continental breakfast of sorts on the bar for the guests who were checking out this morning and Blue had a few pieces of Louise's cranberry loaf and a day-old cinnamon bun to settle his stomach. He was downing his third cup of coffee, waiting for the pain meds to kick in and his headache to fade, when front door opened and Star burst into the lobby.

For such a small package, Star could be hell on wheels when she was worked up. Blue started to smile, but it hurt too much and he groaned quietly instead. She saw him immediately and blew into the bar, scarves flying. "You're alright!"

He could hear the relief in her voice. He nodded. That hurt too. "I'll survive."

"I went in to work at the café and everyone was talking about the accident. Pete was in—he towed your truck—said the brakes failed."

"That's what it felt like." That answered the question of what had happened to his truck. He just hoped there wasn't too much damage.

"Poor baby. You've got a big bruise on your cheek. Come over to the café and I'll put some ice on it."

He didn't want to go to the café and face all the people who were bound to be talking about the accident. He wanted to take a load of carvings to the shop, but although the shop was just through the woods behind the resort, he didn't feel up to carrying anything. He needed the truck. Actually, he just wanted to go home to bed. But he needed the truck for that, too.

"Maybe later. I have to talk to Max and see about my truck."

"Okay. I'd better get back to work. I'm glad to see you're still in one piece."

She gave him a kiss on his unbruised cheek, but he had to admit he was relieved when she left.

He also had to admit he was surprised to see Sean with him that morning at the house instead of Louise. He was pretty foggy about what happened last night after they left the hospital, but he knew Louise had been there and he'd sort of thought, sort of hoped, that she'd be with him when he woke up.

But deep down he'd known that he'd lost her when she took off in Marco's car. He gave a hoarse laugh that went straight to his throbbing temples. Truth was, he'd never really had her at all.

The reporter from Seattle dropped her bags in the lobby and walked into the bar. She stopped when she saw him and he suddenly remembered she'd asked him to have dinner with her in town last night.

"Wow," she said. "What happened to you?"

He gave her the abbreviated version.

"Well then, I guess you're off the hook for standing me up last night. Makes my crackers and cheese in my room sound okay after all."

His chances for an article about his carving in the Sunday supplement magazine were probably quashed, but at this point he didn't care.

She put a cinnamon bun on a plate, grabbed a cup of coffee and sat down across the table from him. "What are you going to do now?"

"My truck is smashed, but there's probably nothing I can do about that today. I think I'll just try to catch a ride home."

"I'll drive you," she said, draining her cup and wiping her lips.

"I'd appreciate that." He rose painfully from his chair. Home sounded perfect.

"I hope you recover soon," she said as they made their way to the door. "I'll call you when the story comes out. Maybe we can get that dinner next time you're in Seattle." She flicked her hair over her shoulder and smiled.

So, the article was still a go. Well good. And who knew, maybe he'd make that trip to Seattle after all.

* * *

At some point during the night, Louise must have fallen asleep because she woke to sunlight penetrating the branches and shining weakly through the bedroom window.

The clock said nine, so she dragged herself out of bed, pulled on her clothes and shot across the icy porch to the bathroom, surprised to see blue sky and calm water. In December, a day like this was a gift. Although she was sad about her decision to end it with Blue, coming to a decision about her future felt good. The black cloud that had followed her for so many years had dissipated and the air was crisp and clear around her. Looking up at the luminous sky overhead, she knew what she had to do.

Coffee and a muffin later, woolly scarf around her chin against the nip in the air, she climbed into the Jeep. First things first. She had to clean up the mess she'd left at the resort last night when she'd made her hasty exit from the Artisan's Show.

There were a few vans in the lot and in the dining hall, a few of the participants were dismantling their booths.

She was surprised to find her table mostly clear. Brandy and Amber must have cleaned up the kitchen. She'd have to remember to thank them later and give them their share of the proceeds from the sale, which, come to think of it, she'd ran off and left under the table last night. Amazing how a family crisis puts everything into perspective.

She lifted the tablecloth but the cash box was gone.

Max walked into the dining room. "I didn't expect to see you here so early."

"I didn't want to leave you with a mess. Do you know what happened to my cash box?"

"It's in my office. Steph says your Dad's going to be okay."

"Yes. I hope so. I'm going to the hospital to see him when I'm finished here."

"Sean's been in. Blue's going to be okay too."

She pressed her lips together and nodded. He'd survived the accident and he'd survive her too. In fact, he'd be better off without her screwing up his life.

"I'll be back for the Christmas brunch."

"Do you think you could bring some of those cinnamon buns?"

She smiled. "Of course."

Max hurried away and Louise packed up the leftovers from the show, putting some fruit loaves and cookies in the refrigerator for the Christmas Eve brunch. There wasn't much else left. The show had been an unqualified success for her.

The table decorations from the show would be perfect for the brunch so, with a one box of goodies in her arms, she started for the lobby to retrieve her earnings.

As she crossed the dinning room, heading toward the arch, she saw Blue shuffle through the lobby, hunched over, one hand clutching his ribs. Her first instinct was to call out to him, but then she remembered what she planned to say and decided it would be better to catch him alone. Not in the lobby of the Fortune Bay Resort.

Then the reporter ran up behind him. "Don't forget your hat," she said, and laughing, pulled his knit cap onto his head and took his arm. "Poor Baby."

Well. She obviously didn't have to worry about Blue. He seemed to be having no trouble moving on. It hurt, though, to see him with another woman. Was this how he had felt for all those years when she'd been dating other guys? She hoped not—because she'd never meant to hurt him that way. She'd never meant to hurt him at all.

Chapter 32

Once the coast was clear, Louise retrieved her cash box and went straight to the hospital. When she got to her dad's room, Henrik was lying back on the raised pillows of the hospital bed, his unfinished breakfast tray on the table at his side. Belinda was there, and Louise hung back at the door.

"How are you this morning," Belinda asked Henrik. Louise could hear the love and concern in her voice.

"Better," he said. "I could go home now."

"Not yet. They said maybe tomorrow. What's this? You haven't eaten your breakfast."

"That sludge? That's why I've got to get home. I'll starve in here."

Belinda looked in the bowl on the tray. "Porridge. That's what the doctor suggested in the meal plan she gave me last night."

"I'm not eating that pig slop."

Belinda put her hands on her hips. "Yes you are, Henrik Ingstrom. We'll have no more fooling around and not following the doctor's orders."

Louise took that as her cue and walked into the room. "Hi Dad."

His face brightened. "Louisie."

She bent down and kissed him on the forehead. "You're sounding pretty feisty. Glad you're feeling better."

He turned his head on the pillow toward Belinda. "See, Louisie's on my side."

"I'm always on your side, Dad. That's why I agree with Belinda. This time you are following the doctor's orders to a T. And if that means eating porridge, you'll eat porridge."

"They've got me outnumbered," he grumbled.

Henrik soon leaned back on the mound of pillows and dozed off. Louise and Belinda went out to the corridor and watched him sleep through the glass partition.

Louise turned to face Belinda. "I've never really given you a chance. I'm sorry."

Belinda tilted her head thoughtfully. "It was certainly a challenge to move into a house with so many memories. At first I thought it was empty. You two seemed like zombies moving around and through each other every day, but not connecting. Then I realized that your mom was still there, too. I tried to reach you, tried to bring a bit of happiness back into the house, make it a home, but everything I did seemed to just put your back up more."

Louise sighed. "It did. I felt like you were an intruder, that you didn't really love my dad, but I see now that you do.

"My dad took my mother's death really hard. I hung in there for years though, waiting for him to come back to me, for us to be a family again. And then, when he finally stopped drinking and I thought he was getting over it, that he and I could start again, suddenly you and Brandy were there too."

"That must have been hard. I should have been more sensitive."

"I guess I was still clinging to the memories of my mom—although I didn't realize it at the time. I thought my dad and I could go back. I didn't want anyone taking her place.

"I miss her a lot. She was a wonderful person," Louise said staunchly.

"That's what your dad says."

Louise looked at her in surprise. "You talk about her?"

Belinda nodded. "It worried me at first, I thought he was comparing me to her, but eventually I realized that one thing I could do for him was let him talk about her. He'd had no one to talk to."

"He had me," Louise argued.

Belinda smiled sadly and shook her head. "He said when he quit drinking, came out of it and looked for you, you had drifted so far away he didn't know how to reach you. I think he felt very guilty about that.

"When we first got together he talked about your mother a lot. I worried that I could never live up to his feelings for her—but gradually he stopped mentioning her so much and I like to think he put the memories to rest. He still has the photo album by the bed, though, and every so often I see him pull it out and look through it."

"I'd love to see it again. I don't have any pictures of my mom."

"Ask him to bring it out next time you're over."

"I will. But now I think I'll go home—I don't want to tire him out. I'll come back tomorrow and help you get him home."

Louise was too churned up to go back to the cabin, though, so at the last minute she wheeled into Maddie's driveway. Rex walked stiffly half-way out to the car to greet her, his fluffy tail up and wagging. The new pup gamboled around him. She reached down to pat the old dog while the youngster leapt up and licked her cheek. "Cold weather getting to your bones, boy?"

Maddie opened the back door, concern etched on her face. "How's your dad?"

"He's okay. For now."

Maddie tapped her chest and blew out a breath. "Thank God. Come in for tea?"

Louise took off her coat, hung it on a hook behind the door and sank into a chair. The kitchen smelled like gingerbread and as Maddie poured her a cup of hot tea, the buzzer on the stove rang.

Pulling on oven mitts with white-bearded Santas on the back, Maddie pulled a tray of gingerbread men out of the oven. In the living room, the Christmas tree twinkled in the corner, the sprawling pile of presents beneath reminding Louise that she hadn't finished her Christmas shopping.

"We've gone through the first batch of cookies already," Maddie said. "And there's still three days to go until Christmas. Sarah was helping but she's taken off." She grinned. "That's okay. It's faster this way."

She popped the last tray in the oven and sat down, focusing her attention on Louise. "Now, tell me about your dad."

"He's stable, for now. I left him sleeping at the hospital. They say he can go home tomorrow, but he'll probably have to have surgery." She heaved a sigh. "It's not over yet."

Maddie covered Louise's hand on the table with her own. "I'm sure it's a comfort to him, and Belinda and Brandy too, to have you here, for now."

"It's more than 'for now'. I'm staying."

Maddie beamed. "Well good, I'm glad you finally came to your senses. And what about Blue?"

"Blue's okay. Two cracked ribs—'"

"No. I mean, *what about Blue?*"

Louise blew out a rough breath. She put her fingers over her mouth and shook her head. "After last night, I don't think I can risk it. Not now. Maybe not ever."

"That's too bad. Have you told him?"

Louise breathed out a sigh that left her hollow, then she dragged herself out of her chair. "You're right. I have to tell him."

* * *

Louise tapped tentatively on Blue's door. Sean had said he was at home, recuperating, and while she hated to kick a guy when he was down, she felt they had to settle this one way or another.

Well, one way. There was only one way.

He wasn't answering. He was probably sleeping. She should go—

And the door swung open.

"Hi. Whoa. Oh no, you look terrible." Not a nice greeting but, man, he looked bad. The bridge of his nose was swollen and he had two black eyes. "Go back and sit, that must really hurt. I brought you some cookies." She held up the bag.

He stared at her, at the bag, back at her, then he turned around, walked back into the living room and sank onto the couch.

"Okay. I'll just leave these here," she said, setting the bag on the kitchen counter.

He winced as he settled on the couch. "What do you want, Louise?"

"I just wanted to know how you were doing—"

"I'll survive."

"Yeah, well. Good...We should talk."

He didn't say anything, just stared blankly at her.

She cleared her throat and started again. "I'm hoping we can go back to the way things were. The way they've always been. You know." Her voice dropped to a whisper. "Be friends."

He looked at her for a minute. Two. She was afraid to say any more. Her knee started to bounce. She put a hand down to stop it.

Then he said, the pain evident in his voice, "I can't just be your friend, Louise. I can't live like that anymore. I've been waiting for you for more years than I can count. Why can't you, for once, just choose me."

"I can't."

"Why the hell not. Aren't I good enough?"

"No. That's not it." She moved over to the couch and reached for his arm but he pulled it away. "My relationships never last. And I couldn't bear to lose you."

"That's bullshit, Louise, because you're losing me now. Tell me the real reason. For once, just be honest with me."

She took a shaky breath. Tears sprang to her eyes and she wanted to look away, but if she wanted him to believe her, she had to look him in the eye.

"It's me. I can't make a relationship last for more than two months. You know that. And with you, well, I know that if we were together and broke up, we'd never be able to stay just friends."

"Well I don't think I can be your friend now, either."

"Maybe after a while we'll forget, you know, what it was like, and just go back to the way things were."

He thought for a moment, then shook his head. "I'm not one of your easy-going *friends*, Louise. It's all or nothing from now on."

He was right. She couldn't go back either. *It's all.* She wanted to say it, *it's all,* but couldn't seem to form the words.

"Okay. I get it." He leaned his head back on the cushion and closed his eyes. "Please, just leave."

His cold dismissal was like a slap in the face. Louise couldn't talk, couldn't cry. Couldn't believe this was the end.

But he continued to sit with his head back, eyes closed, as if she wasn't there. She searched his face for signs of her old friend Blue, but with the bandage on his nose, the blooming black eyes and his newly shaved cheeks, he looked like a stranger. After a moment, she got up and left, quietly closing the door behind her.

She'd done what she'd always tried to avoid. She had broken his heart.

And, in the process, had broken hers as well.

Chapter 33

Louise drove away from Blue's house, the black fog trailing her like a comet's tail. Even though it was barely noon, she went back to the cabin and straight to bed. Except for getting up to keep the fire going, she stayed in bed all day, hunkered down under the quilts, alternately crying and dozing.

Eventually she managed to sleep and when she dragged herself out of bed the next morning it was already nine o'clock. Brawny was complaining loudly that it was time to go outside. She couldn't spend another day in bed. She'd been here before, it was a slippery slope, and in the past when she'd succumbed to the depression, weeks had disappeared into the fog.

Today her dad was getting out of the hospital and she had planned to be there to help. It was time to tell them about the baby, before they heard from someone else, a definite possibility considering how many people she'd told and the way people passed around secrets in Fortune Bay.

So she forced herself into the shower, then phoned Belinda to see what the plan was for bringing Henrik home.

Brandy answered and told her he'd called at eight that morning to say he'd been cleared to leave, and where the hell were they. So Brandy and Belinda had hustled into town, brought him home, and now Henrik was settled in his recliner, asking for Louise.

Grabbing her coat, Louise pulled a tam over her wet hair and rushed to the car.

Belinda met her at the door.

"How is he?" Louise asked as she took off her coat. Through the doorway to the living room she saw her dad relaxing in his chair.

Belinda smiled. "Feisty."

Louise was beginning to see that this unpretentious woman had a spine of iron. Even in the face of illness and possible death, she could still smile.

"How do you do it?" Louise asked, keeping her eyes on her dad and her voice low. "I know your first husband died, and now this. What if it happens again? How do you keep going?"

"I just take it day by day. That's all you can do. After my first husband died, I didn't know if I could go on. But I did, I had to, for Brandy.

"Then I met your father and he taught me to look at each day as a gift. You take it as it comes. The important thing is to share it with someone you love and, for me, that's your dad and you girls."

"But after your first husband died, how did you have the courage to try again with my dad, knowing how much it could hurt in the end?"

"I wouldn't give up the years I've had with your father for anything. Just because they are going to end one day is no reason to pass up the opportunity for love. There is no guarantee of happiness in life, so if you see even a glimmer, you have to grab it."

Louise had never seen a glimmer with Marco, but she remembered a definite shimmer between her and Blue.

The lines of worry returned to Belinda's forehead. "But your dad is so stubborn. He listens to you, Louise. I'm really going to need your help."

"Don't worry, I'll be here. I'm not going back to the city right away."

Belinda's face brightened into a smile. "That's wonderful, dear. Your father will be so happy."

Louise hesitated to tell her the other news. Belinda was kind of old fashioned and would probably want her to get married, and Louise was determined to do this on her own, without Marco. She wasn't sure if her relationship with Belinda had changed enough that she would be on her side.

But if she was going to tell her dad in his present condition, she had to have Belinda's support. If she didn't want to be responsible for a family brouhaha that might put her dad back in the hospital, she had no option but to tell Belinda straight out.

"I have news." She felt a rush of excitement to finally be telling her family.

Belinda raised her eyebrows, encouraging Louise to continue.

She had to get it out before she lost her nerve. "I'm having a baby."

Belinda's mouth fell open and her eyes sparkled with tears. "Oh honey, that's wonderful. And the father?" she asked hopefully.

"No father," Louise said firmly. "I'm doing this on my own."

"Well, you won't be completely on your own," Belinda said, folding Louise into a warm hug.

No, she wouldn't be alone. And now she could see that really, she never had been. They had all been right there, waiting for her to ask. Waiting for her to let them in.

"Your father will be so happy." Belinda laughed, a light trilling sound. She glanced into the living room where Henrik was watching a game, seemingly unawares.

"I'll be a grandmother," she whispered excitedly.

"But should I tell him? Now? I don't want to upset him."

"Upset him? This will be the best medicine there is. Something for him to work towards."

"Okay." Louise gripped Belinda's arm, thankful for an ally. "Let's tell him."

When the women walked into the living room, Henrik made a move to hoist himself up from his seat. "Louisie."

She hurried over and gave him a hug. "Hi, Dad. I'm glad you're home."

"There was no reason for me to stay in the hospital. I'm perfectly fine." He was obviously hoping it was over and everyone would just forget about the attack.

"Well, let's make sure there isn't a reason for you to go back. I'm going to be watching you."

He snorted. "From Seattle?"

"No, from right here. I'm staying, Dad." His face flushed with happiness and tears squirted into her eyes. *Damn hormones.*

"Oh, Louisie, I'm so glad."

She sank into a chair beside her father. "And I've got more news." She glanced at Belinda who gave her an encouraging smile and a slight nod.

"I'm going to have a baby."

Brandy shrieked from the doorway, scaring Louise half out of her chair. She put a hand to her thumping heart and laughed as Brandy bounded in and hugged her.

"Are you having it here?" Brandy asked. "Are you staying?"

"Yes."

Brandy shrieked again and danced around the living room. "I'm going to be an aunty."

"Who's the father?" her dad asked, wiping tears from his eyes. "Is it Blue?"

Louise almost laughed. *Hope springs eternal.* She'd been gone for months and Blue had been right here the whole time.

"It's not Blue, and the father is not involved. I'm doing this on my own."

Belinda put a hand on her shoulder and smiled. "I told her she wasn't alone." Then she slipped out of the room.

Brandy danced over and hugged Louise again. "I'll be totally here for you."

Louise hugged her back. "I'm counting on it."

"So I guess you're going to move back in then," her dad said gruffly, his regular ploy to hide his emotions.

Not if I can help it. "I don't think so, Dad. Not right away. I'm not sure yet what's going to happen."

Belinda came back into the living room with a faded gold photo album in her hands, the one Louise remembered from her childhood. In her teens, she'd steal into her dad's bedroom when he was out and study the pictures of her mother, burning them into her memory. They'd never looked at them together, though.

She stood up and took the album from Belinda. "Thank you."

"Your mother would have been so happy."

"Want to look at this with me, Dad? It's been a long time."

Henrik clicked the remote and turned off the TV. "I haven't looked at it for a while either."

Louise pulled her chair up tight to her dad's and opened the book over the upholstered arm between them. Belinda went into the kitchen, but Brandy found a spot behind Henrik where she could lean on the soft back of the recliner and look over their shoulders.

Henrik patted Louise's hand. "You'll make a great mother, Louisie."

"I had a good teacher, Dad."

Chapter 34

After Louise returned from her dad's house, she lay down on the couch. Nothing else held any appeal. She felt a bit better than she had the day before, but her estrangement from Blue still weighed heavy on her heart.

She pulled the quilt up over her chin. She'd be happy to stay right here until winter was over, curled up on the couch in front of the fire with her cat on her chest. Not talking to anyone. Not having to see Blue ever again.

Or she could go away. Far, far away. That would work too. Except she wanted to stay. Have her baby here in Fortune Bay, be there for her family and let them be there for her. But not if she had to worry about running into Blue at every turn.

So, in other words, she was screwed.

Darkness had fallen when she heard a knock. She groaned and rolled over, turning her back to the door. It opened anyway.

What was wrong with these people? Couldn't they see she wanted to be alone?

"Louise?"

It was Frankie. "Go away."

"I can't. I've come to get you."

"Get me for what? I'm not going anywhere."

"It's our winter solstice night at Maddie's. We already put it off last night because you wouldn't answer your phone. Don't worry, it'll just be the three of us. And Colleen. Whatever is bothering you, we'll talk it out."

Then Frankie materialized beside the couch and was tugging off the blanket. As she pulled Louise to her feet, a disgruntled Brawny rolled off the couch, protesting with his squeaky-gate meow.

"Hi, boy," Frankie said, and gave him a pat as, tail in the air, he headed for his soft spot behind the woodstove.

"There's nothing to talk about. Leave me alone."

"There's always something to talk about. Come on. Maddie's waiting. Colleen's already there. Candles are burning. Chop, chop."

"Chop, chop?"

But Louise allowed herself to be towed to the door because if nothing else, Maddie would have food.

She pulled on some outdoor clothes, grabbed the last box of now-stale, chocolate cookies and stumbled outside.

The full moon reflected on the lake, highlighting the waves in silver. The air was cold. Very cold. She shivered and pulled her collar up around her neck. An iconic winter solstice night.

Frankie prodded her from behind. "Let's get moving."

They walked through the trees, along the shore and a minute later came out into the field where Maddie and Jake had built their house. A soft light glowed in the kitchen windows, but other than that, the house was dark.

Following the path across the field in the moonlight, Louise's boots crackled the frozen grasses that lined the way. An expanse of stars scattered across the sky over the lake, disappearing into infinity. They made her problems seem very small. Small, but still painful. He didn't even want to be her friend.

Rex hobbled out to meet them.

"Hi, boy," she said, scratching his ears.

Maddie met them at the door in a long black gown, her red hair pulled up in a loose knot on top of her head.

"Good. You found her. You can't just disappear like that. We worry about you."

The winter solstice marked the darkest day of the year, the turning point to increasing light, and they always celebrated by candlelight. In the dimly lit kitchen, candles burned on every flat surface, the dancing lights reflecting in the dark windowpanes. Maddie finished lighting the candles grouped on the table with a long white taper.

Frankie took a seat. As usual for their quarterly gatherings, over her jeans she wore the blue silk robe Stephanie had batiked for her.

Colleen swung into the room, calf length skirts swirling over high boots, a large silver moon-shaped pendent hanging around her neck. "There you are. Good job, Frankie."

Louise collapsed onto a kitchen chair. She picked at the frayed cuff of her oldest sweater, wishing she'd taken the time to change. She'd been wearing the same clothes since her final showdown with Blue.

Colleen pulled out a chair and sat, too. "Thanks for inviting me. I've always wondered what you do on these nights."

"We're pretty informal," Frankie said, taking the tarot cards out of their embroidered velvet bag and starting to shuffle the oversized deck.

"It's a time to regroup, hash over the past three months, set a few goals for the coming season. The tarot is just a jumping off point. It raises questions to think and talk about."

"It's mostly been an excuse for a woman's night with wine and chocolate," Maddie said, wincing slightly. "And seriously, it's okay if you two want to open a bottle of wine. Just because Louise and I can't drink is no reason for you to abstain."

"I'm good," Frankie said. "There are enough goodies. I brought whipped cream for the hot mocha drinks."

Colleen nodded in agreement. "We don't need wine. And I have to drive later."

Louise watched Frankie slowly shuffle the cards, and

gradually felt herself relax. When Frankie had first bought the deck, Louise hadn't been a believer. But when Frankie said she'd read the cards in college, she made it sound like a fun activity for their solstice and equinox parties, so Louise had gone along.

She had never wanted to delve too deeply into her psyche, or jim-jam, or whatever it was the cards tapped into, but she'd seen how spot-on the readings had been for her friends and tonight, for the first time, she was eager to hear what the cards had to say to her.

No one could make her decisions for her, she'd take the reading with a grain of salt, but that didn't mean she couldn't use some guidance right about now.

The hair on her arms stood on end. "I'll go first."

Frankie raised her eyebrows, but otherwise didn't comment, just continued to shuffle the deck.

Louise concentrated on the soothing motion of Frankie's hands. Gradually her heartbeat slowed.

Then Frankie put the brightly colored deck on the table in front of Louise. "Think of a question, then cut the cards. The tarot knows the question in your heart."

What exactly was her question? She'd had so many in the past few weeks, but had resolved most of them one way or another. To the question of if she should have this baby, the answer was a definite *yes*. And she had decided to stay in Fortune Bay, which was actually quite a relief. And soon she would talk to Max and, hopefully, could work at the resort.

So, the only question that remained was, *could she win back Blue's friendship, or had she lost him forever?*

"Ready?" Frankie asked.

Louise nodded.

"Okay, we'll do a five-card spread." Frankie set the deck on the table in front of Louise. "Pick five cards, one at a time, and place them face down on the table.

"In the center, a card that represents Your Present. The second card, on the left, is Your Past. The next card, on the right, is Your Immediate Future."

Louise chose the cards, one by one, placing them where Frankie indicated.

"Lay the fourth card above. It's the Impediment. And the last card, on the bottom, is The Possible Outcome."

Although Louise had done this before, she'd never felt this shaky. Of course, previously she'd never had so much at stake.

As Frankie turned over the center card, she said, "The Present."

It was The Tower, a picture of lightning striking a tower on a mountain top, setting it on fire and flinging people headfirst out the windows.

Louise laughed out loud. "Well, I asked for it. That's exactly what my life feels like right now."

Frankie smiled. "The tower signifies upheaval and change. Everything you thought you knew before is suddenly up for grabs. It signifies a major change of perspective—and sometimes a change in your situation. But even if it *seems* bad at the time, the outcome is ultimately for the best. That's not to say it won't be difficult, though. Hard to wrap your head around."

Louise nodded. "You can say that again."

Frankie turned over the card on the left. "The Past."

It was the Three of Swords. On the card, rain pelted down from black storm clouds overhead onto three swords piercing a blood red heart. The black fog and the miscarriage. Could it get any clearer than that?

All three women stared at the card in silence. Finally, Louise said, "My past." She nodded grimly. "There were a few rough years."

She tried to spark a smile, but didn't feel too successful. She shrugged. "We all have our baggage."

"Right. And that's the past," Frankie said firmly. "Moving on to the Immediate Future card which is—the Hanged Man."

"Oh come on!" Louise objected, huffing a laugh as she studied the young man on the card, hanging upside down from a post, bound by a rope around his foot.

"No, it's good," Frankie insisted. "He's alive—and smiling—just seeing things from a different perspective."

Louise laughed. "You're not kidding."

Frankie nodded. "It's all about changing old patterns and letting go. Something we all have to learn. And it's a good omen in this position, right before The Impediment card."

She turned over the card at the top of the spread and Louise was pleased to see a woman dressed in white patting a friendly male lion. She twisted her head to read the upside-down card. "*Strength.* That looks good. Look, he's licking her hand."

Frankie grimaced. "Right-side up, this card represents conquering fear, but upside down, like this, it means, *letting fear reign.* It's saying that what is holding you back from your potential is that you let fear control you." She pressed her lips together and raised her brows questioningly.

"I may have had a few rough years, but I don't let fear run my life," Louise said defensively.

"Possibly not," Frankie murmured, moving on to the last card.

"This is Your Potential. The Queen of Cups. Now *that's* a good one. She's warm and nurturing and often, in a reading, is, uh, ..." Frankie gave a little cough to clear her throat. "Nudging you to take a chance and open your heart."

There was a silence as the women contemplated the cards. Louise reached out and picked up the Three of Swords. "This is uncanny. Three swords piercing the heart. First I lost my mom, then my boyfriend, and a pregnancy.

A baby. One, two, three."

Maddie put a hand on Louise's arm. "Oh, honey."

Louise nodded. "It does kind of follow me. I know it was a long time ago, but I've been thinking a lot lately about the miscarriage. I guess being pregnant has brought memories to the surface.

"After it happened I felt like a black cloud moved in on me. Sometimes, even now, it wraps itself around me until I can't think or move."

"What happened?" Maddie asked softly.

"I was sixteen, it was just before Christmas, and I was in a bad car accident with my boyfriend, Tony."

Colleen whispered, "I remember."

Their eyes met over the candle's flame, and Louise nodded.

"He'd been drinking, it was snowing and we skidded off the road. I had just found out I was pregnant. This was shortly after my mother died, when my dad was drinking pretty steadily. I felt so alone and thought Tony and the baby would be a chance to have a family of my own.

"I know it was a childish dream—it could never have worked out the way I thought with Tony—but the baby seemed like a gift at a time when I needed a family.

"Tony died at the scene of the accident and I was thrown from the car, into the ditch, and lost the baby." She closed her eyes. "I'll never forget the blood on the snow."

She gave herself a shake and opened her eyes. "At the hospital, I gave them Blue's number. He came to Majestic to get me, sat in the clinic all night while they patched me up, but then they wouldn't release me to him because we were both minors. So he called Stephanie. She came and they took me back to Steph's."

There was silence around the table as the women contemplated the nest of flickering candles.

"I had a miscarriage too," Colleen said.

Maddie pursed her lips and nodded, compassion in her eyes.

Louise drew in a surprised breath. "I never knew."

Colleen gave a twisted smile. "It's not really something you talk about, is it? But you're right, it still hurts to think about."

She reached out and took Louise's hand. "I feel badly that I didn't do more for you when your mother died. We all knew you were having a rough time, but no one knew what to do. I didn't know about the miscarriage, though."

"Blue got me through. He's always been my rock. Has always been there for me. Other guys have come and gone, but Blue was always there. Waiting."

"Why didn't you two ever get together?" Frankie asked.

"I don't know. I thought if we ever got together I would lose him in the end, and I couldn't bear that. I couldn't take the chance."

Louise looked around the table at the circle of caring faces lit by the flickering flames.

"We never should have slept together. Now that we've had sex, I'm afraid our friendship is ruined. That we can never be friends again."

"Maybe that's where you've been going wrong," Maddie said thoughtfully. "Sex and friendship aren't mutually exclusive. Jake's my best friend and since we've been sleeping together, our friendship has only gotten stronger."

Louise shook her head. "I can't risk it. I have a terrible record with men. I can't seem to commit. I think two months is my record. And if Blue and I got together, when we split up, unlike the others, we could never stay friends. I'd lose him forever. I don't think either of us would survive."

There was a silence as the women considered her argument. Then Colleen said, "Has it ever occurred to you that maybe the reason you can't make a go of it with the other guys is because *they aren't Blue?*"

Louise was silent. Then her jaw dropped. Could Colleen be right? Had Louise had it backwards all this time?

Her eyes flashed around the table. Frankie and Maddie nodded their heads in agreement.

Louise closed her eyes and slapped a palm against her forehead. "I'm so stupid. All this time." She groaned. "I told him we couldn't be together. Told him to forget about me. I thought it was the best thing for him."

Colleen shook her head, her long black hair shimmering in the candlelight. "Well, you're the only one."

Louise was taken aback. "You knew?"

Colleen laughed. "Honey, the whole town knows."

Louise looked at Frankie and Maddie. "You *all* knew?"

They both smiled and nodded kindly, as if she was, indeed, a little slow.

"We've all been waiting for you to come to your senses," Frankie said.

Of course they knew. Louise groaned again and hid her face in her hands. "When I went to his house, he told me he built the kitchen for me."

Colleen nodded. "He probably did."

Louise raised her head, horrified at how she'd laughed it off when deep inside she'd known it was true.

"It's too late," she whispered as the realization of what she'd done sunk in. "When I left, he wouldn't speak to me. He wouldn't even look at me." She shook her head. "I don't think there's anything I can do. I'm afraid I've lost him for good."

Frankie smiled kindly. "After twenty-five years, I doubt that's true."

"But I was brutal. I told him we couldn't be together. I was afraid of losing him, so I pushed him away. And now I *have* lost him." She rested her forehead on her fingertips. "So stupid."

At the memory of their last meeting, she squeezed her eyes shut. "He's always been my best friend, but he said he couldn't do that anymore. Couldn't go back to being just friends."

"Is that all you want him as?" Frankie asked. "Just as a friend?"

Louise thought about the feelings he stirred in her. The ease, the joy, the passion.

"No. Not anymore. I want it all." She turned to Maddie and Colleen. "I want what you've got. The home, the children. If I must, I could do it alone, but that's not what I want. I want him."

Maddie took both her hands. "Well then, you'd better tell him."

It was late when Louise got back to the cabin, but the white and blue lights blazed on the porch. She stopped for a moment and absorbed the light, like a message of hope from her mother.

"Do you remember her, Augusta? I think you must. What would she have wanted me to do?"

Muddle on through.

Louise laughed. "I can do that."

She went inside and although it was late, she couldn't sleep. Instead, she went to work on a therapeutic batch of Cranberry Loaf with Sharp Lemon Glaze, and the cinnamon buns Max had requested for the brunch the next morning.

She felt jazzed, the nerve endings under her skin popping like fireworks, as if she'd been drinking coffee all evening instead of cranberry juice. As she worked she went over her plans in her head.

For one thing, she was staying in Fortune Bay. How could she have considered anything else? It was her home base. Her support network was here and it was time she started giving back to the community who had supported her for so many years. She wasn't the only one who had problems. People were counting on her now. The baby, her dad, Brandy, Amber—*cripes*, she was just getting started with Amber.

And Blue. She'd been horrible to Blue. Mean spirited and selfish.

As she put the loaves into the old turquoise oven, she remembered the beautiful kitchen he'd built for her. Because Blue loved her, really loved her, and all this time he'd been planning a home for her. All he wanted was for her to choose him and instead she'd stomped on his big vulnerable heart by always, *always*, choosing someone else. Well, never again.

She stopped. But could she trust herself to love him the way he deserved? Did she even know how?

Colleen's words came back to her. "Maybe the reason you can't make a go of it with other guys is that *they aren't Blue*?"

That was so true. He'd always been the one. And she was an idiot for not seeing it before. The question remained, though, how to win him back. She needed a sure-fire strategy because he'd looked pretty firm, if sadly defeated, the last time she saw him.

Good going, Louise. She may have finally convinced him not to take her back.

Chapter 35

When Louise awoke the next morning, the cabin was frosty, so she snuggled down further under Augusta's soft quilt. The air had a faintly metallic tang, a crisp, damp cold that made the hair on the inside of her nose stand on end.

The first thing she saw when she opened her eyes were fingers of pale, crystalline frost creeping up the window, and a cool blue light that could only mean one thing.

Snow for Christmas.

She jumped out of bed and swallowed a shriek when her feet hit the icy linoleum. Tossing the clothes she'd been wearing since her fallout with Blue into the laundry basket, she dug down in the dresser drawers for clean jeans, a heavy red sweater and thick woolly socks.

As she pulled on the clothes, she noticed a *clickety-click* coming from the other room.

Clickety-click, clickety-click. Cautiously, she peeked into the kitchen.

The big room was bright, bathed in the cool light that reflected off the snow. Through the picture window, she saw six inches of white powder covering every branch and twig, the porch railing, the steps and the ground, right down to the stones on the beach.

The sight was so amazing— they were lucky if they got one good snowfall a year in Fortune Bay— that it took her a minute to realize there was a second, more subtle light source in the room.

A woman was sitting in a kitchen chair, knitting. Knitting and glowing. Louise rubbed her sleepy eyes, but the ghostly figure remained.

Merry Christmas.

Definitely a hallucination, but she heard the words clearly in her head.

Louise walked over to the photograph at the foot of the attic stairs and studied the face of the woman waving out the car window, then looked back at the old woman sitting on the kitchen chair. She'd aged, but it was the same woman. Which meant that she was a ghost.

"Merry Christmas," Louise said, her words ringing loudly in the cold air. Did you talk out loud to a ghost? Augusta's lips didn't seem to move, so how did you know if they were her words or your own imagination?

But the lady in the rocker, hair in a tidy knot on top of her hair, knitting something with pale pink yarn, was definitely real—although Louise could tell from the aura of light surrounding her that she wasn't human. Or at least not alive.

Louise rubbed her icy hands together. Her breath came out of her mouth like white smoke. She spun around to the woodstove in the corner, needing something normal to do, something real.

Kneeling in front of the stove, she opened the door and saw that the fire had burned away. Filling the stove with crushed paper and kindling, she reached for the tin of matches before remembering she'd used the last one the day before. Stupid! But she'd had so much on her mind.

Allow me.

The paper burst into flame, and Louise watched, wide eyed, as the cedar lying on top of it caught.

"Ah...thank you," she said, putting two quartered logs on top of the flames and closing the door.

The *clickety-click* started up again behind her.

Taking a deep breath, Louise spun around on her knees. Augusta was watching her, smiling. She knit without looking down, the needles moving in an almost mechanical way that seemed disconnected from her grandmotherly smile.

"What are you making?"

The needles stopped and she held up a tiny pink baby's sweater that seemed to be knit all in one piece. *For the baby. Every baby is a gift to be treasured.*

Louise smiled. "I bought a blue one."

You will need them both.

Louise's jaw dropped. "Two?"

Augusta smiled, her needles working like a machine at her lap.

Louise stood up and walked over to the kitchen table and collapsed on one of the chairs.

"How will I handle that?" she murmured.

You'll do it together.

"I'm doing this alone. The father's not interested."

You're not alone. Just open your eyes. What are you afraid of, dear?

Louise thought for a minute, then said, "Love is fragile. Life is fragile."

Life's not fragile. It's rugged and tough, and you must be tough, too. Fight for what you want and then hold on tight. It's guaranteed to knock you down a few times, but I never took you for a quitter.

"I'm not." Her voice dropped to a whisper. "But what if I, *we*, can't make it work?"

We never know what is around the corner in life, but hiding, protecting yourself so that you don't experience everything you can—well, that's just a waste.

The needles clicked for a moment more and then Augusta asked, *do you love him?*

The image of Blue, as strong and supportive as his big bear came back to her. He'd been there every time she'd stumbled and fallen. Every time she'd reached out and every time she'd pushed him away. And he still loved her, unconditionally, whether she deserved it or not.

It was time she gave him her trust in return.

"I do. I should go." She hesitated, not wanting to leave Augusta.

The old woman smiled. *What are you waiting for?*

Louise pulled on her winter coat and grabbed the bag of cranberry loaves from the counter and the tray of cinnamon buns that were rising in the refrigerator, finally stopping to snatch the Pretzel on her way out the door.

Outside, she felt like she'd stumbled into a winter wonderland painting, even more magical because it happened so rarely. Every cedar and fir branch was heavily lined with snow. The snow came halfway up the sides of her boots, and she brushed the fluffy snow off the windows of the Jeep with her gloved hand and climbed inside, switching into four-wheel drive to plow her way out to the road.

She had to get to the resort. Max had invited half the town for brunch. But surely Sean would find the rest of the baking in the refrigerator in the resort kitchen and set it out on the tables. She had something more important to do first.

There were tire tracks on Blue's driveway, but she couldn't tell if they were coming or going. Clumps of snow plopped down on her windshield as the Jeep hit the weighted branches in passing.

His truck wasn't there, but she didn't know if he had even had it repaired yet. Smoke rose from the chimney, so she raced to the porch and knocked on the door, stomping her feet and rubbing her hands together.

She knocked again. "Blue!"

No answer.

Jumping back in the Jeep, she sped down the driveway, the backend fishtailing when she made the corner onto the road to town. *Slow down, girl. You've got to get there in one piece.*

Minutes later, she pulled into the pristine parking lot at

his workshop. No tracks of any kind marred the snow. She was half afraid she would find him there, with Star.

Star answered her knock, bundled head to toe in a greater than usual amount of her funky knitwear.

"Hi, Louise. Come on in." She held open the door and Louise stepped inside.

Star's smile wasn't quite the elfin grin Louise was used to, maybe because even with the stove going full bore, it was still freaking cold in here. The station had not been built to live in. Certainly not on the coldest days.

"Merry Christmas."

Star's smile brightened. "Merry Christmas to you too. Don't you just love the snow?"

"I do. Is Blue here?"

Star shook her head. "No. He hasn't been here for days."

"Oh." Louise hesitated. "I thought maybe, you know..."

Star shook her head. "We're just friends. He's all yours. Always has been."

"I hope that's still true. I've been such a fool. Blind to what was staring me in the face."

"He's probably at home."

"No. I checked. He must be at the resort." Louise headed for the door, but stopped with her hand on the knob. Star stood alone in the middle of the frigid station. "Do you have plans?"

Star smiled, a little less twinkly than usual. "No. Just a quiet day at home. It's okay. There is nowhere I have to be."

"Come to the resort. Everyone will be there. And I could use some help with the brunch."

Star hesitated, but her eyes lit up and Louise could see she wanted to go. "Come on. I'll give you a ride."

Star's smile twinkled. "Just let me slip on my boots," she said, tugging on her turquoise cowboy boots.

A few minutes later, Louise pulled up in front of the resort. Her eyes searched the crowded lot and when she found Blue's old truck, her heartbeat quickened. Climbing out of the Jeep, she grabbed the bag of sweet breads, handed Star the tray of cinnamon buns and together they hurried across the snowy lot.

The giant noble fir dominated the dim lobby, colorful lights glowing and the star twinkling on top. Through the carved arch into the dining room, Louise could see the broad back of her Santa, sitting in the crowded dining room, head bent, listening intently to the child sitting on his knee.

Star took the bag of baking out of Louise's hands. "Don't worry, I'll get the buns in the oven. You go get him."

Max stepped out of his office and when he saw Louise, his face lit in a smile. "You're here. I was getting worried. Sean put out the baking he found in the kitchen and has already started on breakfast."

"Yes. Hi. Sorry I'm late, but could we talk a minute? I'd like to apply for the pastry job, if it's still open."

His smile widened even more. "That's wonderful. So, you're staying?"

She smiled. "I am." It felt good to say it. "But I have to tell you—I'm having a baby."

He grabbed her shoulders and gave her a fatherly hug. "Congratulations." He pulled away. "That's a good thing, isn't it?"

She laughed. "Yes, it is." Then she got serious. "The baby is due in the summer, but I think I will be able to get the kitchen running smoothly by then—"

"We'll work it out."

"I can get Brandy and Amber to help me for the summer—"

Max put his hands on her shoulders again and looked her straight in the eye. "We'll work it out."

Taking the Pretzel out from under her arm, she placed

it on the check-in counter. "I thought I'd keep this in the kitchen."

Max beamed. "The Pretzel. Of course. We'll give it pride of place, put up a special shelf for it. Now, let's see how it's going inside."

He headed into the dining room and Louise blew out a relieved breath. Another obstacle dealt with. That left only one more. The big one.

She stepped into the dining room, where everyone she knew and loved were sitting at tables watching the main attraction, Santa greeting the children.

Maddie was at a table with Jake and the girls. Louise touched her shoulder as she walked by and Maddie's face broke into a smile.

Amber and Brandy raced up and Amber threw herself at Louise in a hug.

"I told her," Brandy said. "I hope that's alright."

Amber pulled herself away. "I know we're not related, but can I be an aunt, too?"

"I'm counting on you both to help me with the baby, and here at the resort as well. I took the job."

The girls squealed and rushed off to spread the news.

Frankie was sitting with Stephanie across the room and gave her a thumbs up as Louise made her way to the quiet corner table by the windows where her dad and Belinda were sitting.

Belinda's hair was shorter and shiny and a new, rich shade of chestnut brown. Louise ran a hand over it gently. "I love it," she said, making Belinda blush.

Then Louise took a deep breath and turned to the man in the red suit who was seated with his back to her in the center of the room.

Blue grimaced under the fake beard as a little girl with wispy brown hair squirmed on his lap. He'd thought that, despite his injuries, he felt well enough to play Santa today as promised, but his ribs couldn't take much more of this. Luckily, this seemed to be the last child.

"Santa, what happened to your face?"

"The reindeer dumped me right out of the sleigh."

"Ouch!" She winced.

Blue laughed. "Yeah. Ouch. And what can Santa bring you for Christmas?"

"A remote-control drone."

"How old are you, anyway?"

"I'm six."

The girl's parents were making exaggerated, negative gestures behind her back. "I'm not sure I can come up with a drone on such short notice. The elves have already packed the sleigh."

She puckered her mouth as she thought. "Then, maybe just a doll with pretty clothes and long hair."

Her mom gave him two thumbs up.

"Okay then." He slid her off his knee. "I'll do my best." He looked around. "Anyone else?"

Louise slid onto his lap and put her arms around his neck. "Hi, Santa."

There were whistles from the crowd. The kitchen doors swung open and Star and Sean stuck their heads out to watch.

Louise wiggled on his lap trying to find a good spot and Blue felt himself harden. Some Santa he was.

But what was she doing? He thought he'd been clear. No more stringing him along. She had to leave him alone.

She nuzzled his ear and he felt his cheeks flush as she whispered, "Can I talk to you privately for a minute?"

He narrowed his eyes at her over the fake beard. "Not now, Louise."

She blatantly batted her lashes. "Please, Santa?"

"Go for it, Santa," Sean called from the kitchen

doorway.

Blue felt his temper rise. He wasn't going to get into it here with Louise. Not today. "What are you doing, Louise?"

Slipping off his lap, she took his hands and pulled him reluctantly to his feet. His ribs yelped, but he suppressed the groan as he let her pull him through the arch of swimming salmon.

The lobby was lit by the colored lights of the giant Christmas tree and a dim light over the check-in counter. Blue whipped off the all-in-one snowy beard and Santa hat with the fringe of white hair, and tossed it onto the counter.

Crossing his arms on his chest to ward her off, he lowered his brows seriously. "Say what you have to say, Louise."

Louise's mouth suddenly went dry. He still looked mad. Really mad. What if he said no? She'd screwed him over so many times, he'd be justified to say, *No way.*

Catching her lip in her teeth, she looked around the lobby for inspiration. Her eye fell on the Golden Pretzel, glowing under the light at the desk.

"I won this award at the Academy," she said.

He looked at the statue for the first time. "You won this? You never told me."

She nodded. "I know. We have a lot of things to talk about."

The jaunty sound of Jingle Bells played on an electric piano echoed out of the dining hall, children's voices joining in with the words, and somewhere in the back of her mind, she knew it would be her old elementary school teacher Ms. Bowden at the keyboard.

Louise took a deep breath. The aroma of cinnamon buns baking in the kitchen gave her the courage to go on. "I'm staying, Blue."

His scowl deepened. Not the response she was looking for.

"You know I'm having a baby."

His eyes softened and dropped to her belly. "I know."

"I want this baby to have a father—a good, caring father. I don't want to do it alone."

No response. "And you're the only man I want."

Still nothing. "To do this with me." Man, he was making this hard.

"I mean, I know it's not your baby, but you're right, it's not really Marco's baby, either." Her voice softened. "I never loved him. We just got caught in an awkward situation. He doesn't want it and I don't want him in our lives."

Blue squinted, looking her right in the eye. "What exactly are you saying, Louise?"

She knew what he wanted to hear, and that he'd wait until she said it. Well, that was okay. She could say it now. And mean it.

"You're the only one I've ever loved. I was stupid not to see it sooner. So now, I choose you—the baby and I choose you."

He took her hands, his eyes glistening, and it gave her the courage to go on.

"You were right. I was afraid to love. Afraid I'd lose it all again. But that's just a waste of life.

"I want to spend every day with you. I'm ready to start over, off on a new adventure with you. If you'll have me. Me and the baby."

She wrapped her arms around him and lay her head on his chest, feeling the soft red velvet of the Santa suit against her cheek and hearing the strong, steady beat of his heart.

Santa's arms came around her. "To me, it's always been your baby, Louise. I'd be honored to make it mine, too." He tipped her face up to his and drew her into a long, deep kiss.

When he pulled away, she felt the delicious burn of his new two-day whiskers on her chin. She reached up and rubbed both hands on the stubble on his cheeks where the beard had been.

"I've wanted to see this face. Wanted to touch you ever since you shaved."

His beautiful soft lips curved up and his dark eyes twinkled. "You can touch me any time, Louise." He pulled her up onto her toes and kissed her again.

When they finally eased apart, she said, her voice hoarse, "And just for the record, nobody has *ever* kissed me like that."

He laughed—Blue laughed—and the tight knot in her stomach unfurled and she knew it would be okay. This was all she wanted for Christmas. She was finally home.

"Will you marry me, Blue? Let me live in your house and bake in your kitchen. Be a family with me and our baby?"

The carols drifting out of the dining hall changed and voices picked up the words to *White Christmas.* Outside the big glass door, it had begun to snow.

Gently, he cupped her face with his hands. "I've loved you forever, Louise. Since we danced together the first time..."

Putting a hand over his heart, she whispered, "Sean's thirteenth birthday party." She'd always known.

Then she remembered. "But there's one more thing you should know."

He groaned. "What now, Louise?"

"There might be two."

His brows contracted in confusion. "Two what?"

"Babies."

A slow smile transformed his face. "Even better."

Blue peeled the Santa jacket and pants off from over his

clothes, and grabbed his plaid jacket from Max's office along with a scarf Louise had never seen before, knit in every colour imaginable.

She laughed. "What a God-awful scarf. Let me guess. Star."

Blue fingered the lumpy rainbow knit around his neck. "It was a Christmas present. I have to wear it."

Louise grinned. "Well it could have been worse. It could have been leg warmers."

Blue put an arm around her shoulders and turned her toward the dining hall, where stains of *I'll be Home for Christmas* drifted through the doorway.

He whispered, his breath warm in her ear, "The legwarmers are for you."

* * * * * * *

I hope you enjoyed reading Louise and Blue's story in **Home for Christmas.**

Read on for a sneak peek at Family Matters, a bridge novella that catches us up with Frankie and Sean.

Judith Hudson
www.judithhudsonauthor.com

Spoiler Alert!

Be sure to read *The Good Neighbor* before reading
this novella!

Family Matters
A Fortune Bay Bridge Novella
by
Judith Hudson

Chapter 1

Sean geared down his Miata and cranked the wheel,
turning into his mother's driveway. Slamming the gearshift
into park, he sat, hands gripping the steering wheel and
listened to the rain drumming on the convertible roof as he
tried to pull himself together. No sense tackling his daughter
Amber in his current mood of... what? Anger? Frustration?
He blew out a breath, trying to force the hot ball of anxiety
out of his chest. He couldn't lose her again.

But what was wrong with the girl? He'd lost his baby girl
when he was sixteen and it had been eating at him ever
since. Now he'd finally found her and had full custody but
from there, his plan had gone off the rails. It wasn't the fairy
tale scenario he'd dreamed of; she wasn't the sweet little girl
he'd imagined. The real Amber was tough, a scared,

damaged fifteen-year-old who for some reason seemed to be fighting him every inch of the way, when all he wanted was to make her life easy. Give her everything she'd been denied before, starting with a safe, secure, loving home. If only she'd let him.

He opened the car door and made a dash for the house, kicking his wet shoes off inside the door.

"That you, Sean?" His mother's voice echoed down the hall.

Living in each other's pockets was wearing thin, but he couldn't have managed without her these past five months.

Stephanie Murphy sat at the cluttered kitchen table, a mish mash of her art supplies scattered before her, having a quiet before-dinner drink with her good friend, Sean's boss, Max.

He felt bad about disrupting their quiet interlude, but there was no alternative. "Where's Amber?"

Stephanie's eyebrows went up. "She's not home yet."

Sean clenched his jaw and ground his teeth. This was becoming a bad habit he hoped he wasn't going to pay for in future dental bills. He blew out a breath and forced himself to relax. "The school phoned. She's been skipping classes."

Stephanie's shoulders fell. "Not again."

Sean ran a hand through his short, cropped hair. "Where the hell is she?"

Stephanie glanced at the clock. "I assumed she went over to Brandy's."

"We can't assume anything with her these days. I bet she's out with that boy."

The back door opened and Amber stepped into the kitchen, stopping in the spotlight scrutiny of the three adults. "What?"

"Where have you been?" Sean snapped. Stephanie winced.

"At Brandy's. You said I could go there after school if I was home for dinner."

"How did you get there?"

Her eyes flashed away then back. "School bus."

Sean's eyes narrowed. He didn't think so, but short of calling Brandy's mom, he couldn't prove otherwise. And checking up on her like that, like he thought she was lying, was no way to build bridges.

He chose a different tack. "The school called. They said you weren't at your afternoon classes."

Amber's face hardened. "I went to class all morning, but that's all I could stand. It's just too hard. My brain gets tired. I have to get out."

"What's too hard, dear?" Stephanie asked.

"I can't concentrate for hours on end. Sometimes I just have to get away."

Sean stepped toward her. "Well you can go up to your room now and do the work you missed in class today. And come directly home after school every day this week."

"Fine!" Amber stormed out of the room. Sean stared down the empty hall, his back rigid, until her bedroom door slammed upstairs. Then he slumped into a chair and rubbed his face with the palm of his hand.

Stephanie held up her glass in a toast. "Welcome to the wonderful world of teenage children."

Sean shook his head. "I blew it. But what does she mean, *it's too hard?* If she'd go to class, it might not be so hard."

"There's bound to be a transition time when you change schools." Stephanie said. "And she's changed more than schools. Her whole life has changed. Give her a bit more time."

"You're right." Sean looked at her out of the corner of his eye. "Mind if I go out for a while? We probably shouldn't leave Amber alone."

"Sorry," Stephanie said, downing her drink and rising a

bit too eagerly from her chair. "Max and I have plans. We won't be late."

Sean sighed. "I know. She's my responsibility. I am doing my best."

Stephanie put her hand on his shoulder as she walked by him. "I know you are. Don't be too hard on yourself. You two are still getting to know each other. You have no history to go by, no way of knowing what she'll do next. Or why. Give yourself some time, too."

"You're right," he said, but without conviction as the older couple got their coats and went out into the rain, leaving Sean in the quiet kitchen.

His mother's kitchen. He'd moved back in when Amber showed up on their doorstep last fall, thrilled to have found her and grateful to his mother for offering them a haven. Neutral ground where he'd hoped they could slowly get to know each other.

But five months in and he was no closer to understanding this girl. *His girl.* Her outright rejection of the love he was trying to give her was tearing him apart.

He pulled out his phone and called Frankie. He wasn't seeing nearly enough of her these days, but between his responsibilities with Amber, and the new job...

"Hi." Frankie's bright tone turned the hurt in his heart into longing. A longing that wasn't going to be sated tonight.

"Hi."

She waited a beat and when she spoke, the fun had gone out of her voice. "Oh, no. Not again. What now?"

"The school called. She's been skipping again."

"Not my class." Frankie taught English at the local high school and Amber was enrolled in her tenth grade English class this semester.

"She probably knows I'd find out about that right away."

"How did you deal with it?"

"Grounded her for a week."

"Hmmm. Want me to come over?"

"Yes. No. Mom went out and Amber's sulking in her room. I should probably go up and talk to her. Not that I know what to say or think it will do any good. We haven't had dinner yet, either."

"Okay," Frankie said, the disappointment in her voice pointing to one more failure in his life. He felt he was failing Frankie, Amber, his mother, everyone.

"Hey, I'm really sorry. This is not what I want for us, either."

"I know. Maybe tomorrow?"

"I'll try. I love you."

"Yeah, me too," she said, but the warmth in her voice he remembered was missing, and then she hung up the phone.

He hated to put Frankie on the back burner, but what could he do? Before Amber had shown up on his doorstep last fall, he'd had plans—a house, marriage, a family with Frankie. He'd tried to bring Frankie and Amber together, but Amber had resisted all of Frankie's overtures of friendship. Sometimes he wondered if she was jealous of their relationship.

He was tired of juggling these balls in the air, and wasn't doing a good job of it, either. Every other day one of them burst into flame and he either burnt his hands or dropped it completely. Then he was back at square one.

He'd gotten what he wanted, his daughter back, but hoped it wasn't at the cost of the woman he loved.

* * *

Thank you for reading Fortune Bay books!
You can find Family Matters, a bridge novella, in print
and ebook format on Amazon.
The Fortune Bay Series

Available on Amazon as eBook and paperback.

Lake of Dreams
Get this free prequel e-novella when you sign up for my readers group at **bit.ly/freeFB-e-book**

Summer of Fortune
Book One
Maddie wasn't looking for romance. Could a summer of freedom change her life forever?

The Good Neighbor
Book Two
Sean hates to see Frankie and her father estranged. He'd give anything to know where his own daughter is.

Home for Christmas
Book Three
Blue's carried a torch for Louise his whole life, but this time he's not sure he can wait around to pick up the pieces.

Family Matters
A Sequel Novella
Things are at a low ebb for Frankie and Sean. Be sure to read *The Good Neighbor* and *Home for Christmas* first!

Starting Over
Book Four
After a horrific motorcycle accident, Marshall's life seems to be over—until Lily knocks on his door.

Starlight and Tinsel
A Christmas Novella
Star finally gets her chance to shine in this Christmas novella.

Also by Judith Hudson
Writing as J.M. Hudson

The Rocky and Bernadette Mystery Series

Temple of the Jaguar
A Mayan Murder Mystery
A travel cozy mystery. A travel writer and a photographer's
first job together in the Yucatan quickly unravels when a body
is discovered in the crocodile lagoon.

Home for Christmas is a work of fiction. Names, characters, places and incidents are entirely the product of the imagination of the author or are used fictitiously. Any resemblance to actual events, locales or persons, living or dead, is entirely coincidental.

Copyright